GH00643794

CRUEL
PINK

DEBRA
ANASTASIA

Library of Congress Cataloguing-in-Publication Data
ISBN 979-8-218-07710-5

Editing: **Paige Smith Editing**
Photo Credit: Igor Madjinca

Printed in the United States of America

DebraAnastasia.com

For T, J and D
All things I do are for you. I love you.

CRUEL PINK

I'm just a girl, standing here, falling in love with my best friend's older brother.

Totally kidding. I've always been in love with Austin Burathon.

Effortlessly cool. Wears nail polish. Flirts with everyone. When he rescues me in the middle of the night, I see a side of his life that I never knew about.

I thought he had what I didn't.

Perfect homelife. Supportive parents. And he does, but he's fighting a war in his apartment.

Austin's ex-boyfriend, Endgame, takes gaslighting seriously and thinks it defines love. Plus, he's refusing to move out.

Endgame wears pink when he plans on breaking Austin's heart – and he does it often!

He may wear pink, but he has me seeing red.

I'm going to protect Austin, any way I can. I'll do it over and over again, even if it means risking my own heart.

I couldn't make out the writing on the Post-it notes that were
stuck to my ceiling in the dark. I could barely make out how
many there were. The ceiling and walls of the dorm were
completely covered. Her handwriting had a manic scrawl to it.

The roommate from hell was lying on her bed less than ten
feet from me, buck ass naked. She did it just to make me uncomfortable.

It worked. I was uncomfortable. It was her goal and she succeeded.

I rolled over and faced the wall. This sucked. College sucked. Living with a complete weirdo really sucked.

Randomly assigned roommates was a horrible idea. At first, Roberta had seemed nice. She hadn't responded to the email I sent when we were assigned, but when I moved in, she was all smiles. Of course, I had my crew with me then, so all my football playing friends and some of my bestie's brothers were milling around in the common room. Her smiles were fake. Or for them.

For me? As soon as everyone hugged me goodbye, and Peaches fake sob cried, and then cried for real, that was the last I saw of Roberta's smile.

When I was unpacking my stuff into my closet, I tossed her some easy, small talk questions.

"So, where are you from?" I tucked my tank tops next to my underwear.

From behind me I heard what would most likely be described as a growl.

I waited for a few seconds before I turned around. She was standing in front of her now opened closet with her hands on her hips.

"Um. Hi." I had two more tank tops in my hands.

Roberta's eyes were slits, like a shark's, and her lips curled downward.

"Enjoying that closet?" She slid her gaze to my new closet and all the empty space inside. Well, *all* was a strong word. The closet was far from generous.

"I guess so?" I wasn't sure what the correct answer was. I looked past her into her closet that was jammed so full of stuff it resembled a shipping container.

"That was my closet." She pointed at the offending space with her pinkie.

I glanced around, confused. Clearly, Roberta was on her side. Her bed was on her side, and she had a footlocker on her side. But it was cluttered. Like really cluttered. Like she had brought far too much stuff for the size room she was assigned kind of cluttered. It was giving me flashbacks to home and the things that gave me hives.

"Aren't we in a shared dorm room?" I held my tank tops out like they had the answers she needed.

She snatched them out of my hands. I looked at my now empty hands and tucked them under my armpits.

"Oh, you're funny now? Now you're the funniest girl? You know, when you were moving in, I thought to myself, *maybe she's sweet. She has a stuffed animal.*" She pointed my tank tops at the teddy bear on my bed. "But ever since I've met you, I've got a bad feeling." She shifted her shoulders around like she was low-key practicing a TikTok dance.

"We met like an hour ago." I pulled my phone out of my back pocket. Okay, an hour and thirty-four minutes, but still.

"Yeah. Exactly." Roberta took my tank tops and crammed them in her closet. I was surprised it didn't burst from the added material.

Oh no. Roberta was an angry person. I was living with someone that didn't want me there at all. I had to reach out an olive branch. "Uh, if you need to put some of your stuff in the closet..."

I was careful not to call it mine.

Roberta's eyes got wide. "Yeah. Ya think?"

And that's how I wound up rolling all my dresses into my one suitcase and jamming it under my bed. Somehow, Roberta filled up two closets to the brim with her bullshit. And she was still mad.

That was four weeks ago. Four horrible weeks ago. I found out from our suitemates that Roberta had lived in our dorm room by herself for a full year. She was technically a sophomore.

Oh, and my suitemates? They steered clear of me. I was a marked woman. Roberta would make their lives hell if she caught them talking to me. That information was whispered to me when

I was in the shower, so I didn't get to know who had bent a little in the kindness-to-Taylor direction.

I was miserable. Even Teddi and Peaches, my two incredible friends, were worried. They were busy, though. Peaches was in school in Michigan, hoping to become a veterinarian or a police officer. Teddi was in school as well, staying with friends. She hadn't declared a major yet, but she was so driven I was sure it would happen soon.

I heard Roberta fart. A naked fart, with her whole ass out of her comforter. Then, there was a knock on our door.

I rolled over and Roberta stuck her tongue out at me, then spoke up, "Come in, babe."

Our door opened. Roberta had it rigged so it couldn't lock so that Peter could come in whenever he wanted.

It was Tuesday at 2:00 a.m.

He took off his shoes and his shirt as he stumbled in the door. "Smells like burning cigars in here. Ugh."

The smell hit me as soon as he said it.

Roberta pointed at me. "She farts all night. Get me the Post-it notes."

Peter put his hand on her dresser and came back with the bright yellow notes. In her accusatory scrawl, Roberta spoke while she wrote, "FARTS ALL NIGHT!" And then she slapped the note on the space next to her.

Peter leaned over to take off his socks and grabbed his ankles with his butt facing me. "I got you, babe. No worries." Then Peter farted in my direction.

I snapped. I snapped, I snapped, I snapped. I had had enough. I was sick of Roberta's bullshit. Her blatant bullying and her naked ass crack.

I tossed my blanket aside and picked up my backpack. In it I tossed my essentials—my phone and charger. My wallet was already in the front pocket. I grabbed my teddy bear and keys and yanked the door open.

"Oh, she's mad now. Look what we did, Peter. She's leaving."

I put my hand to my forehead. I couldn't knock on any doors because everyone here was afraid of Roberta. My resident assistant? Also afraid of Roberta. I had only one person in the city I could call at this time. On this night. He was a nuclear option, but I was about to blow.

I slammed the door on my way out. All my shit was still in that room, but screw it. I pulled out my phone and scrolled to the one name that set my heart beating every time I saw it.

My bestie's older brother, Austin Burathon. I hit the button and the ringing started.

FINE, I had a crush on him. Fine, I'd had a crush on him my entire life. Fine, I wasn't over it. Wasn't planning to get over it either. *But*, and that's a huge but, I was never going to step over the boundary beyond harmless flirting.

Which was why he was the nuclear option. Who was Austin? Austin was, first and foremost, Teddi's older brother. And when you're really young, four years older can seem like a lifetime. I mean, when he started driving, we were twelve.

He drove us a lot. He was good like that. Being Teddi's friend came with perks. Instead of her parents picking us up from cheer practice, sometimes it was her piping hot brother.

What was it about him? Girl, sit down. You wouldn't under-stand the amount of fuck-hot sexuality that poured off this man. He wasn't even fair. Just swoon and yum and exotic while also being the realest person you spoke to all day. He was a flirt. You could be a boy or girl. He'd flirt. It was so hot. He was like a beau-tiful movie star in the midst of us normal people. He'd wear skirts sometimes and nail polish other times. He was the first real human boy I ever saw wearing eyeliner and it sculpted how I viewed my dream guy. The confidence to put that on and just...be himself? Everyone wanted to know him and be around him. And I was lucky enough to have that happen quite a bit.

Austin was super involved in his family's affairs. They seemed to be collecting teenagers lately. First, it was Gaze, just a year younger than Austin, who was a foster kid for the last few years of his teens. Then, Ruffian showed up on the Burathons' doorstep, and like the superheroes they were, they just folded him into the family.

Ruffian fell in deep love with my friend, Teddi. Later on, he robbed our friend-enemy, Meg. It was a little complicated, but the good news was, he was out of prison and Teddi was still in love.

I did a stint at community college while living at home, and now, finally, I was transferring my credits to college in Loveville City, the same city as Austin.

I got a text message back from him:

AUSTIN: Stay in your foyer. I'll be by in a few minutes.

And that's how I was in the vestibule of the dorms in my Wonder Woman pajama set waiting for my dream man.

I wasn't sure what car to look for when a figure walked up to the door and rapped his knuckles on it.

How did this feel so personal? Well, usually Teddi was involved, and now it was just us. Austin and I.

"Kitten. What's up, baby?" When I opened the door to let myself out, his arms were waiting.

I just shook my head slowly in his chest. He wrapped his hands around my back and my head.

"There, there. This city can be an ass buster. I'm sorry. Let's go back to my place." He put his arm around my shoulders. And even though I was scurrying out of my dorm room in the middle of the night, I still felt a thrill. People walking by would think we were together. Like *together* together.

"Wonder Woman's having a tough one?" He pulled out his phone and ordered us a car service. He took my backpack and slung it over his shoulder and we strolled to the nearest stoplight. I finally took a look at him. He gave me a soft smile. His eyeliner was smudged, and I was pretty sure there was glitter in the crease of his eyelid. He threaded his fingers in mine. "We have to wait for like four minutes. Do you want to talk about it?"

I didn't have to as the window three stories up cranked open. "Run, bitch, run. I told you you couldn't hang."

Austin took one look and then glanced back at my face. "Oh. She's expanding the window a little. Don't look now. That's her butt crack. Sweet Jesus. Her butt crack."

I wiped at my eyes with the back of my hand. "I know what her butt crack looks like better than I do my own. Literally, she's naked so much. It's so uncomfortable."

Austin pulled on my hand and I buried my face in his chest.

"Oh? You got a boyfriend now? Tell him how you can't put your shoes away and you steal phone chargers in your spare time!" Roberta's voice echoed off the surrounding buildings.

"She's charming." He turned his head to shout up, "Hey, wild person, can you stop freaking yelling and put some clothes on?"

Roberta's voice was fired up now. "Oh, really, pretty boy? You want to come up here and say that to my boyfriend?"

"No, sweetheart, I don't do deliveries. But if he comes down here, I'll be happy to kick his ass." Austin pulled me in closer.

"Don't get in trouble because of me." I turned my head and saw a car approaching. Judging from the blinker, it was getting ready to stop near us. Most of the road was deserted. Even in a city, this late at night on a weekday was quieter. "Uber's here."

Austin turned me by my shoulders and opened the back door. "Hop in, angel cake. I just want to tell these two assholes something." He shut the door and hollered a few more things at Roberta and her boyfriend before coming around the side of the car to get in the backseat near me.

"I can't believe I hate those people so much. And I just met them." Austin gave a middle finger out the back window while telling the Uber driver his address.

7

"Thank you." Sitting with him now, I realized how tense I was in the dorm room. He was a bit of home and it made my emotions bubble up inside.

"Come here." He put his arm around me and pulled me in.

I rested my head on his chest. He smelled good, like the outdoors and a muffin. He was cuddling me like he did his sister, Teddi, all the time. If I wasn't so freaking discombobulated and tired, I would have loved to take a selfie. And maybe get a shirt made with the picture on it.

I had issues. He was wild to be close to. My heart was beating so hard. Austin knew I needed hugs—ugh. He was so intuitive.

The Uber pulled over. Austin gave me a quick squeeze before opening the car door and throwing my bag over his shoulder in one swift movement. He held out a hand like I was royalty or dressed for the Oscars or something. I took it and held it still after thanking the driver.

Austin pulled out his phone and led me toward the front door. He tipped the driver on the app and swiped to his key for the building app without letting go of my hand.

Why was he so physical? I was eating it up. I was feeling so safe. Lord, help me, this man was too much.

After the app granted us entry, Austin pulled me along to the elevator. The doors opened immediately.

"Why were you out?" I was realizing he'd appeared so quickly—

he had to have been close by, and not at this building.

"I was partying with friends. Tuesdays can be Saturdays, if you know the right people." He winked at me.

My ovaries found a way to clap for joy inside me.

"Just a heads-up, though. My roommate and I were fighting —although he was gone when I left earlier, he might be back now. Just ignore him. I pay all the rent, so he gets no say in who comes and goes."

I nodded, feeling bad for interrupting. "I'm sorry if this is a rough time for me to be here for you."

"Baby, you're family. You need help, you get help. No other choices." The elevator dinged on the tenth floor and Austin reached out a hand to hold the door open. His rings clanked against the metal.

I was grateful to be given this out, but part of my heart kicked rocks because if he and I were family, we weren't ever going to be kissing buddies.

Austin opened his front door with a code and stepped inside, propping the door open for me to enter behind him. His place was so freaking awesome. He had a very lucrative social media platform, and his apartment was the set for many of his videos and pictures. The furniture was all curves and block colors. Some sharp pieces with black and white were edged in. A wall had all different ring lights and filming equipment hanging on it like art. The whole place had a musky lavender scent that I associated with Austin.

"Have a seat. You need a drink? Hungry?" He set my bag next to me.

"I'm good." Was I feeling out of place? Was I feeling rescued? All of it.

Austin went to the fridge that was painted with a subtle pattern and filled up a glass with ice and water.

He came and sat down next to me, holding out the glass. I took it gratefully, tipping it back to quench my thirst.

"See, angel? I knew what you needed." Austin reached over and moved some of my hair away from my face, the edge of his finger skimming my temple.

Did he know what that touch did to people? I couldn't imagine that the whole world wouldn't feel that tender contact in both their soul and their naughty bits at the same damn time.

There was a gentle tone from the front door. Austin mumbled, "Shit."

The door flung open before he could explain. Stumbling in the entry was a tall guy, his face scribbled with tattoos all over it.

When he snarled in our direction, I could see some of his teeth were capped in gold.

"That's how it is. Quick, right?" The door swung closed and slammed from the weight.

"Taylor, please ignore everything he's about to say." Austin moved my bag and slung his arm over my shoulder, holding his hands over my ears. It didn't matter, I could still hear perfectly.

"Oh, Taylor? She's hot. Fuck hot. I bet she's perfect for you. Into you." I was gathering this was the roommate from the earlier fight. He was latching onto my name and just rolling me into their fight. The man looked me up and down. "Young for you, though."

"She's my little sister's best friend. So maybe be a little respectful, asshole." Austin stood and held a hand in front of me, signaling for me to stay put, I was assuming.

"Oh, so picking up some trash from home, I see." The roommate stepped forward and squared up with Austin.

He was for sure wobbly, like his executive functions were off. Drugs. I bet he was on drugs.

Austin's eyes flared and his hand shot out. He had the man's jaw in his hand as he hissed, "*Respectful.*"

I'd been around plenty of boys in fights in my day. Teddi and I had run with the football players and her brothers our entire life. But there was something different about the way this guy and Austin were threatening each other. It was almost...sexual.

Oh. Then I figured it out. They were roommates and possibly lovers. Hence, the extra anger and tension.

The other guy gave Austin a harsh, hollow chuckle. "So you haven't been able to replace me after all, then. What did I tell you? My leftovers are tainted. You won't find anyone to love you."

I felt my eyes go wide. This guy was straight up gaslighting Austin. And this sure, headily awesome human that had so much confidence was knocked down a peg. I watched as the man's words hit Austin's self-worth.

Austin shook his head and hissed, "Mind your business."

Pushing up from the couch, I strode over to Austin. He wasn't getting told that he was less than in front of me. I stepped between the two men, and Austin let go of the man and put his hands on my shoulders. I saw embarrassment and concern swimming in his eyes.

Wrapping my arms around Austin and rising on my toes, I did something I had been dreaming about all my life. I kissed Austin Burathon. I kissed him with how much I wanted him. I kissed him with how hot I found him. I made sure my lips told him I was awed by him, and his kindness, and his bravery.

He kissed me back. Austin kissed me back with such skill that I literally swooned and he had to steady me. His lips tasted so good, his talent so sure. I was dying. I was dying right here.

The only thing that snapped me out of it was a hard slam of a door.

I jolted back from the shock of the noise. I had been instantly transported to another world in Austin's kiss.

I covered my mouth as the realization of what I did hit me. Oh God. *I kissed him?* I kissed him!

He looked over my head in the direction of the door and then gave me a sad smile. "I guess we're busy saving each other tonight, huh?"

"I'm sorry. I'm sorry I kissed you. It was the only thing I could think to do because I'm pretty sure that dude would not have been affected by a punch from me." I thumbed the indication over my shoulder. "And I had to do something. Fuck him. Wow. Fuck him so much."

Austin shook his head and held out his hand. I took it. "I've fucked him a lot, angel. It doesn't change who he is—I've tried."

"Who is he?" I followed Austin as he stopped to grab my backpack and I got my water glass.

"Him? That's Torin." Austin opened his bedroom door and I was treated to another magazine layout. The furniture was all low and minimal. The brick wall behind his bed towered to a high ceiling.

He set my bag on top of the dresser.

"Endgame," I offered as the stories shared by Teddi flooded my mind. She never referred to Torin by his name, only Austin's complicated ex-boyfriend that everyone called Endgame. Austin and he were so much in love, but Teddi didn't like Endgame at all. She felt he was a toxic hanger-on that didn't value Austin. The last I'd heard of Endgame had to be my senior year of high school.

"Teddi told you." Austin sat on his bed.

I sat next to him. "She's not a fan."

"I know. My sister is opinionated. It is what it is." He flopped backward onto the bed and a sliver of his toned stomach peeked out from under his shirt. There was a hint of a tattoo there.

I flopped back as well, both of us staring at the ceiling. "Yeah, she hates the hell out of him. I hope I didn't make things more awkward by kissing you." The entire kiss replayed in my mind—a flashback of literal minutes, but I was grateful to have the memory nice and clear. I'd revisit it for the rest of my life.

"Nah. The kiss was fire. Thank you for that. He and I were likely to get into a hate brawl anyway. It was a total mood diffuser." He turned his head to look at me and I kept my eyes firmly on the ceiling.

The last thing I wanted our kiss defined as was a mood diffuser.

He propped up on his elbow and turned his hips toward me. "So what are the implications of you walking out tonight? You had to be in a rough spot."

And just like that, Austin switched the moment to be about fixing my problems and ignoring his own.

I let him move the conversation in that direction because I was still hurt that the kiss hadn't meant the world to him. The moon to him.

I sighed. "Roberta, the roommate, had a single dorm room before I came along. I guess it was luck of the draw or whatever. She really wanted it to stay that way." I turned to pop up on my elbow, facing Austin. Lord, he was pretty. Sexy.

"And she decided to make your life miserable so she can have it back that way again," Austin correctly surmised.

"Yeah. And I like to imagine I'm tough, but when her boyfriend farts at me in the middle of the night? Apparently, I bounce the hell out." I ran a hand through my hair as amusement hit Austin's face.

His unrestrained smile was lighter fluid on my heart. It started clodhopping around in my chest. I was the one that made him smile, and I knew I was addicted to that whole feeling instantly.

"So can you find a new roommate?" He asked me.

He narrowed his eyes like he was trying to plan my future for me.

"It's difficult because I'm on two scholarships. And they are tied to my room and board. The college is super picky about the awardees maintaining a proper decorum. Roberta knows this and has threatened to tell the whole college all the ways I'm evil. She has literal fistfuls of Post-it notes with my flaws wallpapering the dorm room." I touched my neck.

"Oh, I'm so sorry. Crap." He held out an arm and we hugged briefly, on our sides. "That's so rough. Fuck her so much."

"Yeah. She's really like all of my problems right now." I rubbed my thumb on his comforter.

"Listen, stay with me. What can they do if you just move out?" He tilted his head.

In every crush dream I had about Austin since I was old enough to fall in love, this conversation would happen over and over. "Really? That's a lot to ask."

"Nah. You and I can be boyfriend and girlfriend, which keeps me away from Endgame and him away from me. Plus, you can live here and not have that stress from Roberta and her revenge farts." Austin held out his hand for a shake. A special deal. A secret. I wanted to lick his hand, but instead, I shook it.

I was going to live with my dream man and pretend to be his girlfriend. I knew the long-term damage was going to be substantial to my heart, but there was no way in hell I was saying no to him.

"You've got a deal."

SLEEPING WAS EASY, and I wasn't expecting that. Leaving a dorm room in the middle of the night was exhausting. Austin had me in a cuddle. He was a touchy guy. Hell, it wasn't even the first time we'd ever cuddled.

I tried to etch the feeling of the weight of his arm on my hip. Too bad a feeling couldn't be a tattoo.

The alarm on my phone went off. The trill of a pop song was like a knife to my eyeball nerves. I clamored out of bed to silence it. I stood there, trying to get my act together. I glanced down at my Wonder Woman pajamas. I couldn't wear those, even a little.

Austin rolled onto his back and put his arms behind his head. I was distracted by him. The way he was muscled was my favorite. He was so complete and so well hidden under clothes, but when I got to see his chest, it was sigh-worthy. He had more tattoos than the last time I had been face-to-face with his bare chest at a pool party Teddi had in senior year.

"Kitten, you look lost. You okay?" He propped himself up and reached inside his end table drawer. He popped a piece of mint gum into his mouth. I covered my own mouth. I forgot my toothbrush.

"I need all my stuff. Like all of it. I'm supposed to go to class and I'm wearing this." I waved my hand in front of my body.

"How much time we got?" He flipped the covers off and got out, stretching.

How was a girl supposed to talk when he was doing...all that? He was wearing black fitted boxers and still had on his chains.

I looked down at my phone's screen like it had the answers. "Class is at ten. It's 9:45."

"I got you." He tossed me the pack of gum and I slid out a piece.

He rushed into his closet and I realized it was far more than what I was expecting. It was a full-on extra room, which made sense. Austin made money on social media. He was known for fashion and eclectic ways of framing everyday items. Most people my age were following him on TikTok. He was pretty good at shielding his actual appearance, so he had found a way to be sort of mini-famous without actually having too many of the pitfalls.

I trailed behind him. He had all kinds of cameras, makeup, and clothing, and it was meticulously organized. I felt every girly part of me swoon.

He studied me up and down in a way that seemed clinical, and then he flipped through the options. "I'll drive you. What building is your class in?"

I caught the soft, long, black skirt he tossed and slipped it on over my shorts. Then I had a tank top and a sweater to manage. Next, I had a pair of boots. The outfit was quick and effortlessly perfect for walking in the city. "Parker, Eastside."

Austin grabbed a ponytail holder and a makeup case. "Let's go."

While he was picking out my stuff, he'd been building his own outfit. Jeans, a white sweater, and a slouchy beanie were all I could see. I grabbed my backpack and phone as Austin threw open his door. A wall of weed smell hit us.

Austin peeked over his shoulder, mouthing, "Sorry."

There were so many actual humans in his living room. I was counting at least five. Two of them were naked.

Endgame was slouched in a chair holding a glass, swirling the caramel colored liquid inside it.

His eyes were mostly red. His voice was quiet and meant for only Austin, but I heard him anyway. "Done with her that quick?"

"Shut it," Austin bit out his reply and I had no idea why his words made tears prick in my eyes.

Endgame rolled his eyes.

Austin opened the door and held it for me. I hustled through it. Once I was in the hall, Austin leaned back in the apartment and hissed something I couldn't hear.

He closed the door before I could hear any response. I knew I was madly in love with Austin, but moving in with him while he navigated a breakup might be a poor choice.

The girl in love in my head stomped her feet. She didn't care if anything made sense as long as she could be near Austin.

He held out his hand and I took it. We ran through the hall and down a set of stairs. Austin reached for my backpack before taking the burden from me. When we hit the garage, we all-out sprinted, still holding hands until we skidded to a stop at his vintage white CRX. I heard the doors unlock and grabbed the passenger door. Austin had the car in reverse the second my door was closed.

"You'll be a few minutes late, sugar." He pushed up the sleeves of his sweater while he waited for the parking garage arm to let us out.

I rested my head back and watched him. I woke up with Austin Burathon. He dressed me and was driving me to school. Teenage Taylor was dying one thousand deaths of happiness.

"Thank you." I watched as he navigated the manual transmission like a boss. *Why were his forearms so defined?*

"You wanna get your stuff after class? What time do you get out?" His warm brown eyes met mine and he offered me a small smile.

"I don't know if I'm ready to battle Roberta and her boyfriend yet." I unzipped my backpack and slipped my phone into the front pocket.

"Oh, sweetheart, they won't be allowed to talk to you. I'll be there and I'll have some of my friends with me." He double parked in front of the Begonia Building, which was near the Parker Building.

"Okay. Eleven-thirty is when class ends." I opened the car door while the drivers of the vehicles behind us laid on their horns.

"I'll be in this exact spot then. I'm going to sit here the whole time so these bastards get so mad their panties light on fire." Then Austin winked at me and we had a date.

I closed his car door and headed to class.

This was all great. Super awesome. I was so happy and confused that all I wanted to do was talk to my best friend, and she was Austin's sister.

I texted Peaches. She was my best friend, too. But she was the ridiculous one. Good ridiculous, but still ridiculous.

ME: So I left my dorm last night.
PEACHES: OMG! Why?
ME: The bitch and her screw buddy hit my last nerve.
PEACHES: Where are you? R U ok?

Now Peaches was sounding like Teddi, who would one hundred percent be involved in finding me housing options and a lawyer.

ME: Austin picked me up
PEACHES: NO! TAYLOR FANCY BOLAND!

She used my full name.

ME: Yes
PEACHES: No!
ME: Yes
PEACHES: Did you literally cream your pants?
ME: Yes!
PEACHES: No! AUSTIN BURATHON of the FUCKHOT GUYLINER and SUAVE AMAZINGNESS!!?

Okay, both Peaches and I had had middle school crushes on Austin. She grew out of hers, preferring the football players in our class. I never grew out of it, and Peaches knew it.

PEACHES: CALL ME
ME: I can't. I'm in class. Then after class Austin said we're getting my stuff.
PEACHES: I wanna come visit soon.
ME: Pffft
PEACHES: Soon, TAYLOR.

I put my phone on airplane mode and tried to focus on class. I couldn't let my grades slip during this upheaval. My scholarships depended on it.

I USED my phone's camera to check my hair and redid my messy bun. Then I wondered if that's how Austin would style me. God, how I wanted him to style me.

After I got my backpack together and wrangled up all the butterflies in my chest that were excited to see Austin again, I headed out. The door was being held open for me.

As I thanked the guy for the service, he tipped his chin in my direction. "No worries, pretty girl."

I felt myself glow at the compliment. I'd been in this class for months, and this cute guy picked today to talk to me? Maybe thinking about Austin was making me put off welcoming vibes.

I'm sure the blond clean-cut guy was just being nice. I hustled back to the front of the building, and sure enough, Austin's car was waiting for me—double parked again.

The passenger side opened up and I saw that the car was packed. Three people in the small backseat and one in the passenger side. The beautiful woman patted her lap for me to sit on her.

I gave Austin a confused look. He had clearly gotten his friends and returned ready to storm my old castle.

He patted the beautiful woman's lap, too. "This is Tinsley. Have a seat. She's stronger than she looks and only bites on the weekends."

Tinsley threw her head back and howled with a cackle. The horns started up again. I didn't have time to question it. I hung onto the roof and swung into Austin's low-set car. This wasn't a safe way to drive anywhere.

The introductions started as soon as Tinsley and I settled into a very cozy situation.

"I'm Fred." Fred was a girl as well, but she was built in a way that I was pretty sure she could punch straight through the roof of the car if she wanted to.

"I'm Caesar." Caesar held out his hand and I awkwardly tried to complete the shake. I felt his lips kiss my knuckles. He was a beautiful man.

"I'm Fiona."

I waved to her.

"Fiona is our ninja. She's in on all the details," Austin offered. "So, is your roommate home now, do you think?"

I let myself rummage through my memories of Roberta's schedule. She seemed to always be in the dorm with her dumb boyfriend. "I honestly don't know if she even goes to her classes. It's terrifying."

"Okay, no problem. We'll plan on them being there. Let us know what's yours and we will bag it up and be out in ten minutes. I have another friend coming with their truck. You didn't have any furniture, did you?"

"Just my TV and my mini fridge." I thought about how Teddi had gifted me the fridge, personalized with my name and cutesy characters hand-painted on the side.

Tinsley pulled her phone out and held it in front of my chest. "I'll tell Parker. What's the room number?"

"408." This was happening. Austin and his crew of friends were going to help me get my shit.

Tinsley used voice to text to compose a message to Parker. "Do we have to sign in?"

"No. Roberta always makes sure the back stair door is propped open for her boyfriend."

"Well, that doesn't sound fucking safe." Caesar scoffed.

"It's not. She couldn't care less." I shook my head.

Austin reached over and squeezed my knee. "It ends today, okay?"

I felt my body go boneless when I met Austin's eyes. "Okay."

When Austin and Fiona started talking about where to park the vehicles, Tinsley whispered in my ear, "I saw that."

I turned my head toward her.

"The way you react to him. Hell, I think everyone in this car has reacted to him that way at some point." She twirled my blonde hair around her finger.

"So obvious?" How did this chick read me so quickly? Then I

looked back at Austin. He was effortlessly cool and welcoming. Maybe everyone fell in love with him as he made his way around the planet.

"You're only human." She laughed a bit and let my hair go, a single spiral lock left as a memento in her fingers' place.

Austin parked his car next to an old white truck. He got out, then I got out and reached back to help Tinsley extract herself.

"Sorry, I smooshed you in there." It was the first time I noticed her five-inch heels.

"Oh, you can sit on my lap, sit on my face, whatever you need, baby doll." My eyes went wide and Tinsley started laughing.

That distinctive laugh caught Austin's attention. "Behave. She's not even been with us twenty-four hours, guys."

Caesar flopped the passenger seat forward and Tinsley and I helped pull him out. Austin had Fiona, the ninja, and Fred didn't need anyone to help her.

Parker, the driver of the truck, was leaning against it. "We kidnapping a college kid?"

If I found out Parker was a movie star, I wouldn't be surprised.

Austin held out a hand to me and I took it. "She's a willing captive. Hell, she's damn near a family member. Taylor, this is Parker. He's one of my models."

I held out a hand and Parker's gleaming white teeth caught the sunlight like he was filming a toothpaste commercial.

Then the passenger door of the truck opened. First, a cloud of smoke, then one old beat-up boot. I looked to Austin just in time to see his face fall.

Endgame.

Endgame tossed the butt of the cigarette onto the ground. "You don't even text me when you send out an all-call?"

The whole atmosphere changed. The tension stilled the laughter.

Austin pressed my hand, but I wasn't sure if it was intentional or not. Endgame had sunglasses on, but I felt like his gaze was burning through me.

"Well, let's go!" Tinsley bounced forward and linked her arm in Endgame's. "Room 408."

As we walked up the stairs, the whole group of us sounded like a slow SWAT team. I felt the need to fill these people in.

"My roommate is probably naked. She's always naked."

"Oh, baby. We know how to handle that. Fire with fire." Austin put one hand in the air and swirled his index finger.

As I was walking behind them, the party of people in front of me started shedding their clothes. I felt my jaw drop as Tinsley and Parker draped their pants on the stairway's handrails.

Fred snorted and pulled her shirt off.

"Oh, we going all the way?" Austin was stripping like this was always the way he and his friends walked upstairs. "Kitten, you keep your clothes on. That'll be the power move."

Endgame was not getting unclothed, but every single one of Austin's friends and Austin were butt ass naked by the time we got to the fourth floor.

And yeah, I looked. I had to look. It was right there.

Then I glanced away. How were these people so comfortable with nudity? They weren't even drunk. Well, maybe Endgame was, but he was clothed and surly.

Austin opened the hall door for me and I became the grand marshal of the most unusual parade of my life.

I knocked once and then turned the knob. True to form, Roberta was naked. Her dumb boyfriend was also naked and lying on my bed.

Roberta's slow, evil smile was soon replaced by shock as Austin and his friends made their very naked way into the dorm room.

"What the fuck is going on here?" Roberta used her comforter to cover her body.

Austin put a hand on my shoulder. "Just point to your stuff. We got you."

And that's how I got to orchestrate a very beautiful group of people around a room while my evil roommate fumed. Her boyfriend had the sense to shuffle to Roberta's side of the room.

Tinsley went to the closet. "All of this?"

"None of it. She wouldn't let me have a closet." I pointed under my bed where I had a few bins full of the clothes that I had been forced to move.

"Oh, that's some hard bullshit." Fred shook her head and squatted low to grab a few bins.

Austin stood on my bed and started rolling one of the two posters I had. "So all these Post-it notes? These are complaints about you?"

I nodded. Fiona walked over to Roberta and her boyfriend. I didn't hear what she said, but both of them recoiled.

"I think we need to keep all of these, Taylor. This is good evidence for you to get your dorm deposit back. This is some next-level stupidity."

Parker and Endgame started the process of snatching the Post-it notes from the walls. Parker made sure to get the ones on Roberta's side. His man business was swinging all over the place. Endgame lit a cigarette and pulled a multitool out of his pocket. He managed to get the TV off the wall. He stuck the wad of Post-it notes to the screen.

Austin and his friends were the most efficient stuff gatherers. Using a throw as a bag, they gathered all of my loose things. Everyone had an armful, Endgame with the TV. If it was a full ten minutes, I'd be surprised.

"Where can I find you when I figure out what you stole from me?"

Apparently, ten minutes was long enough for Roberta to snap out of her shock and be an asshole again.

Fiona stepped closer to Roberta. "What did I just say?"

Roberta's dumb boyfriend pulled on her arm. "Yeah, maybe just be quiet."

And for once, Roberta swallowed her words.

Austin motioned for me to go out first, and I didn't have to talk to Roberta again.

There was a crowd now. Some were gawking, some were taking video. I was happy that Austin's friends were covered up with my belongings, except for their butts. And they all had great butts.

When we got downstairs, they put my stuff in the bed of Parker's truck before we went back up the stairwell and they got their clothes. Everyone redressed while Endgame and I stayed with the vehicles.

He still had his sunglasses on.

"Thanks for helping with this." I broke the awkward silence.

He barely nodded.

Parker was the first one back in the parking lot, followed by Austin and Tinsley.

The laughter was catching on. Once Tinsley got going, everyone fell in, and even Endgame cracked a smile.

"Let's get out of here before the cops come." Austin unlocked his car and everyone went back to the spots they were in before, except Tinsley. She got in between Parker and Endgame in the truck.

We were on the road, back to Austin's place, when Caesar was finally able to stop the fits of laughter. "This is the most fun I've ever had during the week, in the sunlight."

Austin tilted the rearview mirror and smiled at Caesar. "You guys are fucking awesome. I love you all."

Fred clapped Austin on the shoulder and Fiona smiled.

Caesar leaned over to her. "Fee, what the hell did you say to them?"

Fiona shook her head. "That's between me, them, and the devil."

Austin caught my eye. "See what I mean? Ninja."

Caesar leaned forward and covered my hand with his. "That was a toxic situation, Taylor. You okay?"

"Yeah. I mean, it was pretty screwed up. She really had me in my head." I picked at some lint on Austin's skirt.

Fiona covered Caesar's hand on top of mine. "You can't give them your sanity. She's an emotional vampire. I hate people like that."

"You have such great friends," I complimented Austin.

"I do. They're ready for anything." Austin switched gears and put on his blinker.

After we were parked, with Parker's truck right behind Austin's parking spot, we all got out.

Tinsley started picking through my stuff, finding things to carry. "Do we have to be butt ass naked to move her in, too?"

We all started laughing again as we brought my stuff inside.

Thankfully, we had time to use the elevator. It was weird to have all these very new-to-me people holding my stuff. I was pretty sure Caesar had a t-shirt stuffed with all of my bras and underwear. Endgame took the TV up, but after it was set in the living room, he disappeared into his bedroom.

Tinsley and Austin shared a pointed glance. He directed the group to put my things in his room.

After another trip, we had everything. Caesar clapped his hands loudly. "Well, this has made me a thirsty guy. How about a drunk lunch?"

Tinsley whooped. "I'm all in, baby."

Caesar held out his arms to her. She hopped in them, straddling him.

Fiona and Fred were down as well, and Parker had to bow out because he said he had a job. I looked to Austin. I was spent, but I couldn't imagine him passing up a chance with all these amazing friends.

Austin stepped closer to me and slung his arm around my shoulders. "Taylor and I have some stuff to work out."

There was a collective groan and some good-natured cursing launched in our direction.

"You know that we'll be drunk stupid later this week." He appeased them as he herded them out.

"Thank you, thank you so much," I called after them.

Once the door was closed, I watched as Austin contemplated Endgame's closed door. I reached out and held his wrist.

He gave me a sad smile before scratching his head. He let his hand drift down his neck to his chest. "Let's organize your ass. It's moving day, kitten."

3

My job was folding my clothes and placing them in the bottom dresser drawer. Austin was hanging up my dresses in a section of his wardrobe room. I sat criss cross in front of the dresser with my phone next to my knee.

I felt bad that I had to infiltrate all of his neatly organized things. Okay, that's a lie. I was freaking delighted. I was in his room. I could take a look at his tall, sexy self anytime I wanted to.

This man had lived in my dreams, in my fantasies, and all my hopes for as long as I could remember.

I shoved my underwear and bras in the back corner of the dresser. When I took another glance, Austin had paused and was pulling his long hair into a messy bun. He caught me looking.

I pointed to my head. "We match."

He gave me a smile, but I felt like the emotion didn't reach his eyes. *Endgame.*

That was what I was sensing. He had had an orgy's worth of people here this morning but still managed to get himself to my dorm to help.

There were layers to all of this and I wasn't ashamed to say I didn't feel sophisticated enough to noodle it all out. Not in just over twenty-four hours anyway.

Once my stuff was put away, Austin sat on the floor next to me. "Are you okay with living here? I mean, I know it's different and everything from the dorm. And maybe you want to live with kids your own age."

"You're only four years older than me." I actually knew that it was four years and ten days, but he didn't need to know that I had done that math more than a few times.

"But we can for sure get you back into the dorms. Fiona and I can really make a case with those Post-it notes."

Panic filled me. Austin titled his head. "Don't worry. If that's something that scares you, we won't do it."

"How did you know I was scared?" I picked up my phone as it started to vibrate.

"I've known you a long damn time. Remember the bees? I'm intimately acquainted with what your features look like when you're spooked." He reached out and touched my cheek.

"The bees? Oh, I remember. It's actually a huge recurring dream for me. Whenever I'm stressed, it's you and me and the bees all over again."

"You mean nightmare, right?" He rested back on his hands.

"Sure. Yeah."

That was a lie. It was a dream. I was twelve at the time, on a camping trip with Teddi and her family. The kids had gone on a hike around the lake, and Milt, the middle Burathon kid, and Teddi had started to race ahead. Austin had waited for me.

I was a few paces behind when I stepped on a hive of ground bees. I froze in place as the bees swarmed me. The buzzing near my ears felt like it was shaking my brain.

Austin rushed to me and swooped me up into his arms, running with me to avoid the bees. We both got stung repeatedly. I clung to his neck as he thundered us to the shore of the lake and plunged into the water.

The lake water was ice-cold, and he made sure he was touching my hand at all times. When we bobbed together, we saw the bees at the edge of the lake, swarming in an ominous cloud.

Austin had taken care of me, even though his face was swelling.

We treaded water near each other. "Are you allergic?"

He nodded once.

"Why would you save me then?"

"I could never not save you, kitten."

I'd had a crush on him before the bees, but I'd love him for the rest of my life after the bees.

At twelve, I looped my arm around his chest and told him to relax as his eyes swelled shut.

"I've got you. Just lay back. I just got my water safety certificate." I wanted to be a lifeguard at the local pool as soon as I was old enough. Until then, watching for water safety was my job in my house.

I swam us both diagonally on the lake, Teddi waving her parents over as we got closer.

"Bees! Austin got stung!"

The Burathons splashed into the water, and there was a medic involved. Once Austin had Benadryl in his system, the swelling went down quickly.

"Buzz, buzz, baby," Austin interrupted my thoughts.

"You were irrational to be willingly stung. I'm not allergic. I was hating it, but I'd have been okay." I pushed myself to stand.

"When you call for help, I'll always show up." He stood up next to me.

You know how you can see perforations in paper? You know where it will break once there's enough pressure put? That's how my heart was right then. Anyone could predict how this would pan out. The inevitable tear. But this man had ruined me for anyone else.

I was stubborn and set in my ways.

AFTER A SHOWER, where I dipped into Austin's luscious smelling conditioner, I put on leggings and a t-shirt.

When I walked back into his bedroom, he was on the phone. I made sure to pad around quietly as he conducted his business.

"Sure, I get that vibe. We can make that happen." Austin turned and looked me up and down again. My skin lit up with his attention. Maybe I should've put on something fancier. "I actually have a perfect model for that."

After he ended the call, he came close to me. He reached out and touched my hair, then pushed it behind my ear. "Do you think it would be okay if I took pictures of you? With you?"

My heart was beating in my mouth, my ears. "Um. Yeah. Sure."

"This brand wants a really dynamic ad campaign and you would be perfect. Classically, almost old Hollywood gorgeous. You'll be fantastic." He snapped his fingers near my face and took off into the wardrobe.

I covered my mouth. He called me gorgeous. Buzz, buzz. All over again.

I heard my phone vibrate again. I picked it up off of Austin's dresser. The text message from Teddi was all caps:

TEDDI: UR DATING MY BROTHER?!!

"Oh no." I felt my stomach stop. I mean, I didn't even get to explain to Teddi anything about the situation.

"Oh crap." Austin emerged from the wardrobe. He had a white silk dress draped over one arm and was holding out his phone to me. There was one word, all caps. My name.

"I think we have to FaceTime Teddi before she flies here on pure rage."

I nodded. Of course, that made sense. Calling her would make sense. The one problem I had was Teddi could read me like a book. We'd been friends for so long, she knew my thoughts before I had them. I couldn't hide my feelings for Austin from her, not even if I tried really hard.

The tones for the ringing FaceTime made my fate's choice for me.

"Hey, Teddi Bear." Austin stepped in front of me and moved to the side so Teddi could see me.

I wiggled my fingertips in her direction.

"You need to tell me when, what, and where." She was dressed up. Behind her were massive deep orange curtains.

"How's the meeting going?" Austin ignored her questions.

"Fine. We're on a break." She glanced over her shoulder.

I racked my brain for what she was doing. Teddi had the energy and drive of eight people. There was the nonprofit she was starting up under the name of her boyfriend's late mother, Ivy. Then there was the under-the-radar store of necessities she was working on with the local mafia boss and his crew.

She was a busy lady with a daily planner that rivaled a billionaire's.

"Are they going to donate the space?" Austin moved over to

the bed and patted the spot next to him. I sat down. He put his arm around me.

Teddi's eyes went wide. "Of course. I could talk a fish into buying land. They're going to donate food to the women's shelter, too." She leaned in closer to the screen. "Are you two f-ing with me right now? I mean, I know you're in the same city, but like, why is Endgame texting me a picture of the two of you?"

Austin side-eyed in the direction of Endgame's bedroom, then met my eyes. I squinted at him and the pain I saw.

Endgame was texting Teddi to tell on Austin?

"He was drunk. And he has no idea that Taylor literally grew up in our family." Austin clenched his fist.

She nodded. "I gathered that. He was like, here's how quickly your brother replaces me. I'm still living here and everything."

Austin swallowed hard. "Taylor and you need to talk. She'll catch you up."

He passed his phone to me. "I'll be back."

He stormed out of the bedroom, slamming the door behind him.

"Oh no." I turned my attention back to Teddi as the painting on the wall shook.

"What's going on? Why are you at Austin's?" She narrowed her gaze. I heard Austin knocking on a door in the apartment.

"Open. The. Door. Goddammit." His voice echoed through the crack under the door.

Teddi's anger morphed into concern. "Endgame texting me is freaking weird. Taylor? What's going on? Please tell me. I have to finish this meeting and I won't be able to think."

"Roberta and I... It wasn't working." I glanced at the door as I heard a loud bang. It sounded like someone was kicking in a door.

I stood and went to the doorway, opening it to peek out. Just as I did, Endgame's door swung closed. The living area was empty, so I knew Austin had gone to confront his ex-lover.

"In the middle of the night I needed help, and Austin came to get me. Things here are a little complicated." The screaming back and forth started up. Cursing. *Shit.*

"Hey, are you okay? Is Austin okay?" She was centering her laser focus on me.

"He's pretending that I'm his girlfriend to make Endgame mad," I whispered to her as I closed the door.

"Oh. *Oh.* That is something else. Okay. Wow. Okay, I hate to leave, but I need to go." She focused past her screen.

"We're okay. I'm safe. Austin's having it out with Endgame for texting you, I think. Go do your thing. I love you."

"Okay. I love you." She looked reluctant, but the video ended.

I wanted to give Austin privacy, but my little cheating heart really wanted to know what the hell was going on. I turned back to the door and opened it another crack.

I couldn't hear exactly what was going down, but the heat and anger were as clear as a bell.

I closed the door again and made my way back to the bed. The fighting was taking me back, making me want to be small. I was at the Burathons' house a lot as a kid. They were very kind to let me come over as much as I did.

I never invited Teddi to my house, and we ignored how weird that was. She had a pool. She had all the kids over all the time. Her parents seemed to love kids. They seamlessly enveloped me into their family vacations.

My house was not the same as theirs. My parents fought. They fought each other. They fought us kids. It wasn't until I had stayed with the Burathons for a week that I knew adults didn't have to fight all the time. Picking what was for dinner wasn't a federal case. No one threw a vase at anyone else's head.

I took a deep breath as the panic started to claw at my chest. It was like this for me. This way I handled the feelings, feeling like they were zooming out of control. That was my job at my house. Keep my sister, Raven, out of the parents' way. If they roped you into the fight, you were bound to become part of the battle. You'd have to listen to lectures and shouting, sometimes the same topic over and over again.

Sometimes when I was at the Burathons' house, I felt guilty that I was leaving Raven to fend for herself. She was so much younger that Mom would often be caring for her. Until Mom set her down one day and left, never coming back. The daycare Dad invested in was a priority for him afterwards. It was a considerable cost, but Raven really enjoyed it. She had a bunch of friends. I'd feel guilty trying to get her out early, because I'd be bringing her back to the house that was not relaxing at all. So, my sister was there more than she was with us.

You've got to handle your stuff however it makes sense. The shouts of Endgame and Austin brought me back. A place I never wanted to be. Never wanted to have to live in twenty-four seven ever again. Don't get me wrong. I love my family, but just having to spend time with them was exhausting. Not relaxing. As we've grown, we all have our peculiar ways of interacting. Because it wasn't healthy—all the fighting that used to happen before Mom left.

I heard smacking sounds followed by a groan. A door slammed again, and before I was ready, Austin stormed back into the room.

Tears rimmed his eyes. He had a very clear imprint of a hand on his cheek.

He held his open palm up. "I'm so sorry, kitten. This isn't cool."

I left the bed, letting the phone drop. I gently reached out my hand, holding it just above the mark.

"Did he do this? To you?" And then it was rage. Pure, unadulterated rage. The thing was, in my family you had to learn to fight. To stand up for yourself. To scream louder than everyone else sometimes, well, before Mom left and everything was quiet.

Austin grabbed my wrist and lowered my hand. "Don't worry about it, baby."

"He can't hit you. He can't." I tried to walk around Austin, and he put his hands on my shoulders.

"It's over. Nothing to think about." He stepped to make sure I was staying put.

"You need ice." I tilted to see the rest of his mark.

"I'll be fine. Let's talk about when your classes are. We can set alarms so we don't miss anything." He attempted to smile.

"You always try to take care of everyone else, huh?" I stopped trying to maneuver around him.

He shrugged. "Listen, you've seen a very carefully curated version of me, but here? In my world? I'm the draft. I'm messy. I make mistakes. I make the same mistakes over and over."

"I get that." I stepped backward and then moved to the bathroom.

I grabbed a washcloth and let the tap run cold. I heard the bed squeak under the weight of Austin sitting down.

Once the washcloth was wet, I wrung it out. When I got back to him, he looked defeated and I hated it. Hated Endgame.

I put my finger under his chin and gently lifted his face. I slowly applied the washcloth, holding it gently in place. He kept his eyes on the floor and spoke quietly. "You shouldn't have seen this."

"And you shouldn't have had to get naked and peel hundreds of Post-it notes listing my faults off walls, but here we are." I lifted the washcloth and flipped it, to get the cold again.

He lifted his eyes and stared at me. "You're not a little kid anymore."

I nodded. "Haven't been for a long time."

He covered my hand and took the washcloth from me. "Thanks, kitten."

He lay back and pulled on my arm so I had to crawl on the bed next to him. I rested my head on his chest.

I wanted this more than anything, but knowing that he and Endgame had fought took the filter off the dreamy fairy tale in my head.

AUSTIN FELL ASLEEP, and I didn't. I knew he was a heavy sleeper. It was a Burathon inside joke that you needed a bullhorn to wake Austin up when he was tired. When I pushed myself up to move, his breathing was deep and steady.

It wasn't my place, maybe, but Austin had been mine in my heart for so long, I had no other choice.

I slipped out into the living room. It had to be dinner time now. There was a low bass in Endgame's room, with the door closed. I gasped when I saw him sitting in the living room. There was a glowing orange tip tapping in his hand. The lights were out, but he was silhouetted enough that I could see him. Endgame.

I crossed my hands over my chest.

"Say what you're going to say." His voice was gruff.

"You hit him." Each word snapped off in my mouth like brittle branches.

There was a hollow laugh. It infuriated me more.

"Don't act like you know him. You've been here for a day." He put his drug on the coffee table.

I let my hands fall and took measured steps until I came right up to his toes. "I've known him my whole life. And you may be big. Hell, you could probably knock me out, but I'll make sure that there's a reason you're coming to the hospital with me."

"You're messing with shit you don't understand, little girl."

"And you're messing with the life of an incredible guy, asshole."

Endgame stood up and towered over me. And I was pretty tall. He puffed out his chest. "Maybe don't threaten a guy in his own place."

"If it makes you uncomfortable, move. I'm staying." I tipped my chin up and refused to look away. I wasn't a fighter anymore, but I knew how to fight with Mom. Thanks to my upbringing, I could go to war with this guy emotionally, physically, whatever was needed.

"Pfft." Endgame stepped to the side so he wouldn't touch me. He walked past me and opened and closed his bedroom door.

I glanced down to the mug, his cigarette still burning. It was reckless—that little act. Leaving something burning and not caring said a lot about a person. I lifted the butt and tossed it into the kitchen sink, letting water turn the embers black.

I was starting to think I was here for a reason. I might be the only person allowed to see this side of Austin's life, and it was scary. I sure as hell wasn't going to let him go through it alone.

4

Austin

I woke up and it was three a.m. I had a blanket tucked around me and Taylor was close by, her hand resting on my shoulder. The washcloth on my face was cold, so she must have replaced it recently.

I lay still, thinking about what had gone down with Endgame. From the very start, when I first laid eyes on him, I knew he was trouble. He was a mistake. He even told me as much. Of course, that made me more determined to fix him. To save him.

He was getting arrested when we first met. I was in the park, working with a model, one of my long-term clients who needed a picnic-themed shoot. All of a sudden there was a guy with face tattoos pretending to be my assistant.

"Um, do I know you?"

My model was perched on one of the large boulders the city had carted in for the park's landscaping.

"Just go with it, okay?" He leaned down and started to mess with one of my bags.

"Go with what?" I held up a hand to my model. The sunset was due to hit in just a few minutes and I didn't want to miss the lighting.

Just then two bicycle cops came on the scene. "There he is!"

As the man stood, I stuck out my foot and he tripped/sprawled on the ground.

One of the cops was on top of his back and the other wrangled out some cuffs.

The guy on the ground gave me as much of a dirty look as he could. "Thanks. You're a real stand-up guy."

And then when we caught each other's eyes, it hit. I knew. I knew I had known this man in another life. There was no other way to explain it. The whole world stopped breathing and slowed. One beat at a time, until his face was imprinted on my soul. And even though we didn't say anything else to each other, I knew I'd see him again.

And I wasn't wrong. When I got home and unpacked my stuff, I found what had to be a half a pound of cocaine.

The criminal had hid his stash in my bag. I set it aside in my closet. I wasn't sure how to dispose of it. I didn't have to wonder long, because that very evening, Mr. Criminal was at my door.

"You have something of mine." He lifted his eyebrow.

"I think it's a gift, being that you stuck it in my bag." I stepped back as he stepped into my place. I knew he was dangerous, but I

let him close the door to my apartment. "How come you're not in jail?"

He walked into my place like he owned it and sank into the chair. "Because they can't charge you for possession if you don't have anything on you."

"And did it occur to you that I could go to jail? Just because I was in the wrong place at the right time and you're a douchebag?" I'd be angry if it didn't feel like this man's whole being would fit into my own.

"Nah. They'd never test you. Look at you. You got nail polish on and half that stuff you're wearing is designer shit. You got money." He kicked his feet up on my coffee table.

"So what do you want?" I crossed my arms. Chances are that a guy carrying that much cocaine would have a...

He slid a pistol onto his lap. "Just need my stuff. Then I can get going."

I didn't know why I did it. Well, sure, when I was a kid, I'd had my share of haters. Bullies and stuff. Kids didn't take kindly to a difference. And I could French braid all the girls' hair by fifth grade and did so on the playground for Pokémon cards, so I had an ingrained instinct to make jerks' lives hard. Or harder if I could.

"Nope. Sorry. Fed it to the squirrels. You know, city rodents are really into that kind of thing. We can probably see the little disco balls from their rave from here if we look hard enough." I pointed with my pinkie out the window.

"I have a gun and you have a wise mouth. Not that smart, huh?" He stood up and walked to me.

I held my ground. In all the years I took beatings, I learned flinching or backing down made it worse.

The man put the gun to my temple. "You wouldn't be that stupid."

"You'd be surprised how stupid I can be." And then I leaned forward and kissed him.

Endgame and I had our first make-out session with his loaded gun pointed at my head.

If that wasn't a forewarning of times ahead, I didn't know what was. And now I was here, pretending to date my little sister's best friend to put distance between him and me.

There's not a friend I had that couldn't say I told you so. That they all told me dating a drug dealer—hell, letting him move in with me was a horrible idea.

God bless them, they put up with him. And some of them could even see it. The crackle between him and me. It bordered on hate. It could be confused for love. He'd hurt me so many times. Cheated on me more than I wanted to admit.

I allowed it to continue because I was addicted to that feeling. The freefall of danger. How wrong it was to let him in time and time again. To believe that he was changed this time. That it was real. The way he would act like I meant everything until he treated me like garbage.

Endgame had a horrible childhood. You couldn't even call it a childhood. He was hustling on the street while I was learning to ride a bike.

The backstory kept changing now. The only constant in them was him. His mother was a saint that was addicted or a narcissist that got off on hurting others.

I watched Taylor stretched out asleep. Bringing people into our homes was something in my DNA. My parents had done it before me. Because of them, I now had an adopted brother in Gaze and his girlfriend/fiancée Pixie was family as well. Ruffian, Teddi's boyfriend, was living with my parents now, too.

I sat up and ran my hands through my hair. Endgame and I had traded insults and hate, even coming to blows when he called Taylor a slut and slapped me. I punched him in response, and he smacked me back. It had been a first. Not the fight—that had happened before. Not the violence—that, too, had taken a dark turn I wasn't proud of. But the fact I was stone-cold sober when I hit him.

The fact I had defended Taylor had cracked him. Because all the times he cheated on me, I was loyal to him. He had not had to deal with seeing me with someone else.He probably thought he had a lock on my heart.

He did. That much was true. But pretend dating Taylor was freeing me up a little. Letting me breathe a smidge. Endgame was too much. Too much of everything. The way my loyalty was built and the way his self-sabotage was built-in had gone from a match in the worst way to poison.

He had slapped me and I'd punched him. Then he pulled me in hard and kissed my mouth. I kissed back before I regained my senses.

It was a tactic. Calculating. He knew that I was a sucker for the swing of emotions. I reacted to them. Endgame knew it took very little to push me from fighting with him to in bed with him.

I looked down at my phone. I hadn't plugged it in last night to charge. Four texts from Mom.

MOM: What's going on?

MOM: Why is Teddi so mad at you?

MOM: Oh no. Taylor? Is everything okay?

MOM: You need to text me or call me or your father and I are driving up.

I picked up my phone and called my parents while repositioning myself on the bed. Taylor didn't move.

"Austin Thomas Burathon, what in heaven's name are you doing up there?" Mom's voice was already shrill.

"Good morning. It's all fine. And Teddi is better. She's probably sleeping, right? So she didn't get a chance to fill you in."

I was doing my best to murmur, but despite my efforts, Taylor was rolling around. I reached out and stroked her hair to soothe her. A soft smile curled her lips.

"You're right about that. She burst into our bedroom and dumped all her concerns on us and woke us up. And I was pacing all night." I heard her harumph on the other end. "So what happened?"

"Taylor texted me that she was having a housing issue, so I stepped in. I learned it by watching you, so maybe you're not allowed to be angry." I glanced over to a drawer in my desk. I knew it had pictures of Endgame and me. They used to be displayed, back when he lived in this room with me, but now they were hidden under some junk mail and a few invitations.

"How is she? What happened?"

I filled Mom in on Taylor's situation and how my friends and I moved her stuff in at my place.

"Am I on speaker?" she asked.

"No. Regular phone, why?"

"That poor girl. You know she was always at our house because there was so much drama at her place. That she had to face all of that—I'm so glad you were there." I could hear my mother's smile. She was right. It was good that I had made sure Taylor was out and safe, but I was having severe misgivings about exposing her to Endgame and me and the wreckage of the relationship we once had.

"Yeah. She's a good kid. She'll be here with me for now. First, we come down from this whole debacle, then she and I can talk about alternate housing." I thought I saw Taylor's eyelids flutter, so I changed the conversation to dinner Sunday night. We were celebrating Dad's birthday, so I checked in with Mom on the menu.

"Oh, it's just hot dogs and hamburgers, but we'd love for you to make your famous mac and cheese. That's honestly all your father wants to eat." She sucked on her teeth. I was guessing Dad was in the room and she was giving him the business.

"That stuff is delicious, and I'm not even ashamed that I crave it."

"You got it, Dad. I'll bring Taylor with me, too." I didn't want to imagine leaving her here to deal with Endgame on her own. She was already getting over living with awful Roberta and her boyfriend. She didn't need to get into my issues. It was bad enough she'd nursed my wounds with cold washcloths last night. I slipped off the bed and padded into the bathroom. Under this bright light, the mark from Endgame's slap was still obvious. I wondered if I had marked him as well and snarled at myself when I got a little thrill that he'd have to explain it to any of his lovers in the near future.

See? Sick. Not okay. Not healthy.

"Okay, big guy, you take care of both you and Taylor and we will see you Sunday. I love you," Mom offered.

"Love you, too, Mom." After I ended the call, I brushed my teeth and washed my face. I was procrastinating going into the living room to make coffee because I didn't want to face Endgame. Not yet.

BY THE TIME I was dressed, and had a scarf around my neck, I felt like I either needed to have coffee or kill someone. I chose peace and opened my door. Taylor was still stretched in the same position, so I closed the door carefully.

The living room was a mess. Endgame was passed out on the couch, hand on the center of his chest.

Cigarette butts were scattered on the floor next to him. And that was a good night. The worst nights had drug paraphernalia and bottles.

He was broken. I knew he was broken. He could suck the life force out of any person he settled his laser focus on. I hated that he was still here. A testament to the fact I was still allowing him to dictate choices in my life.

I went to the hall closet and opened up a grocery bag. I needed to tidy this place before Taylor was up and about. I started gathering up the dishes and plates, then I moved to the plethora of rubbish around the couch. While standing over Endgame, I saw that he did indeed have a mark from our fight last night. A nice black eye on his left side.

His eyes opened, and he registered no surprise at my presence. He went from sleeping to perfectly awake.

"You the maid?" He scratched his chest.

"No." I wasn't getting into it right now. I had two meetings and a product placement ad to shoot. There was no time for a drag-out fight not even eight hours after our last one.

"Where's your new girlfriend?"

He knew where she was. I didn't answer; instead, I resumed placing the empty pizza box into the bag.

As I turned my back, I felt his hand on my hip. I stilled while he stood behind me. "You're just not going to talk about it? That's cool. You do you."

Endgame stepped around me but only removed his hand when he ran out of arm's reach. He didn't help put the dishes away. He didn't offer to run the vacuum. Just went back to his bedroom and closed the door.

I sat on the couch he just vacated. It was still warm from him.

I had to get him out. I had to make him move. Taylor being here was the only good excuse I could come up with. Even though I didn't like the idea of her roommate making her living conditions horrible, I was grateful to have a reason to evict Endgame. Because if it was up to me? He might have me trapped here forever.

5

W hen I got dressed this time, it was in my own clothes. My belongings were piled around my TV. It was still on the floor, long cord coiled like a snake.

Austin was at the desk in his room with his noise canceling headphones on. The screen showed at least ten people in their own prize screens. Both his meetings were on Zoom, so I did my best to sneak around the outskirts of the webcam's view.

After fussing with my hair and adding a smidge of perfume, I finally made my way into the bedroom. Austin looked at his image on his screen and I was reflected in the distance behind him. He spun his head and took in my outfit and hair from head to toe. I found myself holding my breath while I waited for his approval.

He gave me a nod and a subtle thumbs-up. *Why did I care?* I'd been dressing myself for years before I came here to live with Austin.

I waved at him. After I got my bag together, I slipped out of the bedroom and into the living room. Endgame was not around. I was grateful I didn't have to confront him, and before I knew it, I was on the ground floor of the apartment. The doorman tipped his hat at me. I nodded back because I had no idea what was expected. I felt around my skirt for pockets full of cash. This skirt didn't have pockets. I missed my pockets.

I knew a tip was customary—I just wasn't prepared with bills on the fly like this. Would I have to tip him every time I came in or out of the building? That could turn out to be pretty pricey right there.

The doorman didn't mention any compensation, and if I found out that I had inadvertently stiffed him, I'd make it right. I'd have to ask Austin about it.

My class was packed, but I was able to snag the seat of a student that got up the second the professor started lecturing. The anthropology class was instantly boring and mind-numbingly useless for my field, but credits were credits. Two rows down, I saw the back of a very annoying head. Roberta and her boyfriend, Peter, were slouched in their chairs.

I vaguely remembered her talking about switching her classes, that the chemistry professor expected too much.

The college had so many courses, I found it odd that she was in this very one. She pushed forward in her chair and put her head on a swivel. I dropped my gaze when she got near me. She was looking around, and then I put it together. She would pick this class because I was here. In her head, I bet I'd be doing her work for her and her dumbass boyfriend.

Maybe it was a jump and I was slightly paranoid, but as the professor went over the last chapter, Roberta shifted in her chair. Peter looked equally out of place.

After class ended, I tried to hightail it out of the lecture hall, but Roberta was standing at the end of my row.

I turned to go in the opposite direction, and Peter was on the other end. They both walked toward me, and the theory I had been thinking about seemed like more and more of a possibility.

"Your naked ass friends made a mess of my room." Roberta crossed her arms under her boobs.

"It was our room, and there's not a thing in the world that I do that you approve of. So maybe move on."

Peter started patting on the backs of the chairs behind me like he was playing a drum solo to a song that only existed in his head.

"My room. I never asked for you to move in." She sneered at me.

"That's not how any of this works. If you wanted a single, you should've asked the college for that." I had to take a roommate. Single rooms were an expense that was a luxury.

"Well, you need to pay me back for all the cleaning I had to do." She started tapping her long, pointy fingernails on her forearm.

"I do not." I put my messenger bag over my shoulder.

"All you need to do is study with me a few times a week. That's all you have to do."

"It's only fair," Peter spoke up behind me.

"I can't even get my head around how you can do the mental gymnastics to make that a normal thing to think." I realized that I was hemmed in by them, but I had long legs. I stepped over the back of the lecture hall chair, not caring if they saw my underwear as I made my move. Roberta reacted like I was an escaping pet guinea pig, skittering back out of the row to try to catch up with me.

I stepped over two more rows before moving toward the center aisle.

Peter was following Roberta's lead and trying to catch up with me.

The anthropology professor stopped his meandering pace out of the hall to watch us over the top of his readers. "Everything okay?"

"Yeah. She owes me money, so I'm letting her pay me back." Roberta had the lie ready really quickly. "The college is raising my payments because she dipped out."

The professor looked from her to me and back again. "Bill collecting is for another time."

He waited, and I glanced at Roberta before shrugging. "He's right. And I don't even owe you money, so we can just be done with this. And you."

Roberta and Peter stuck around long enough that it was beyond awkward before heading out the door.

My professor pushed his readers up. "Young lady, I've been around a lot of youths for a great length of time in my life. You didn't want to talk to them, of that I'm sure."

I nodded slowly. I didn't want to bring him into it, but I was really feeling angry that they had decided to be in my class right after I thought I had put an end to dealing with them.

"How about I walk you out?" He held out an elbow and I took it.

I couldn't predict Roberta other than she was like a mean dog with a bone—and they don't give up easy. Sure enough, Roberta and Peter were sitting on the small brick retaining wall outside the doors of the lecture hall.

Professor Quigby ignored them as he led me to the quad. Once we had enough people around us as classes changed, he offered, "It's easy to get lost in the crowd. You should be good. Please do be careful."

"Thanks, sir. I really appreciate it." Before the crowd could disperse, I threaded through them, not daring to look back to see where Roberta and Peter were.

When I got back to the apartment, I had to knock. Austin opened the door and waved me inside. He still had his headphones on and was having a very animated discussion about a spring line and the vibes he wanted a shoot to have.

I came through the apartment and set my bag down in his room. Then I sat right on the floor. I felt out of place. The last thing I wanted was dedicated bullies. I put my hands in my hair and rested my elbows on my knees.

I heard Austin end his call, then I felt his arm around me as he sat down, too. "What's going on, kitten?"

I rested my head on his shoulder. Without him, I didn't know what I'd have done. He felt like home. His comforting voice settled me.

"They decided to switch to my class and then waited for me outside the lecture hall." I looped my index finger around one of his leather bracelets.

"The Dickbag and the Douche wash?" He brushed my hair off my forehead.

"Yeah. She says I owe her money for damages and stuff. Plus, they want to raise her housing cost because now she has a single. I need to talk to the RA. I got that email this morning. College sucks." And as depressed as I was, being in the same room as Austin and having him dedicated to me was a rush.

"Okay. You're getting the full crew now. I don't like that they are still in your day." He pulled his phone out and started a group message, typing with one hand so he could keep his arm around me.

His phone started pinging with responses. "They're all in. Tinsley will set up a Google calendar with your schedule and we will make sure you're covered."

"Covered how?" I turned my head and rested my temple on my knee.

"Don't you worry your pretty little head. We got you, girl."
He set his phone next to him on the floor.

"I really need to make sure I handle my stuff. It's what makes
an adult." I was wondering how hard I could lean on these people
before I became too much of a burden.

"Baby, you met some of the crew, right? Damn near all of
them have had to deal with getting their ass handed to them at
some point growing up. That's the beauty of adult life—the
cliques of high school are done. You don't have to take it
anymore. We all make sure that we support." He pushed himself
up and held out his arms. I grabbed his phone, and with the other
hand, allowed myself to be pulled to standing.

I had been in Teddi's crew growing up. She was popular and
not a jerk. She dragged every single group in school together to
help with the kids with cancer charity, Me Party, that she
established.

But here on my own, I didn't have anything to do but get
angry by myself. I had to take this. Plus, Austin deciding to keep
me close was always on my to-do list.

"Hey, what's your classwork look like? Can you come home
with me this weekend?" Austin picked my bag up off the floor
and moved it to his bookshelf.

His handsome, earnest face waited for my answer. Like I'd
ever say no to him. "I can make it work. What's going on?"

"Dad's birthday. I'm glad you'll come. You hungry? I'm about
to grab lunch." He went to the closet and I was treated to a shirt
change. He was the kind of ripped a guy got from being really
physical, not bench-pressing all day. His tattoos were perfect.
They highlighted the muscles in his chest and arms. They were
also statement pieces.

Once he was covered, I realized I was just standing there like a
deer in headlights. I looked at Austin's face to see him grinning at
me. The crackle of him knowing I was checking him out made me
flush.

I tucked my hair behind my ears and then turned so he

wouldn't see my red cheeks. I started digging in my bag for my phone, but then realized I should just carry the whole thing as a purse. It had a charger, my money, my ID, and an umbrella. I took my laptop out and set it on Austin's desk.

After he slipped his shoes on, I watched him notice the computer. "We're going to have to lock that up."

He pointed to the big drawer in his desk and then went to a book on the shelf. He moved a book, and between the volumes, there was a small key. He tossed it to me and I snatched it out of the air.

I'd not even locked up my computer in the dorms with stupid Roberta. I waited to see if I'd get an explanation. I didn't. I was willing to bet it had everything to do with Endgame.

After my laptop was secure, Austin locked his bedroom door behind us. Oh, something was definitely up. Endgame's door was closed as well, but I could hear some low bass coming from deep inside the room.

Austin's eyes flit to the doorway and held for a beat, before he strode to the door and held it open for me.

I wasn't sure if we were asking Endgame to come with us. It was going to be tricky, because he'd showed up to help move my stuff in the Great Naked Migration. Was he part of the friend group? If they were broken up, why was he still living here?

Instead of asking those burning questions, I let Austin close the door behind me.

Austin

Taylor set her shoulders back and readjusted her backpack. She had questions, I could tell. Hell, I had questions. I was glad she decided to come to the birthday party so I didn't have to explain to her that she would never be able to stay in the apartment with Endgame alone. It just couldn't happen.

Endgame was not a good man. Not even close. Part of what drew me to him was the fact I knew I should stay away. I had to lock up valuables, for fuck's sake, because I had things go missing. Sometimes they would turn back up, but sometimes they didn't.

Endgame's "friends" were a dicey group from way back in the day. Some he met in jail, some he met selling drugs, but all were shit at making good choices. Taylor's rose gold MacBook Air would certainly find its way out the door.

The text response to my all-call about watching Taylor's back was heartening. I knew it would be, though. No one wanted to see a younger kid get in too deep. And the goddamn bullies could smell weakness. Not that Taylor was weak. Actually, she was a pretty tough kid, but without her friend group to rally around her, she would have to be adopted into mine. For now. I'd work on finding her a better living arrangement. Endgame just had too many issues to ask her to take those on while she lived away from home for the first time.

When I mentioned we were headed to the bagel store, I had a few replies saying they would meet us there. After I held the door open for Taylor, the smell of hot fresh bread hit me in the stomach.

"Best bagels in town, right here." I motioned to the menu. I'd pay for her stuff, even though I knew she'd fight me. When she was growing up with Teddi, Taylor always offered to pay her portion of whatever my parents had taken us to do. See a movie, go to a waterpark, etc. And even though my parents always said no, Taylor always asked.

She slid in next to the girls, and I leaned over the table to get her order. Hot chocolate and a sesame seed bagel with cream cheese were mentally added to my order. A few of the guys and I got in line and waited.

"What's she dealing with?" Caesar asked.

"That naked roommate still busting balls. They had a class together, and she and her boyfriend were waiting for Taylor after class."

"Oh, that's bullshit. So we all gonna take turns walking her to class? Because my weekdays are very tight." Caesar gave me a somber look.

Parker snorts. "Not too busy to get our asses to Bagel and a Roll for lunch, though."

Caesar grumbled, "Well, we all have to eat."

I leaned forward, closer to them both. "No worries. It'll be fair. And I'll see how much I actually need other people. Her schedule might meld with mine."

Caesar nodded. "You're all in on this one, huh?" He flashed toward the table that held Taylor.

"She's been a part of my family for years. She's like a little sister to me."

"I'm glad she's not like a sister to me, because damn," Parker offered.

I peeked over at her, trying to see her as if I didn't know her. Taylor was almost as tall as I was. When she was younger, she'd hunch her shoulders, but eventually she must have come to terms with her height. And now? Shoulders back, head high. High cheekbones and plump lips—she would photograph like a dream. Taylor was hot. Maybe it was the confidence paired with the classic beauty, but it was causing a stir. People in the bagel shop were gawking at her. Had I never noticed that before?

Parker lifted an eyebrow. "Thanking some gods that you aren't actually related now, huh?"

I contemplated the table.

"He'd never mess with his sister's best friend, right?"

Endgame. He'd got his ass up and followed us here.

Parker's happy face slid into a passive one. He pulled a chair over from a table nearby and straddled it. I hated him on sight. How his face and his edged tone called to me—I didn't know. Was there something that was the opposite of soul mates? Hate mates?

Taylor saw Endgame sit next to me. Her eyes flared with rage.

Parker tapped his fingers. "Just managed to be here when you don't normally see daylight?"

"I was hungry." Endgame reached over and grabbed half of my bagel, taking a bite.

Taylor excused herself from where the girls were chatting. Then she stepped up on a chair like it was a stair, then used the tables to get to our booth.

I held up my hand for her to take. She stepped down onto the booth's chairs and slid right between Caesar and me.

I turned my head so Endgame couldn't see and smiled at her. She reached over and took the rest of my bagel, broke it into a manageable piece, and then fed it to me.

I let her see my gratefulness for her outrageous behavior.

Endgame made a very disgusted noise and then pushed away from his chair. "Yeah, that makes me sick, so I'm gonna go."

I made sure not to watch him leave.

Taylor's defiant glare turned soft as soon as Endgame was gone. "You okay?"

She touched my cheek. I leaned against her hand. "Yeah. Thanks."

"I'm not a fan of his." She put her arm around me.

"You're not alone there, sweet cheeks." Parker held up his coffee cup as if to toast her.

They were right. I wasn't sure why I let Endgame keep this poison-tipped knife in my heart, but I knew it was still there.

6

Austin's friends were amazing, loud and hilarious. It took me back to hanging with Teddi and my friends from home. It was crazy how college and adult life divided us up. A lot of the guys had partners now, and holidays were spent visiting family more and less time with each other.

At home, during the semesters I went to community college, my life felt a little like a ghost town. Once I had secured my scholarship, I was excited to go to college. And honestly, Austin being in this city had glamorized it for me.

All Austin's social media was eye-catching and cool. I know now it was how he framed things that made them that way. On your own in this city was somehow the loneliest, most crowded place to be. When I had conversed with Roberta before the dorms, I thought she and I would be a great fit.

Obviously, we were not. She didn't share space well.

I watched Austin out of my peripheral vision as he pushed the rest of his food around. Endgame was wrong for him. Like super wrong. It reminded me of how I felt around Roberta. Outside, uncomfortable and self-conscious.

And it was hard to see a guy that wore a skirt on occasion and pretty much always had some sort of guyliner and nail polish on to be anything other than boss-level confident.

I met Parker's eyes. He was a good-looking guy, but I knew that his real attractiveness peeked under a camera. For whatever reason, a lens just magnified him in a way that made you want to look.

"You ever model?" He twirled a coin in his fingers.

"Me? No. I even suck at taking selfies." I left my coffee at the girls' table when I crossed the tops of the tables to get to Austin. I had nothing for my hands to play with.

Austin perked up. "You always look cute in pictures with Teddi."

I tried not to let the word "cute" make me feel like I was sitting in a high chair. It barely worked.

"She coming to the shoot today?" Parker flipped his phone up and thumbed at the screen.

"I'm sure she has work to do. She's in school full-time. Very dedicated," Austin responded before I could give a response.

"Yeah. Makes sense."

The table closest to ours dragged us into their conversation about music, but I had a nagging feeling that Austin had put a stop to something before it started. I'm sure it was wishful thinking, but it seemed a little like jealousy.

Austin

Freaking Parker hitting on Taylor right in front of me. Sure, he knew we were only pretending to date, but still. I wasn't sure why I snipped at him. He had noticed the same thing that I did. Taylor's face and body would most likely really bring lovely things to the shoot.

I was protective of her. She was Teddi's bestie that I had stolen from her dorm room. Draping her in clothing and setting her up with Parker for a sexy shoot just felt wrong.

But then my brain went ahead and did it to her in my imagination. She and Parker could look really special. I let that war die in my mind. Not everything was about making content for social media.

We all stood up and cleaned off the tables. Tinsley told us she had already set up a calendar and sent us a link to our email so we could coordinate with Taylor's schedule.

Taylor had another class. Fred planned to dress like a college kid and infiltrate the lecture hall so she could escort Taylor. Fred always loved cosplay. I guess even the slightly boring kind.

After we all said goodbye, Tinsley, Taylor, and I went back to the apartment so Taylor could grab her computer. When the girls were gone, I was left by myself.

Endgame's door was closed, but I could tell that he wasn't

there. He would stay gone for a few days. Just enough for me to start worrying about him. And there was plenty of reason to worry. When he went on a tear, he went to the lowest of lows. He would find his worst vices and wallow in them.

It was an endless cycle, and I knew it was all games and mind-fucks. It still worked, though. I needed to nut up and make him move out. My empathy for his situation always got the best of me. It was a quality I loved from my parents and siblings, but it had a dark edge to it when it was used against a person.

I hated myself as I pulled up Endgame's social media. And like I predicted, there was a vague passive-aggressive message posted while he was wearing his pink shirt. It was for me. Cruel pink because he only wore that color when he was intending on breaking my heart. And he knew I'd be looking. And I hated that he knew it and hated that I did it.

I needed to stop. He needed to be in my past. When the good was good, it was great. But the bad? It was the kind of shit that ate at a person's well-being.

The first time I broke up with Endgame we were both blasted in the club on 8th Street.

I'd heard from Caesar that Endgame had been dealing and was seen groping a very willing guy on the street.

We'd fought. We'd drunk. Eventually, I stormed out and visited Parker. Straight Parker had no romantic interest in me, but I knew his presence made Endgame jealous. Parker was a very, very good-looking guy. His muscles were almost anime-level crazy.

I'd sat at the table, a big round number at first by myself, then with Parker while he was on break from tending bar, and then the booth filled with people. I was quiet and Parker kept my drink full.

I wasn't texting any of my friends. I knew what they would say or do. Unfortunately, Endgame had hurt me enough times that they had all reacted before. Fiona would say she told me so. Tinsley would want to slash Endgame's tires, even though he didn't have a car right now and he had a suspended license for drinking and driving. He was a mess. He was making a mess of me as well.

It was near closing time when I locked eyes with him sitting in his pink shirt.

He'd found me. Not that it was too hard, Parker's bar was a great place to crash.

Endgame tilted his head. The skinny guy next to him was sucking on his tattooed neck like he was drinking blood. It would leave a huge mark, threaded into his ink. Then the tall girl next to Endgame leaned in and whispered in his ear. Endgame started French kissing her.

The last was a girl known for her hilariously public blow jobs. As she approached Endgame, I saw him toss a dime bag to her and point at his crotch.

She looked one way and then the other before sneaking under the tablecloth. I didn't need to guess what was going on, as Endgame tilted his head back. This was how he fought with me.

Not just words. Not just getting physical—he would fuck with my mind. He didn't even like girls, but he was happy to bribe this chick to do him. Right here.

And I should've left, never should have stayed, but I was stubborn. I didn't want Endgame to know he was getting to me.

That's how I ended up toasting him when he met my gaze. The kissing girl had dipped down to his chest and was lapping at his right nipple, his shirt fisted in her hand to allow her access.

Mr. Hickey was going to town as well. All bets were off as Mr. Hickey got to his knees and pulled his pants down.

I could see the feet peeking out from under the table. Endgame was getting a blowie in person while giving a guy a public hand job and having his nipples stimulated.

When he came, he started slapping the top of the table, making a show of it. "Fuck, yeah. This. I fucking love you guys."

And that was the way he sharpened his knives. He told them the thing that he should've been saying to me. That I had been pulling teeth for.

Blow Job wiggled out from under the table, licking her lips. I watched as her fist clenched and unclenched the drugs she had earned.

Endgame pretended to listen to the guy whose dick he was still holding, but his stare was on my face—gauging my reaction.

Parker stepped in between the death glares Endgame and I were shooting at each other. "You know he's a huge, huge douchebag, right?"

I bobbed my chin up and down. Oh, I knew the hell out of that information.

And yet I wanted him still. I wanted to fix him. I wanted him to prove that I was so valuable to him—he should never cheat.

It was toxic and it was apparently cyclical because that night in the club had been over a year ago and Endgame still had a place in my apartment, and a place in my life.

Taylor might be what I needed to move on, if my family didn't kill me for having her pretend to be my girlfriend.

THE REST OF THE WEEK, Endgame made himself scarce. In the group texts, he didn't respond when we made plans to eat at a restaurant. Night after night his bedroom stayed empty.

Taylor was a good roommate. She made sure to keep up with the cleaning and we helped each other cook. She didn't leave hair in the drain and made sure to run the vacuum a few times a week.

Roberta had been delusional. She had a jewel of a person to live with, and instead, she had scared Taylor away.

On Friday as Taylor and I were packing for the weekend to visit my parents, she showed me a text from Roberta and the resident director at the dorm.

"Mr. Peachpower wants Roberta and me to do a mediation." She poked at a link in the words and it launched her Google calendar.

It auto programmed an appointment with Peachpower on Monday morning.

"So you have to be back for that?" I pointed at her phone.

"I guess. I don't know what she thinks is going to happen. I'm not going back. I don't trust her, and I hate the nudity and the Post-its. It's just not happening." She tucked her phone into her pocket.

"I think that's the college trying to protect their asses. They have to make sure they offer all options so they can charge her more money."

"Well, now I feel bad. I mean, she's an asshole, but having her pay extra for a single is rough." Taylor added a pair of Converse to the front pocket of the suitcase.

"That's college, baby. If she wants the privacy, she has to pay for it. Not torture sweet girls until they run screaming in the middle of the night." I added a layer of packing cubes that included some of my more useful pieces.

"I guess." She added her hair dryer.

"No 'I guess' about it. She was making you pay emotionally, and that's not a currency you want to deal in." I added a pair of boots to the pocket with her shoes.

She got on top of the suitcase after I was done placing my stuff inside and sat on it. I had to maneuver around her bottom and legs to zip the super full case closed. I got two full finger brushes of the soft skin on her legs.

I looked up at her to apologize, but was instead met with her slightly parted lips as she focused on my mouth.

It stopped what I was going to say in my throat. She was beautiful. She was safe. She was a sure thing. I mean, I knew she had a crush on me. Had always known. But I had a flash forward of what a relationship between us would be like. She was too young for me, and I was too far in the real world for her to understand me.

Four years was a big age difference right now. I took a step back and nodded to show Taylor we were all packed.

Endgame was six years older than me. I almost smiled with the realization. At no point in our relationship did he or I worry about the age gap. But then again, I was the younger one and I actually cared about Taylor as a human being.

"Do you want to visit your house while we're back?" She hadn't mentioned any side trips even though we would both be in the same area as our families.

She tilted her head down and to her left. "No. I'm good staying with you guys."

I wouldn't press her on it and see how things panned out when we got there. I could take her for a ride if she needed.

Soon enough, we were leaving. I asked Tinsley and Parker to check on the apartment while we were gone. I also had a small security camera above the door in the living room. With my traveling schedule, I had to have a way to keep track of my stuff. And one of the byproducts was also watching for Endgame. When he came back. If he came back.

7

I'd been driving with Austin before. When we were younger and he was carting us around to all of Teddi's Me Party events for the charity. If I scored the front passenger seat, I was happy. I'd pretend that anyone driving by would think he and I were dating. And now, I was in that same position with us both pretending the same thing—well, in some company.

His parents and Teddi knew that Austin was pretending to

keep me from dealing with Roberta and Peter. No one here would think we were really coming as a package deal. I was immediately homesick for the apartment. There he would touch me more, stand closer to me.

The trip home had us swapping favorite songs, going from connecting from his phone to mine. We both added to our playlists. When we got to the Burathons', the driveway was already overflowing with cars. Gaze and Ruffian were playing basketball in the backyard. Gaze had been recruited as a second string NBA player, and Ruffian was just enjoying the game, even though he was good at it, too.

"Ah, my adopted brother and his adopted brother."

I had to laugh at the dynamics of it all. Gaze had been a foster kid in the Burathon home and they eventually adopted him. And then, while Gaze was still in college, his surprise younger brother showed up at the door.

Teddi, Austin's biological little sister, was now dating Ruffian. It made for some hilarious jokes about the family being related to one another.

A huge van painted with splashes of neon colors pulled up behind Austin and me.

"Well, that's it, kitten. We've got the whole shit show in here now. You ready to have some fun?" He opened his door and mine opened itself. There was a guy dressed from head to toe in cosplay.

"Splatoon?" I took a guess. His eyes widened.

"Why yes? Do you play the game?" He held out his hand and I took it. I watched as Austin and Milt, his middle biological brother, hugged and slapped each other on the back.

"I don't play. I win, Bama." I pretended to holster a gun. I knew these guys from all the time I had to squeeze past them on the Burathons' staircase. They were fun background noise when I had sleepovers with Teddi.

"We got a badass over here!" He pretended his hands were an explosion and a few of the friend group gathered around me.

The trunk on Austin's CRX popped open. The cosplay guys dipped in and took out our bags.

After a quick head count, eight guys scrambled out of the van. It was the crew I was used to seeing around. Milt traveled in a pack with his friends. They were all wildly talented gamers. We Play You Pay was their business.

Instead of hiring princesses to come to your kid's birthday party, you could hire We Play You Pay. These guys would come to the house all dressed up in a thematic character. They had Halo, Splatoon, and every Mario character you could imagine. All their elaborate costumes that they'd gone to Comic-Cons in were now serving as work uniforms. Teddi and I had filled in as Princess Peach and Rosalina a few times in a pinch. Seeing these guys at a party was awesome. They could do face painting and balloon animals, but they also would watch a kid play a video game and hype them up. Tips and tricks were shared. It was a hilarious adorable concept. We Play You Pay always pitched in when Teddi was granting wishes to kids in need.

"Are you all staying here?" I leaned closer to Bama so I could hear his answer. His co-employees were starting to chant and jump with Austin.

"Some of us. I'm going to be here. We have air mattresses, so there are plenty of places to crash."

I followed the crew of guys in and made eye contact with Austin on our way up the path. He asked, "You okay?" without using words and I replied, "I'm fine," the same way.

Ronna was at the door, hugging everyone that came in. She had on her paint splattered shirt, so I was guessing she had spent the morning refurbishing furniture. Mike was man slap-hugging the guys, too. When they got to me, Ronna hugged me for an extra beat. Austin's parents were the ringleaders of this open, loving family. It seemed no matter how many kids showed up at their dinner table, there was always a place setting.

"Hey, pretty girl, how's it going?" She leaned back a little so she could look at my face.

"I'm good." I mean, I was okay. Doing fine. Running away from my dorm was not as traumatic a thing when the end result was living with my dream guy.

"I'm glad you're out of there. It sounds like it was a hellscape." She put her hand on my forehead as if she was checking a kid for a fever.

Then Bama was up for his hug and I turned to Mike Burathon to get my hug. Teddi's dad was always ready to have a house full of people. Teddi screamed from the top of the stairs and jumped at me. Mike and I caught her at the same time. She kissed both of our faces over and over.

Austin came over and lifted her off of us like she was a misbehaving cat. She even did grabby hands as if she didn't want to let go. Gaze and Ruffian appeared at the top of the stairs, sweating and panting. Gaze had a basketball under his arm.

Ruffian took in the scene and then smiled. "Shit. I thought someone was getting murdered in here."

After Teddi set her feet down, she bounced up and turned around so she could give Austin a hug like a koala. He supported her with an arm around her waist, but continued talking to Mike as if he wasn't carrying a person at all.

"Made good time!" Mike leaned in to hug Austin and they smooshed Teddi in between them. She did hilarious jazz hands and acted like she was getting compacted.

Austin responded while keeping Teddi trapped, "We did. You know, go fast, pass on the right as Mom always says."

Ronna stepped in and swatted Austin's arm. "You know I hate that saying."

Mike and Austin responded at the same time, "We know."

She put her hands on her hips and surveyed the crowd. "Well, I'm thrilled I shopped in Costco yesterday. Everybody interested in a BBQ dinner?"

The cheers picked up again. The gamers started chanting, "Chicken! Chicken!"

She waved her hands above her head to get them to stop. "Any allergies? Vegetarians? Vegans?"

There were a few things mentioned and she pulled her phone out of the front of her shirt, where I assumed she was keeping it safe during her painting to take notes.

Teddi and I jump-hugged each other.

She was exuberant and gorgeous, as usual. "How the hell are you? I can't believe you're living with Austin. We need to have a sleepover. You're staying here tonight, right? Dad's making a fire, and Milt's guys are going to set up a blowup screen outside. It's too cold for the pool, but it will be fine anyway."

"You're making to-do lists in your head, aren't you?" I put my hands on her cheeks as I watched her rev up into her plan.

"Always. You know that."

We all herded upstairs where Ronna swung into mass feeding mode. We got assigned jobs and Teddi helped her mother dole out supplies and orders.

I was peeling potatoes for a salad and Austin stepped up next to me to join while the pasta cooked for his famous mac and cheese. We both used the peelers and saved the peels for the compost. I tried not to frame us as a happy couple visiting his parents in my head and failed. I had done it so many times over the years. When our elbows touched, I met his eyes and he winked at me. Just us in on our special secret.

When Peaches arrived, Teddi's whooping let us all know like an alarm.

Austin handed me a towel to wipe my hands. "Go. Do the thing. You know you have to."

I set down my peeler and did as he said before turning toward the front door.

Peaches and Teddi were jump hugging and I slid down the banister to join them. We all crumpled on the floor as I hit them like a set of bowling pins.

The laughter stopped us in our tracks. Peaches was the craziest of us all, but it felt super right to be together again.

8

Austin

R uffian and I watched as the girls flopped around on the
floor of the foyer by the door. Rocket, our slap happy
cocker spaniel, was getting in on the action, throwing her tongue
around like it was a gift.

"Wow. I can't tell if these girls are good for each other or
horrible." Ruffian took out his phone and snapped a picture.
Gaze put his arms around us both.

"Yeah, I have a feeling those screaming giggles will be with us all weekend." He tapped our chests.

"I don't know how I wound up with one of them in my place." I felt myself smiling at their antics. My sister's friends were a hoot. They were tighter than a camel's butt in a sandstorm and had a ton of inside jokes. Whenever Teddi had a whim, Peaches and Taylor were there to see that her dreams came true.

Gaze leaned down so I could hear him. "Yeah, so I guess Teddi told Pixie that Taylor moved in? How's that going?"

I turned to face my adopted brother and his half-brother. "She's easy company. Way easier than living with Teddi has ever been."

"Hey! I heard that!" Teddi and the girls had unwound their limbs from each other and she was now focused on him.

"Do you, for one second, think you're easy to live with?" I lifted an eyebrow. She would probably lie right now, but she and I knew she was a lot to deal with. In an amazing way, but still.

"Okay, fine. You got me. But that's your burden to bear, dear brother." She took the stairs two at a time and headed at me. I managed to swing her into a headlock and started to tickle her ribs.

"Oh no. Not fair. Not fair. You have those long spider fingers. No." Teddi went boneless, so I was forced to carry her so as to not hurt her.

Once I had her on the ground, Rocket took it upon herself to jump in Teddi's lap.

Mike and Ronna stood next to each other in the kitchen doorway. The house was just teeming with people.

"Do you think they have a vacancy down at the Holiday Inn?" Mike asked Ronna loudly.

"I doubt it." She swung the hand towel over her shoulder.

"Too bad. Because I think the only sane thing to do now is abandon this house and let these kids take it over." Mike snapped the tongs he used to flip chicken over on the grill at us.

I looked at Taylor after I released Teddi. Her smile was blinding. It went straight to the part of my brain that calmed me. It had been interesting getting to know her outside of being Teddi's friend and right-hand lady.

She was quieter. And lovely. She was truly so pretty. It was crazy seeing her like that now—after so many years of seeing her just as a younger sister figure. I felt a pang of concern over how wholesome she was. Making her deal with my Endgame drama bullshit was wrong. She didn't need to know what living with a drug dealer was like.

As I watched her take back up at the potato station, I started getting into deeper thought about how I needed Endgame out of the apartment. He hadn't paid rent—well, ever—but when he and I were dating, I could find a reason to support him more.

That was before he stole money from me. Before he cheated on me. Before our breakup. Now it would make sense to ask the grown man living in my apartment to pay his way.

I didn't want drug money either. I wanted clean money that he earned in a normal way. And with that guideline, I knew I was picking a future. Endgame couldn't do a regular job. He was a personality that only dealt in extremes. The amount of money he made dealing was too exorbitant, it would actually kill him to work so many more hours for minimum wage. But if Taylor was going to be around for a few months, I had to preserve her giggling, happy personality, Endgame had to go.

I had made a plan standing in my parents' kitchen watching Taylor swing her hips to the music Gaze had playing from his phone. And that made me want to make this weekend last forever. Because facing Endgame and ending whatever it was we still had was not something that would be simple or easy or painless. Not even a little.

TEDDI'S old bedroom had been the site of so many sleepovers in the past, it felt like old times. We had an extra air mattress, and Teddi and Peaches were on her bed. We had taken so many selfies together and recorded a few dances as well. This was how it was for us back then. Talking up a storm until we drifted off at ass early in the morning.

Teddi sat up straight. "I gotta go kiss Ruffian goodnight. Be back in a few."

Peaches held her hand out to me, and when I took hers, she pulled on my arm until I got up on the bed with her.

"No, seriously." She acted like we were already having a conversation. "Living with Austin?"

I buried my head under Teddi's pillows. Peaches started slapping my butt like it was a set of bongo drums. "Talk to me."

I flopped onto my side and eyed her. Teddi knew I loved Austin—well, had a huge dumb crush on him for as long as I knew her. But I didn't get too raving around her. Austin was her brother, it was creepy. But with Peaches? Oh, she knew it all. The stupid amount of times I created Austin and me in role-playing video games to get married and the times I micro analyzed pretty much anything Austin did.

"What can I say? My roommate was unbalanced. Like unsafe." I put my hands behind my head.

Peaches ignored my reason for moving in with Austin and got

73

to the important questions. "Is he that pretty all the time? With the suave and those flirty eyes?"

I gave her a slow nod as I slid my mouth to the side. "All the damn time. It actually hurts my brain. I wonder if I'll get used to it."

I picked at my nail polish.

"We've been around Austin for a billion hours throughout our lives. Neither one of us is used to what a smoke show he is. I think everyone is in love with him. Just everyone. What are his friends like? Is his bed comfortable? Have you felt his sheets on your bare skin yet?" Peaches got a dreamy look in her eyes.

I hadn't told her yet. I glanced at the door, and when I looked back at my friend's face, her eyes were wide. "You have?"

"No. Not yet. No. We kissed. But..."

Peaches screamed and hit me with a pillow. Then she straddled me and put her nose an inch from mine. "Kissed? Kissed!"

I covered her loud mouth. "Peaches Beaches Willmer. Stop screaming *kissed*!"

She started licking my hand and I had to pull it away. I wiped my hand on her shoulder. "That's disgusting."

Peaches got really quiet like we were starring in a horror movie. "Tell me everything. Please."

I bit my lips together for a beat before I unloaded on her. "So, so good. He smells so good. And his lips? So soft. And like, come on, you know how you feel his, like, stare in every part of your body?"

Peaches nodded and sighed like Austin was doing it to her in that second. "Yum."

"Light that feeling on fire. And then toss that in lava. And then have sex with it."

Peaches rolled off of me and exhaled like she had just had a powerful cigarette. "Sex with that man should be a protected sacred right. And we should all get a chance."

We were both silent for a few seconds. I was picturing wrapping my legs around Austin. It was good.

"I bet he's into, like, freaky stuff. Like things we haven't even heard of. He just seems too cool and relaxed, and God, I bet his power motor is long. And strong. We've seen him in gray sweatpants. You remember the gray sweatpants?"

She made her fingers act like they were walking down a set of stairs and added the pinkie from her other hand to be Austin's penis. It flopped and whopped around in his pants like it was trying to get out.

"The sweatpants. I'll never forget the sweatpants." I made my own fingers be the walking legs with the added appendage.

"Those sweatpants made a woman out of me. Remember, they were so low?"

"So low. The V. Fucks out loud the V." I made a V with my fingers.

"And that tattoo we didn't even know he had of the bird with the wings? Ugh. I wanted to lick it." Peaches snapped her mouth shut, cutting our reminiscing short as Teddi opened her bedroom door. She was all flushed and happy.

"My boyfriend makes me so happy, even my downstairs lips are puckering up." Peaches imitated Teddi's voice.

Teddi hopped onto the bed like no one was on it, landing cleanly in the small space between Peaches and me.

"What were you guys talking about?" Teddi looked from my face to Peaches' face and back again.

Peaches spoke up, "How we would both sell an organ for a chance to get railed by Austin."

Teddi made a gagging sound. "Ugh. No. That's my brother. You two are obsessed and always have been."

I had to offer at least a little defense. "Please. He wears skirts, nail polish, and eyeliner. It's not even fair."

Teddi stuck her tongue out. "I cannot even think of Austin with either of you. It turns something in my stomach. Gah. Let's switch the subject."

Peaches propped her head on her hand and gave me an elaborate wink, but asked Teddi about her newest program that was working on getting families in need lunches and breakfasts on the weekend. She pointed out that a lot of the kids miss meals when they are not in school.

Once we got her talking about her charities, she could plan/dream for hours.

I made sure to steer the conversation to her and Ruffian, and when that dwindled down, I grilled Peaches about her new major. Peaches wanted to be a police officer (for now). We fell asleep talking about how scary Peaches would be armed.

In the morning, we all woke up in Teddi's bed like a lump of puppies. These girls damn near raised me, and spending time with them made my soul happy. It reminded me that despite the crap that went on with Roberta, I still had these girls and always would.

After we struggled to get ready in Teddi's bathroom, we made our way downstairs. Mike's fiftieth birthday party was going to be an all-out banger. Between Teddi and Ronna, there were so many to-do lists that everyone could pick a few jobs and march forward in the planning without having to consult anyone.

I felt hands on my shoulders, and when I saw that the right one was littered with rings, I knew it was Austin. "What are you going to pick?"

He dragged his right hand down the list posted on the kitchen cabinet, index fingernail painted black.

"I don't know. Maybe pick up the paper goods and the balloons? The store that had the order was right next to my house. So technically, I could stop in and say hi. I'd have to borrow a car, though."

"I think that's a great idea. It's on the other side of town and we could pop into the deli on the way home to get the hors d'oeuvres. I'll drive if you think my car can fit the balloons." He leaned forward so I could see his profile with my peripheral vision. I nodded once.

That would be great except for visiting with my family. I didn't want to subject Austin to anything that would give him a bad impression of me. And with my family? He could definitely get the wrong idea about me. I'd avoid my house then. Seemed simple enough.

Once everyone started filing out to-do chores, I saw Teddi and Ruffian busy setting up some lawn games. Peaches was swinging on an old tire swing. The branch it was tied to dipped down low with every pass.

"What are you doing?" I paused on the front lawn.

"I'm security. Practicing for my new major and everything." She kicked off the ground to go a little higher.

"Peaches, darling. You go too high on that swing and it will snap like a Broadway star keeping the beat." He pointed at the struggling branch.

"Don't you worry about me, pretty man. I've got reflexes like a ninja and situational awareness that would make satellites look like pussies." She kicked off even more.

"We're headed out for balloons and stuff. You wanna come?" I tipped my head toward Austin's car.

"Nah. Thanks, though. The guys are popping by, so I want to be here to boss them around." She kicked her foot again, and the tire started spinning while swinging.

"Okay. Don't make yourself sick. I'm concerned. That's a lot of motion."

Peaches laughed, the noise funneling upward in a swirl as she moved quickly.

Austin held out his hand and I took it. "Let's leave her be. I don't want her getting all stirred up and then puking in my car."

He waved to a few people with his other hand, but firmly kept my hand in his grip.

Of course, he had done this in the past. And it had broken my brain for a few weeks after it happened every time. And now I had the extra distraction of knowing exactly what it was like to have him kiss me. I mean, he hadn't meant it, but it still mattered— changing things.

He opened the passenger door and shut it as soon as my legs were clear.

When he put the car in reverse, he slung his arm around my seat to get a better look behind him. He was so close I could see how immaculate his eyebrows were. He clearly plucked them into the flattering shape.

I felt the loss of the comfort of his arm when he switched gears and had us going forward. Every little thing this man did, I analyzed how it related to me. It was too much. It was okay to be a boy crazy teenager, but at twenty to be swooning over an almost touch was overkill.

It was hard to stop it, though. He was acting like a boyfriend and accompanying me. I knew he could have hung out with Gaze, Milt, Ruffian, and the gamer crew setting up decorations in the trees, but he picked taking me to the party store. I was an expert at reading too much into things when it came to Austin.

Teenage Taylor would have shined her braces in the drop down mirror and tried to get Austin to play some romantic music. Teenage Taylor was hopeless for this man. He was perfect for her, to her.

But having seen how Austin struggled with Endgame, I knew his life wasn't all perfect and drama-free.

"Whatcha thinking about?" Austin leaned into the right-hand turn at the very end of a yellow light.

"Nothing. Just making sure I keep the notes in my head." I tapped my temple with my index finger.

"Balloons and paper stuff? How many times are you reviewing that information?" He gave me a teasing smile.

"Listen, wise ass, it occurred to me that I didn't have a gift for Mike, and there is a craft store next to the party store. Maybe I can make something that would be appropriate." I stuffed my hands under my legs so I wouldn't pick at the polish anymore.

"It's fine. I can take you wherever you want to go, princess pants." He leaned over and tapped my leg. I felt the nerves shoot up right between my legs like a lightning bolt. This man's touch. I swear on all things good and holy, everything he did seemed sexually attractive.

He tapped the screen on his car and cued up a song. Crap. Now I was going to have a new favorite song.

I looked out the window so I'd stop stealing peeks at him. We motored for a few more miles, and then Austin had to drive down the road that ran behind my house.

When I was younger, if Austin had to drop me off or pick me up for anything with Teddi, it was always at the end of my driveway. It was really long. I never invited Teddi to my house, and she was understanding, and also never pressed it. Maybe it was that her house was such a hot spot of activity, she didn't get too curious to see my house.

Of course, she met my parents over the years. Weird times out in the store when we would run into each other, unplanned.

As I searched through the trees to see if I could get a look at my house, I saw movement along the side of the road.

"Stop!" I put my hand on the dashboard. Austin whipped his head in my direction.

"Are you okay?" He focused on the rearview mirror and then eased off the road.

"It's my dog." I flung open the door and hopped outside.

I made eye contact with Axel, my black Labrador. Normally, people would expect a dog to be happy to see one of his family members, but that wasn't the case with Axel.

His giant pink tongue was lolling happily out of his mouth. He had put on the brakes faster than Austin. He gave me a cautious look. Almost a challenge.

"Axel, come here right now." I pointed at my feet.

I knew things weren't going to have my desired outcome as he turned his head while keeping his gaze on me.

"Don't you do it." I took a step toward him, and soon Austin was out stepping next to me.

"Do you know this guy?" He squatted down. We were a few car lengths away from Axel.

"Intimately." I took another step closer. "His name is Axel, and if you look closely, you can see he's dragging his leash behind him."

Axel gave me a trepidatious tail wag because he knew he wasn't supposed to go joy riding around by himself. Axel had one hundred percent yanked his leash out of my sister's hand. I knew this because he had done it to me on plenty of occasions. Axel was amazing at throwing a wrench in a person's plans.

Once, instead of showing up for my shift at the mall on time, I had to call ahead to tell them I'd be late as I hung part of the leftovers from dinner out my car window to see if he could be baited into coming home.

"Your dog?" Austin tried clapping and snapping.

"Yes. This is one of his favorite games. Run away, find something horrible, roll in it, eat some of it, and then make me come and find him and bathe him. Come here, boy. You're a good boy." Axel stuck both paws out and his butt in the air.

"Playtime?" Austin stood next to me.

"Oh yes. Is this a busy road? Great. Axel will want to play tag, and we are it." I took a step closer and Axel twisted in a circle and barked.

"Does he play fetch?" Austin seemed to be asking me questions for Axel's first day of puppy daycare, not figuring out how to help grab this dingbat.

"Depends on his mood. Sometimes." I folded my arms and looked away. Sometimes if I pretended not to know him, Axel would forgo tag for jump up and slobber—another favorite.

Austin nodded. "Be right back."

He went into his car from the passenger side. He dug around under the seat and presented a tennis ball. He left the passenger door open.

Axel's whole demeanor locked on the ball. Austin noticed, too, and tossed it in the air.

Axel got closer. Austin tossed it up again. Axel bounced around like his legs were made of Tigger's tail.

Austin feigned a toss, and Axel was on his mark. He couldn't be fooled. If you didn't toss it, he wouldn't run.

I sidestepped in Axel's direction.

Austin spoke out of the side of his mouth, "On three, I'm going to toss it into the car. Then you and I are going to make sure to herd him in."

Austin counted it down and tossed the ball. I went to the back of his car and he went to the front. Both of us put out our arms to dissuade Axel from detouring to the road.

Axel hopped into the backseat like it was the easiest thing. He sat up and had the tennis ball in his mouth.

"You jerk. Did you drag Raven's arm out of the socket?" I reached into the car and petted his big dumb head.

Austin came close to me and let Axel sniff his hand before trying to lick him with the ball still in his mouth. "Oh. He's freaking adorable. I love Labs. They are such chaos."

Axel must have been toward the end of his jaunt because he was breathing really hard.

"I'm sorry, he's drooling on your seats." I had no way to clean it at all.

"No, don't worry about it. Making sure Axel doesn't become a pancake is totally worth having to detail the CRX." Austin made sure to block Axel's way out of the car, even though the pup was clearly tired. "You get in, and I'll close the door. Then once you have his collar, give me a thumbs-up and I'll get in the driver's side."

I did as he suggested, and as I gave Austin a thumbs-up, I realized that I was going to have to take Axel home. And it would be the first time any of my friends had ever been at my house. My stomach dropped to my feet. I was all of a sudden very, very concerned.

9

Axel's hot dog breath made me roll the window down a few inches. And that was some sort of a cue for him because he scrambled to his feet and put his head on my shoulder so he could sniff the air rushing in.

"I'm sorry. He loves car rides, only after he's pulled a *Shawshank Redemption*, of course." Taylor leaned closer to me and tried to force Axel's head back. He was still gnawing on the tennis ball I had in the car. I was pretty sure it belonged to him now anyway.

"He's fine. I felt like this shirt was too dry anyway." I headed to the next turn because that would take me on a shortcut to Taylor's driveway. That was a plus and a curse of being a licensed driver in a big family. I was considered part of the transportation solution for all the different social activities any of my younger siblings participated in, so I knew where everyone lived, but I had to visit those places a lot.

"It looks like he rolled in some burrs." I tried picking a few off his paw. They stuck to me and I had to shake my hand to get them to release.

"Oh, I hate those things. Rocket's fur eats them. And then Rocket absolutely hates to get them removed. The only people in my house that have the patience to get them out are my mom, Teddi, and me."

I made a few turns and signaled to pull down her driveway. It occurred to me that I had never seen Taylor's house in all the years we knew her. She was always ready at the driveway's end. That's part of why she was the favorite of my sister's friends. She said thank you and respected the time table I was usually on.

When I glanced over at her, I saw her tense up. She grasped the door handle like I was going off a cliff.

"You good? This okay?" I never wanted to make her uncomfortable. I just assumed that door-to-door service for Axel made the most sense.

"I'm good. And he won't walk now that he's tired. He weighs over a hundred pounds, so I couldn't carry him." She put a finger to her mouth and chewed on her nail.

"Okay." I slowed down. I knew Taylor had a younger sister, though I never met her before.

We passed a small pond and a few ramshackle sheds before the driveway ended.

"Sorry," Taylor offered. I gave her a look that I hoped was filled with nonchalance and lack of judgment.

Taylor's house was a hellhole. The stuff gathered around the property was the most random assortment of shit I'd ever seen in one place. This had to be a hoarder situation. It was a mess of rusted metal and furniture and appliances outside.

She opened the passenger door, and I noticed she was blushing hard. Even her ears were red. My heart went out to her. She was embarrassed to have to be here with me. I wish I could tell her I was just happy we could take her dog back. That was what was most important.

A preteen girl ran up to Taylor and tossed her arms around her. "You're home! I lost Axel!"

Taylor hugged her back and kissed her head. "He's a dingbat, and he's right there." She pointed at the backseat and Axel seemed to take that as a cue to hop out.

"Raven, grab his leash." Taylor pointed to where the leash was dragging behind Axel. The dog acted like he had been separated from both of his ladies for years. Full-on whining and jumping.

Her sister put her hand through the leash loop and wound it around her arm, obviously serious about keeping the wild dog close at hand.

"Where was he?" Raven stepped back and got on one knee. Axel was still the proud owner of my tennis ball. Raven took the dog's snout in her hands and kissed his nose.

"Running alongside the road. He has burrs, so be careful." Taylor pointed to Axel's front paw.

"Oh my gosh. You are going to be the death of me." Raven sounded like a grandma.

"Raven, this is Austin. He's Teddi's brother." She stepped to the side so I could wave. I watched Raven's eyes take in my longer hair and nail polish. Then she gave me a half-smile and a wave.

"He looks like a movie star." She stood up and walked closer to Taylor. "Dad is gonna kill me. You know what he said about Axel being a nuisance." Raven petted Axel, who sat next to her like a perfect gentleman.

"I know. And if he does take Axel to the shelter, I have a

microchip on him. They will call me." Taylor petted Axel right between the shoulder blades, where animals were most likely to get their chips implanted.

"You did that?" Raven's mouth dropped open.

I was surprised, too, but for different reasons. We had an Apple tag, a microchip, and a very elaborate dog tag on Rocket, and she didn't make running away her life's mission like Axel.

"I did. You have to keep it a secret, but I wanted you to know. Even if Dad takes Axel, I'll get him back. You just do your best here." Taylor put her hand on Raven's shoulder. "Where's everyone?"

"Dad hasn't come back yet." Raven turned her head quickly and I soon picked up why. Gravel was crunching under someone's tires.

Taylor groaned. "He's home. Go take Axel inside and see if you can clean him up."

As Raven wrestled the wiggly dog into the house, I caught a glimpse of the inside. There was a wall of what appeared like magazines in the foyer.

When I glanced at Taylor, she was watching me. This was a sore spot. I wasn't trying to embarrass her, but before we could discuss it, the man I assumed was Taylor's dad parked his car alongside mine.

He got out slowly and had to gather a few bags and an armload of mail. I leaned close to Taylor. "Anything I need to know?"

She silently shook her head. There was no prep for this or what this man thought of me. Did he even know that Taylor was living at my place?

"You home? I didn't know you were coming. Gas isn't cheap." He stopped and rocked back on his heels. He took me in from top to bottom. He flinched at some of my more perceived feminine choices. I was used to this. To guys like him. I never tried to fit in, so I was used to having people pass judgment on me. "Who's this?"

I stepped forward and stuck out my hand. My father had ingrained in me since a young age that men shook hands, so I always offered. It was also a nice secret way to throw any haters off-balance. I took my hat off inside, if I had one on. I held doors open for ladies and men. I could play a mean game of hoops. All the things about masculinity that I accepted. A few things. But they mattered to guys like this. Judgment passers. He did shake my hand, though, after shuffling his burden around to free up a hand. It was a hard shake. A warning shake. I held eye contact. He wasn't intimidating me.

"Yeah. It was last minute. Austin, my dad. Dad, this is Austin."

I watched her swallow and then saw anger flare in her dad's eyes. They were having a silent conversation. It had to be about the condition of their place. It was obvious there were struggles going on here.

"Mr. Boland." I made sure to use Taylor's last name to greet him.

Taylor offered, "We were just leaving. I had to drop off something."

She was keeping it vague. I didn't add to anything. Her father didn't hug her. He just nodded.

And then we were headed back to my car. I held the door open for her and she collapsed on my side. I saw that Raven and Axel were waiting at the screen door.

After I got to the driver's side and sat down behind the wheel, I looked at Taylor, who had her head in her hands. "Can we just go? Please. That's not anything I ever wanted you to see."

I reached out and put my hand on her shoulder as I backed out of the driveway. "Kitten, you've already seen my secrets. You have nothing to worry about."

Taylor peeked over her fingertips at me, so I refocused on her. "You sure?"

I felt my empathy rise up. She was nervous. I could tell from how she was clenching and unclenching her fist.

"Yeah, baby. I've got you. You don't have to be afraid of anything. We can talk about it, not talk about it. Whatever you're on board for, I'm here." I downshifted and headed in the direction of the party store.

"Thanks. That means a lot." She took out her phone and I glanced at her screen as we waited at a stop light. *Dad* was the main texts she was responding to. I didn't try to read over her shoulder, though. She'd already shared more of her privacy than she was comfortable with.

She was pensive in between texts. When we got to the party store, she was out of her side of the car before I could help her, and that was fine. It was nice to have something to focus on together. Teddi had instructions on what to purchase and I put it on my card.

"Can we pop in there?" We were at my trunk, putting away the balloons and plates. Luckily, Teddi used balloons in a ton of her party prep for charities, so we had tons in the shed. The guys would fill the balloons when we got there. That would give us room to ride in the car.

Taylor was looking longingly at the craft store. I shrugged because we were probably cutting it tight on time after dealing with Axel, but I took an encouraging step anyway.

In the store, she found a giant five and a giant zero. "I bet I can use Teddi's craft stuff to make something cool out of these."

We stood in line. I put my arms on both shelves on either side of us while we waited in the long queue. Taylor leaned back against my chest. I turned my face toward her and kissed her cheek.

"It'll be okay, baby. Just relax."

She nodded, her hair moving up and down on my shirt.

After putting her items onto the checkout counter, I opened my wallet. "I've got these."

Taylor shook her head no and whipped her credit card out of her pocket. "No, you don't. This is my gift to your dad. I have to pay for it."

I tried to outmaneuver her and jab my card into the slot before she could, but she was quicker. The cashier snorted. "The two of you are too damn cute together. When are we getting you in here for wedding supplies?"

Taylor declined the bag and shook her head.

I wasn't sure what compelled me to do it, but I answered, "As soon as I can get a ring on that finger."

I put my arm around Taylor's shoulders. Her face and ears were red again, but I was confident it was the kind of color that didn't hurt her essence.

10

I started sketching out the rough draft of what I was thinking for Mike's present on the number five. It was a cardboard, hollow character. I was hoping I could get something decent done in time to gift it to Mike at the party.

I tried to block out that Austin had seen my house. Met my dad. Met my dog and sister, too. But most importantly, he saw where we lived.

The Burathons were not rich, but they didn't ever want for anything either. They had new cars, and all the kids got cars. Their holidays were ginormous displays of affection and spoiling.

I had it different. We were living in the house that my mother's parents gave to her when they went into a retirement home together. It was in poor condition. There were so many things wrong with it that getting started seemed fruitless. My room was spotless for as long as I could remember. I didn't know when I got obsessed with keeping my space "normal," but it was a clear decision I made very early. Mom liked to joke that the nurses switched me at birth for someone else's kid before she left.

Having the house be the way it was gave me enormous stress. Living there was pretty rough. If I tried to move my need to clean outside my room, my father would have a fit. He would say I was ungrateful when I scrubbed the kitchen counter cabinets free of their years of slimy grim.

Dad seemed to buy into the delusion that if we didn't have people over, or no one saw how we lived, that we didn't actually live that way.

Raven did her best. She was not a clean freak like I was. She was also content to stay home while I had the exact opposite response. I tried to get away as often as I could. I noticed she liked to spend downtime in my room. Maybe the lack of chaos soothed her.

Peaches entered the room, back from her jaunt with some of the boys to secure alcohol. She tossed her bag onto the floor and did a flying belly flop onto Teddi's bed with me.

"I saw you and Austin left together. How did that go?" Peaches leaned over me to grab a green ink pen. I really enjoyed trying to draw, but Peaches was talented at it. She was doing a quick sketch of Mike with a birthday crown on in the zero.

"Well, when we were driving past my house, Axel was running down the road so we had to save him and take him home. All the way down the driveway." Imagining my house through Austin's eyes gave me a deep wave of shame.

"All the way?" Peaches stopped drawing and stared at me.

The funny thing about being kids is the unspoken stuff feels really weird when it is spoken about finally. Peaches knew I didn't have people over. I didn't have people drive me to my door. So although we had never discussed it, she knew this was something that was an issue for me somehow.

"Was your dad there?"

"He wasn't and then he was. He and Austin shook hands."

Peaches flipped on her back and studied the ceiling. "Ugh, he met your dad. That's right out of our middle school dream journal. Remember when my mom found that book and forbade me from pining over a dude in a skirt?"

"I do remember that. And I remember you standing up pretty strongly to your mom."

Peaches nodded. "And you know what else? Mom saw Austin like last month mowing the lawn and she came home and said, 'I get it now.' Such a hypocrite, but then again, maybe it's best that Austin was an adult when she noticed this."

"Yeah, it's one hundred percent more acceptable that way. I don't know how it's going to go down when I go back home in the future. I think Dad was more insulted that I didn't come and stay at the house when I was in town. Mostly, I just wanna make sure Raven is doing okay. She was pretty shaken up that Axel had run away."

"Isn't that like Axel's main focus every day besides eating dinner?" Peaches twisted her torso so that she could draw again.

"Oh yeah. He absolutely loves to eat his dinner and find something disgusting to roll in outside." I added some balloons.

"Well, I hope she's all right. How old is she now?" Peaches switched up the pen from green to brown.

"She's going to turn thirteen next month." I added a few slices of cake to the five.

"Tough time of life. Those teen years are brutal." Peaches put her pen in her mouth, pensive.

"Hell yes. And she doesn't have a Peaches and a Teddi right

now. All she has is Axel since her bestie from elementary school became a jerk. So now she's headed into high school next year and having to figure out a whole new circle of friends. I wish she and I had been closer in age so I could help her through that." I noticed all the empty space on the five and the zero and then inspiration hit. "Hey, we should get everybody to write a sweet note to Mike on here! We can get as many people as we can before the gifts are passed out."

I ran my finger over the inside of the zero. This was the perfect use for the giant five and zero balloons.

"We can hide it in here and make sure Mike stays out. Perfect." Peaches put a few squiggly hairs peeking out from under Mike's party hat. Then she dumped the pen she was using back into the bin where she had taken it from.

Path decided, we set the five and the zero up on Teddi's bed with the tools of the craft close by. Peaches had the foresight to add a layer of paper underneath so the ink that was used wouldn't bleed onto her comforter.

"We getting dressed up for this or what?" Peaches strode to Teddi's closet and flung open the door. I'd lost count of the amount of times we had dressed from either Peaches' closet or Teddi's throughout the years.

Even though we were different heights and sizes, we were always able to make things work. I had brought a long black tank dress that I was planning on cinching at the waist with a thick corset belt, and I was totally interested in stealing a set of Teddi's fancy flats to complete my outfit.

Peaches seemed more unprepared to actually stay over. She even had to borrow a bra because she had workout clothes on. The sports bra uniboob was not working with any of Teddi's V-neck shirts or dresses.

"And here she is now." I gestured to the bedroom door as Teddi knocked and then opened it.

"Hey, ladies. What're we cooking up?" She put her bags from a local boutique next to Peaches' bags.

"The big five-oh. Literally." I explained my idea to Teddi and she instantly assimilated the coordination it would take to complete the job into her soul. I almost felt guilty knowing that by bringing it up, she would put all responsibility for getting the signatures from the party attendees on her shoulders.

"That will work. The boys are downstairs playing basketball. So maybe while I get dressed, you guys can see if they want to get their notes out of the way?" Teddi finished the last bit over her shoulder and she walked into her closet and closed the door.

I grabbed the five and Peaches nabbed the zero. We both had a fistful of colorful markers. The hardest part would be keeping it hidden from Mike. When we got outside, the pickup basketball game in the backyard had stopped all progress on the decorating.

I heard Peaches sigh. "Skins versus shirts. My favorite teams."

Austin was on skins and I let a small sigh slip as well. Boys playing ball was so cliché. But the ebb and flow of the game was hot, and they didn't even know it.

I hugged the five to my chest while I watched. Austin was dribbling the basketball while planning his attack. Gaze was on his team and Ruffian was on shirts. I noticed a few guys we hung out in high school were here as well now. The good news was everyone was crowded around the court, so we could get the signatures and good tidings. The double good news was Mike was nowhere in sight.

Peaches leaned against my arm. "Are you seeing this?"

I nodded. Austin was in low slung black jeans and high tops. He had a thick chain with a lock around his neck. His guyliner was smudged and running a little low, too. His hair was held back in a messy bun with a flower scrunchie.

"I don't remember that many tattoos on that manscicle before." Peaches pointed a dreamy index finger at Austin.

"Just the butterfly is new." I knew his tattoos better than I knew my own beauty marks.

The butterfly stretched on his lower chest. It was mostly a sketch. Not much color on the image.

I watched the muscles in his back flex as he passed the ball to Gaze. Gaze plucked the ball out of the air like his hands were magnets and the ball was metal.

Ruffian tossed up his hands as Gaze dunked over his head. "This is ridiculous. He never fucking misses."

Gaze bit his smile and then gave Austin a side glance.

"Y'all are working against me."

Things were getting heated. I'd seen this before when Gaze played ball. He was insanely good at the game. Ronna pushed her way onto the court with snacks and drinks. It was clear she was picking up the switch in the vibe. Moms of boys knew the signals to look for, I guessed. Austin grabbed a water bottle and let it run over his forehead and face, then he splashed it on his chest.

"Oh, that's not even fair." Peaches rolled her eyes.

Austin caught my eye and then jogged over to me. "How are you?"

Peaches was making herself scarce. "Me? I'm good." I held a marker out to Austin and put the five on my forearms like they were a table. "Is Ruffian really mad?"

Austin clicked his tongue while he started drawing hearts on the five. "He's just salty because that's like the third time Gaze has dunked on him. I feel bad for him. He hasn't had as many years of having Gaze make an absolute fool out of anyone that plays a game with him as I have. It builds character. He'll get there."

He added his name and a sweet message to his father. I held the five with one hand and waved my other hand in front of his words to dry them.

I didn't add to the conversation because my mind kept replaying my house's front lawn with the rusted appliances on it like a horrible commercial.

Austin caught a towel that was thrown over my head and used it to wipe his face. Then he used the cover of the towel to wipe his eyes. He gave them an expert pirate smear by accident.

He put his hand around my waist and looked deeply into my

eyes. "No, really, I just want to make sure you're okay. You seem sad."

I stared into his gorgeous eyes and felt my heart thumping in my throat at being this close. This touchy-feely in front of the whole damn world.

But my pride was also on a tightrope. "I keep my room really neat. Like super neat, so you don't have to worry..." I let my sentence trail off. Maybe he was concerned that what he saw was how I'd live.

He touched his forehead to mine. "Baby, it's okay. I'm literally just concerned about how you're feeling. Crap, I know having people come over wasn't something you ever wanted. And then when you moved away, you had your stupid roommate. That's a kick in the pants."

I started feeling my eyes well up with tears and my nose getting congested. Austin was going to make me cry with his understanding and empathy.

"Don't. Oh God, I've fucked you up. I'm sorry." He pulled me next to him for a side hug. His body was warm from playing basketball.

He gestured to one of the guys on the sideline. The guy ripped his shirt off like it was on fire, ready to sub in for Austin.

I pulled back on my emotions and somehow cleared my tears without letting them fall. "Don't stop playing. I'm good."

Austin smiled at the good-natured ribbing that Ruffian gave him as he walked toward the back of the lawn with me. When we had distance, he turned and put his hands on my shoulders. Did I ever even have a shot of knowing Austin without having a crush on him? He was so touchy. And brutally hot. My heart never stood a chance.

"Seriously, we can totally go. I know this has been a lot. This morning and everything." He rubbed my shoulders.

"I just can't believe you saw it all. The way it is. It's just been a thing I hid for so long. I mean, that was not normal." I waved a hand at the Burathon residence. "You come from this. Normal.

No dishwasher collection on the front lawn." I choked out the last few words and closed one eye. Austin had seen my deepest fear: knowing how we lived.

"When I saw your place, all I had was concern for you. I can't believe that karma put you in such a shit dorm setup as your first time away from home. You're a great kid and deserve straight happiness." He gave me a half-smile.

I tried not to let the blow that Austin called me a kid show.

"Meh. That's debatable. Teddi is a superhero. The rest of us are just trying to catch up." I moved the five behind my back, which in turn pushed my breasts in his direction.

"You know what's interesting? The whole time I've known you, which is a very long time now, I'd have one hundred percent described you as being a sweetheart. A motivated, community-minded sweetheart. And that's just for the sheer amount of times I saw you leaning over a plan for a Me Party with Teddi. You never let her go it alone. Her friends are a huge part of her productivity."

I got that, I really did. But if there were no Teddi, I didn't think I'd be nearly involved with charity. I mean, Teddi allowed us to participate on such a level that I could probably run my own charity now if I wanted to.

"Thanks. I just kind of want to curl up in a ball." I pulled the five around and hugged it.

"We don't do that. Not when we have each other." He gently bopped me with his elbow.

I'd believe anything this man said right now. Topless and smiling at me in a very we-have-a-secret way.

"Okay. That sounds like the way to go." I turned and faced the basketball game, feeling reassured that Austin didn't see the worst I had to show and now hate me.

"Axel is very much going to run away again, isn't he?" He took a step toward the game.

"Oh yeah. For sure. Probably tomorrow with as far as he got this time." I rolled my eyes. I loved that dog, but he was work.

"Let me see what my lease says about dogs. Would that make your sister's life easier?" He grabbed my hand and we moved faster, both with our feet and my pounding heart.

"I think so. She loves the dog, but the stress of walking him and keeping my dad happy are a little much. I can ask her what she thinks. It'd be great to give her a break at the very least. Are you sure, though? That dog is bonkers." I felt my heart lifting. I'd love to have Axel all the time.

"We have Rocket. Cocker spaniels and bonkers go hand in hand."

When we got back to the crowd of people watching the game, he squeezed my hand once and then lifted it to his mouth to give my knuckles a quick kiss. No one looked at us twice because Austin was affectionate with everyone. But I felt that kiss feed my hopeful heart. Again.

Austin waded through and waved a hand at Fred, who had arrived so Austin could take his break. Then he was back in the game, trash talking the shirts and winking and blowing kisses at people on the sidelines.

He was made of swoon and sex. I loved him so much. He could never know. Teddi could never know.

I caught Peaches' eye and she was giving me the thinking Kermit the Frog smile. All my secret thoughts were right on my face, and she could read them easily. With that, I heard a car door slam. My ex from high school, Brutus, and his crew of friends had just shown up.

11

Austin

Maybe it was being the eldest brother, but I always kept tabs on who was dating who in Teddi's circle of friends. I wasn't a hater of her having a relationship or anything, but I took the job of being her confidant seriously. I used my networking and people skills to make sure there wasn't anything too horrible headed in my sister's direction. Of course, she ended up dating a criminal anyway.

I knew Taylor had dated Brutus. They had broken up on a Me Party weekend, so it had been a group event. I remember being impressed with how Taylor handled it and less impressed with Brutus. He had pouted and stomped around while we all worked to help Teddi make a kid with cancer's day.

I missed a chance to block Gaze's shot, so I tapped out. Once I had a replacement, I went to the water jug Mom had filled on the picnic table by the court.

Taylor was focused on getting the signatures on the number five. Brutus hit his friend and pointed to Taylor. I took her in again as if I was her ex-boyfriend. Short skirt and red lips, she was aging well. Too well.

I splashed some of the water onto my face and wiped my eyeliner off of my cheeks. Peaches flounced over and pulled on Taylor's arm. They gave each other a knowing look.

Ruffian joined me at the water station and took a long swallow before rubbing his face down with a towel. "How did decorating for a party turn into a basketball tournament?"

I laughed. "Because we're all great at procrastinating. And your girlfriend can plan an entire party in her sleep."

"That's for sure. She's way overqualified for a fiftieth." He sat down so he could watch the game.

I stayed where I was so I could watch what was about to go down now that Brutus was here.

I knew Taylor was powering through, but me having been at her house had rattled her. Hell, it rattled me. I felt embarrassed for her, knowing she had expended so much effort growing up to hide how her father lived.

Brutus and Tasker, another one of the football guys Teddi knew in high school, whipped their shirts off as they walked closer. Tasker had a little belly going, but Brutus was ripped in a way that made me think he was dipping into some chemicals to get buff.

Ruffian snorted under his breath. "Looks like some guys from the past found their way here today."

"Seems like. Once the word gets out, you know how it is."

Taylor clutched her pen and number as Brutus came close. He leaned down and kissed her on the cheek before whispering in her ear.

She squinted at him and gave him a forced smile. I was headed in her direction before I had consciously made a choice to get involved.

When I was close, I put my arm around Taylor's shoulders. She shot me a grateful look.

"Austin, good to see you, man!" Brutus slapped me on the shoulder.

I lifted my chin at him.

"You guys here for the game or the party?" I didn't take my arm off of Taylor.

"I guess both. Once the guys started posting about it, we had to swing by." Tasker was bouncing on his toes and stretching his arms.

Brutus' gaze lingered on my arm. I let it stay there so he would have questions. Man code was such that if he thought I was involved with Taylor, he would back off. It was a pecking order. To all of Teddi's friends I was an elder.

He would not move on her if he thought I was in her life like that.

Taylor leaned into me and rested her hand on my chest. Oh, this had been a very good idea then. She wanted to convey the image that we were together as well.

Teddi appeared on the porch, dragging a sound system out with her. Dad's favorite albums were actual vinyl albums, so she was rigging a system to play them outside.

She took in the backyard and stopped at Taylor and me. I gave her a little wave, then watched her skim the crowd until she saw Brutus. Then Teddi gave me a subtle thumbs-up. Brutus and Tasker got tapped into the game and we watched as Gaze made sloppy suckers out of them both.

"Thanks." Taylor patted my hand.

"He and you ended a little hot if I remember correctly?" I stepped away from her now that the guys were playing ball.

"A little. He's dropped enough dick pics into my DMs to make me Pavlovian gag when I see I have a message from him." She admired her five, and Peaches smacked her zero next to it.

"This is literally the cutest gift. So freaking adorable."

Both Peaches and Taylor hid the numbers behind their backs when Dad made his way out from the garage.

The crowd had been coached on "Happy Birthday" that they shouted together. The basketball game tapered off as Mike gamely got the grill started. Gaze and I took over grill duties. We worked together as the dusk set on the day and the fairy lights that Teddi was so fond of illuminated the backyard.

Ruffian and a few of the guys started working on a bonfire in the back. A few girls had their feet dangling in the pool, even though it was too cold for a swim.

While Gaze and I flipped the burgers and the hot dogs, we made sure to keep the vegan options separate on the grill.

Ronna and Mike mingled with the guests. Although most of the people were young, they had a few of their friends as well. One of Mike's friends was opening a brewery downtown, and he brought a keg of his homebrew recipe that was due to be the flagship drink.

Teddi made sure the music was flowing and the vintage sounds of all of Mike's favorites filled the air.

Presents were opened throughout the night, and Taylor's last-minute idea was a huge hit. After flipping the last few burgers, she came close again. I watched as Brutus had his third beer.

"Did he drive here?" I pointed my spatula at her ex.

"I think it was Tasker, and he's only had half a beer. But we can make sure." She started tidying up the area that Gaze and I were using as a buffet table.

"Yeah." I didn't like how often I found Brutus staring at Taylor. It was like he was psyching himself up for something.

After smothering the charcoal, I wiped my hands on a towel.

"Between sweating for the game and cooking over the hot grill, I need a shower."

I ran my hand down the front of my chest. Her eyes followed my fingers.

"Just hop into the pool." She leaned toward the cool water.

"I hate swimming alone. You down?" I bowed to her as if we were at a formal dance.

"I don't have a swimsuit. In fall." She shook her head.

"I didn't bring one either." I set the spatula down and poked at Gaze.

"No, man. Don't." He seemed to already know what I was getting into.

"You go, I go." I started running toward the deck.

"Dammit." Gaze came running next to me. We both took a running shallow dive on either side of the girls that were sitting with their feet in the water.

The cold water was a slap. My brain saw white. I hopped up and the girls on the deck were screaming at the splashes that must have drenched them when Gaze and I hit the water.

I dunked under even though it was a shock, the sweat and grill grime coming off me.

Gaze splashed me when I surfaced. "You're a dick for using that one promise a million years ago against me."

I heard a scream and observed Brutus grabbed Taylor in a fireman's carry. I saw where he was heading and his giant meathead could only do one thing. Toss a girl into the pool, even though she was kicking and slapping him.

I dove under the water so I could get to her just as she hit. When she surfaced, she covered her chest. Her outfit was now completely see-through.

I held out my arms and she walked into me. I had no shirt to offer her, so all I could do was give her my body to help her preserve her modesty.

"Brutus, you're an asshole." Peaches was beating on Brutus

with a towel. He was laughing with a red face. He shot his shot, and it was the wrong move.

She was shivering in my arms. Teddi was at the edge of the pool with a towel for Taylor and a middle finger for Brutus.

"I can't get out." Taylor's mascara was smearing on her cheeks.

"You can. Just wrap yourself around me and keep your chest against mine. We'll get you out and no one will see anything." I felt her legs lock behind me. I kept an arm across her back so that there would be no space between us.

I walked through the water and up the stairs with her on me. Teddi wrapped Taylor's shoulders in a rainbow towel like a shawl. I still didn't put her down. I wasn't taking any risks. I walked her right into the house and up the stairs. Mom hollered after me that we were tracking water through the house, but I knew once I explained what happened, she wouldn't care.

I got her up to Teddi's bedroom before setting her down on her feet. I pointedly closed my eyes so she could have privacy.

I heard her teeth chattering and started to feel the chill myself.

"I'm covered." Taylor had rearranged her towel so it was wrapped around her.

"You okay? You want me to go out there and stuff Brutus' balls up his asshole?"

Taylor's laughter felt like a reward. "He'd probably like that. He was weirdly obsessed with his balls."

"He's drinking a lot and can't stop staring at you." I unbuttoned my wet jeans. I was going to shower downstairs, but the denim was digging into me now.

She swallowed hard. "He's not good at letting go."

"We can make our boyfriend-girlfriend act be a traveling show, if you want. I know he won't touch you with me here. Not that that's fair, just your words should be plenty. But if you aren't in the mood for a fight, it's an option."

"I think that would be preferable tonight. Just take him out of the equation." She moved toward Teddi's bathroom.

"Okay, I'll meet you in the kitchen." I turned and left. It wasn't fair and I was trying not to think about it, but I had seen the cloth plastered against Taylor's breasts in the pool and they were spectacular.

12

Austin had seen me as close to topless as a person could get. I mean, I could see my nipples in the pool, and he had come and been my dignity.

I sighed. Wrapping myself around his body was intense. Chest-to-chest, him in his low slung jeans, easily holding me up. It was effortless for him. I could feel my heart beating against his. We fit so perfectly. I knew we would. My whole being had been betting on that exact thing.

While I took a shower and dipped into the shampoo and conditioner that Teddi kept on the edge of the tub, I let the hot water try to restore my body's temperature.

I toweled off and wrapped my hair in another fluffy white towel. I put on my leggings and a sweatshirt that I had planned to sleep in.

I met Austin in the living room and he had a towel on his hair, too.

He held out his hand and I put mine in his.

"I texted Teddi so she knows we're pretending and she knows not to make a fuss."

I nodded. That was good. That was the right thing to do. It was slightly crushing to think that he freely told Teddi the pretend relationship was just that—pretend.

My heart was going to be put through a cheese grater, but I couldn't stop myself if I tried. Even being a fake girlfriend was still a girlfriend to Austin Freaking Burathon.

We walked out to the porch and I saw Brutus hunched over at the picnic table, another beer in his hand. Austin led me over to the bonfire and pulled me onto his lap when he chose a chair.

Teddi gave me an exaggerated wink. I smiled in her direction. I'd soak this in. Austin was rubbing the center of my back until I leaned to the side. I was going to get bonfire snuggles in.

He wrapped his arms around me and locked them there.

I could smell the nape of his neck. If I had any guts at all, I'd place a kiss there, but I had to respect the fakeness of the relationship. And kissing his neck would be pressing my luck. Instead, I just inhaled.

Austin leaned near my ear. "I think Tasker is taking Brutus out of here."

His low voice near my earlobe was music. A prayer. It made my eyelashes flutter.

"Yup. They're leaving." He sat up now, letting his arms drop. "Mission accomplished and we didn't even have to have sex."

I wanted to trail my fingers across his jaw. Instead, I forced myself to push off of him and sit in the empty chair next to him. "Yeah. We showed him. Thanks."

Peaches came close and dropped my phone in my lap. "Aren't you glad you tossed that at me?"

I checked the screen and it wasn't cracked. It also had a few messages on it. I unlocked it and saw that Peaches had snapped five pics of me with Austin. One was us coming out of the pool that seemed like it could be a book cover. The lap sitting by the bonfire was hard to see, but I knew what it was. I covered the images with my hand. Peaches was a real one. She knew that I'd want to remember these things, and now I'd have a way to do just that.

The evening lasted well into the morning. The stars eventually showed up as the bonfire wound down. Ronna had dragged out blankets and we all covered up, letting the songs go on too long.

Brutus sent me a few more messages and I ignored them. When it was time to go inside, Austin touched my waist and then squeezed my hand.

He went downstairs, and I was already missing him. Never mind that I had spent all day with him.

When we got set for bed, Peaches and Teddi took turns showering.

Teddi was first. "Not all of us had a douchebag throw us into the pool."

Peaches watched her until the bathroom door was closed. Then she was sitting on my air mattress. "Dude. What the hell?"

"I know, right? The cuddling? The touching? I think I'm pregnant." I sighed and let myself fall back onto the bed.

"I think I am, too. It was so hot. Austin, as if he could get more good-looking. Sweet shit, he thinks of everything. Can you imagine what kind of orgasm he doles out?" Peaches landed next to me.

"Oh, that would kill me. I can't even do that to myself."

"It'd last forever. He's the kind of lover that takes all damn day. And I'd bet your left breast that he can find a clitoris with his eyes closed. Or a penis. He just knows like *everything*. I die." Peaches made her hands do elaborate shadow puppets.

"Why do we have to bet my boob?" I turned to face her. She did the same. Our noses were almost touching.

"Because this is all you. Your middle school dreams. Now your full-sized lady parts reality." She smacked my thigh.

"It's going to hurt eventually." I smacked her back.

"So much. I can't even imagine how hard we'll cry." Peaches turned to the bathroom door as it opened.

"Why are we crying?" Teddi came out in her towel.

"Because periods give us feelings." Peaches covered for me as she hop-wiggled to the end of my air bed.

"That's the truth." She scooted past Peaches as they switched places.

I was saved from having to talk about it more with Teddi because she went to her go-to—recording the party. Teddi was meticulous and always made sure to note what worked and what didn't. She usually had a few pages of thank you notes to write as well. But tonight, thank you notes would come from Teddi's dad, right after she forwarded the list to him.

When she climbed up to her bed, we were all more than ready to close our eyes.

THE NEXT MORNING TEDDI, Peaches, and I spent way too long in bed. We scrolled through our phones, showed each other videos, and all looked at the dick pic Brutus had sent to Peaches.

"He's really branching out. I mean, would you lead with this?" Peaches zoomed in on the penis skin.

"He needs a better down there skincare routine, for sure. That's a lot of clogged pores." Teddi put her hair into a messy bun on the top of her head.

"That's a great point. I'll tell him to exfoliate." Peaches started typing away.

"I can't believe he went straight to texting you his man dangle. Sweet lort. Have some shame, you know?" I checked on Austin's social media. He was already out and snapping pictures in the backyard. Everything he put in focus looked cooler through his lens. Pastel, watercolor, and ethereal.

"I can't believe he threw you in last night. What a dick." Teddi adjusted her fluffy socks.

"I didn't see him coming." I glanced at Peaches, who seemed like she was hiding a smile. She knew I was watching Austin take that dip in the cold pool. Hell, all the girls that weren't related to him at the party were watching that routine.

Teddi continued her recounting, "I bet he was sad when he saw you and Austin were," she put her fingers into curlies to indicate quotation marks, "dating."

"He wastes no time. I don't know what happened to him in college because he was a good dude in high school." I pushed myself to the end of my bed and hit the valve to release the air in the mattress.

As I stomped on the mattress to get it as flat as possible, I got a text from Austin.

AUSTIN: Wanna go get your dog?

He sent a picture of himself smiling. I could tell from his surroundings he was right outside Teddi's window. I crawled over Peaches, and Teddi retracted her legs so I wouldn't smoosh her. I got to her window, flipped the locks, and opened it up instead of texting him back.

He covered his eyes from the late morning sun. "Hey, Juliet.

We can't stay too long today, got to get you back to the old homestead."

He was merging the Wild West and Shakespeare.

Teddi pushed her way next to me. "Remember when you used to sneaky smoke out there and thought no one knew, but really, we all knew?"

Austin tossed up his hands. "Are you always this good at keeping secrets, Bear?"

"Hey, if you're rolling up on my girl here, I need to make sure she knows everything about you." Teddi gave me and then Austin a big cheesy wink.

"She grew up in that room with you. I doubt there's very little she doesn't know about me." He pulled his keys out of his pocket and twirled them. He was killing me with a leather jacket and black jeans.

"You've got a very Goth thing going on today." Teddi was really into the ball-busting at this point.

"Maybe you should close that window. There's a huge bees' nest just above it." Austin pointed and Teddi popped her head out to look.

"Oh, shit." She and I slammed the window down together just as a bee flew into the glass.

Peaches screamed like the bee was a horror movie killer, which sent Teddi and me into fits of laughter.

After we stopped laughing and making fun of Peaches, I helped her roll the airbed up before getting dressed. Later, a light knock sounded on the door, and Teddi opened it to reveal Austin waiting, leaning against her door jamb.

I spoke around the hope in my throat. "Almost ready."

Peaches slapped me on the ass before giving me a full body hug, and then Teddi joined in so we had a three-way situation going on. I loved these girls so much. I almost felt teary thinking about how the times together had gotten so few and far between since we were in school.

Austin held out his hand and I grabbed it. After a whole extra round of goodbyes and thank yous, Austin and I were on the road.

"I checked into my lease and we can have one dog. It has to be under forty pounds, but the landlord owes me a favor. So we can just say Axel is on a diet and has his own journey he's going through."

He hit the blinker as we turned toward my house. My stomach clenched with the thought of Austin seeing how I lived again.

"I want to make sure it makes sense for your sister and stuff. This only works if it makes her life easier." He patted my hand.

"I think I have to talk to her about it. It never even occurred to me that I could take Axel with me. With the dorms, that's a hard no." I held my phone with my finger hovering over my sister's contact info.

"Well, we can always come back and get him, too. I have concerns with how far away his furry butt was from your house when he ran." Austin eased off the side of the road, where he normally would drop me off and pick me up when I was growing up. "And I realize that coming back here is a tender subject as well. I can stay here—unless you need backup." He tapped his fingers gently on the steering wheel.

"Thank you. I'll take it from here. I appreciate that. I'll be back either with Axel or not." I swung open my car door and shut it as Austin wished me luck.

I walked briskly toward my house. The condition of the yard and the porch brought a familiar paralysis and dread.

It didn't take long before I had an armful of Axel, leash dangling.

Raven was limping toward me covered in mud. "Axel, you're the devil."

"Funny you should say that. I have a proposition for you." I rubbed Axel's big head.

Austin

I thought it was going to take far longer for Taylor to figure out if Axel was coming with us or not, but it had to be under fifteen minutes when I saw her and Axel loping toward me. Taylor motioned for me to roll down my window.

"What's up?" I waited as she shuffled a bag and the leash.

"Can he go in your car? It's, like, really nice. His paws are muddy."

Axel jumped up, putting said muddy paws on the door. His tongue lolled out the side of his mouth as he tried to see what was going on in my vehicle.

"Hey, boy. You love getting into trouble, huh?" I leaned over and opened the door, inviting them both in. Taylor tossed in a blanket and I draped it over the seat.

"I'll clean the car when we get home. So sorry about that. We should be grateful we aren't taking Raven. She was covered in mud. Axel had dragged her for all he was worth on the morning walk. Raven refused to let go after Axel had been so successful yesterday."

I grabbed Axel's collar and helped direct him into the backseat. I cracked the back window a bit and he immediately put his nose in the gap.

Taylor got in and closed the door before Axel could get any more ideas about being an adventurous wanderer.

"I guess Raven's mud was part of the reason we picked him

up so quickly?" I petted his head and he managed to lick my hand three times.

"Oh yeah. She was super done with his ass." She dug into the bag and pulled out a dog treat. He instantly propped his head on my seat. Taylor gave him the bone-shaped dog cookie.

He munched in my ear and dropped a crumb on my shoulder. Taylor picked it off.

"Did we ask Endgame if he's allergic or anything?" Taylor bit her bottom lip with worry.

"He's fine. He hasn't paid rent ever. He gets no say about a dog. He can take a Benadryl if he needs to." I wasn't sure how he felt about pets in the apartment. I knew he didn't have any growing up and seemed to think the time and effort most people paid to their animals was a waste of time. He hadn't said that much, but it was just a feeling I got from his interactions with any of the dogs and cats we encountered during our relationship.

Taylor pulled out her phone and checked her email. "I have to read this article and then answer questions for my class." She kept petting Axel's nose as he rested it on her shoulder.

"Go for it." I synced my music up on the aftermarket screen I added to my dashboard and let her have the time to do her work.

On the drive, I wondered when Endgame would be back. A huge part of me hoped he wouldn't be. And then, the tiny part of me that seemed to be in charge when it came to any decision about him pinged to the surface, hoping that I'd know he was okay. I had ways I wasn't proud of to get information on Endgame. Like where he was and what he was up to. If I had to I'd tap into that. But for now, I had Taylor to think about and her dog to keep me occupied.

13

Austin

Through some sort of Labrador miracle, Axel's paws did not get the car muddy. The blanket would have to be washed, but at least it contained the worst of the mess.

Bringing Axel into the apartment was easy. He loved new places. As he blasted around the place, I was able to see that it was empty. No Endgame. I tried to see if this was affecting Austin, but his attention was on Axel and his ability to be in eight places at once. He was pure Labrador exuberance. Austin brought our bags into his room and Axel hopped onto the bed like he paid rent. Luckily, his paws were no longer too muddy since most of the mud had fallen away after it dried.

I was concerned until Austin took a flying leap onto the bed and hugged Axel. "We're going to be such good friends, buddy."

Axel took his job of licking Austin's face and sometimes his hair seriously. I went into the bathroom and wetted a hand towel. When I got back to the bedroom, I offered it to Austin.

"He's a lick monster. Always licking. Even if he's asleep, if you put your hand near his nose, he sleep licks. It's hilarious."

Axel finally calmed down enough to let Austin just pet him. He started closing his eyes as well.

"So, was your sister really okay with us taking this big guy?" Austin didn't stop petting Axel.

"She was, for now. I'll check back with her and make sure she didn't just decide that on a whim because she was mad. But it's hard for her without me home to walk this dope." I lay down next to Austin and petted Axel, too. Our hands clashed a bit on Axel's back. Axel flipped over to offer us his belly.

Austin patted him. "He's a handful, for sure. Cute as hell, though. Just like his lady." Austin gave me a wink.

I tried my best not to blush, but my body wasn't taking orders from me anymore. I didn't want to bring up Endgame, but his lack of presence hung in the apartment.

"Did you finish your work?" He gave Axel a final pat and kissed him on his nose.

"I have to get to the questions. Thanks for reminding me." I patted Axel, too, who just stayed on his back, legs in the air.

"It seems like this will work for him." Austin went to his suitcase and started to unpack.

"I'm going to do my stuff after I get these questions in to the professor." I pulled my laptop out and set it up on Austin's desk.

"Yeah, go for it. I have to put away the leftovers Ronna sent us home with." Austin took a Tupperware dish from an insulated bag.

I turned my back as I powered on my laptop. I had a feeling that Austin was going to check on Endgame. And I also wondered if he was the only one that did that.

I PUT the food from Mom in the fridge. It looked the same as when Taylor and I left the day before. Which I was expecting because I had the camera trained on the front door, though Endgame would sometimes climb through the window, usually when he was high and feeling paranoid that people were following him.

As I closed the fridge, I remembered standing in this exact place when Endgame climbed through my window for the first time. The noise had set me running to the living room as Endgame fell over an end table and broke a glass sculpture I had on it.

"Shit. Sorry. I was coming in here and everything. You weren't supposed to hear me." He picked up some of the jagged pieces in his hands. Then he dropped them as the pain from the cuts he was earning hit his nervous system. *"Shit."*

This fucking guy. The same one that planted drugs on me, held me at gunpoint, and the one I had kissed was back.

I flipped on the light and left to get the broom and dustpan from the laundry room. When I came back, he was propped against the couch, sitting on the floor. His leg was bleeding, the red puddle under his knee alarmingly growing while I watched it.

I abandoned the broom and ran to the bathroom for towels. I made a pit stop at the kitchen for scissors as well.

After I kneeled next to him, he held up his two bloody palms. "I got shot. A few blocks from here. And you know what? I thought if I'm gonna die tonight, I want that man's lips on mine one more time before I go."

I ignored him and started cutting his jeans so I could find the source of the bleeding. "I'm going to call 911." I paused to dial and he snatched the phone and tossed it across the apartment.

"Nah. Those meat wagons are expensive as shit. And they'll want to know what I'm on. And who I am. I ain't got time for that. I'd rather die than end up owing some asshole money to put me in a dress with my ass hanging out." His pupils were dilated.

I was at a loss of what to do. I went back to cutting his jeans. Eventually, I found the source of the blood. The wound near his outer thigh was deep but on the surface. I put pressure on the wound and he hissed.

"Shit. You got to be pretty and hurt me all at once? Figures. Life's never easy." He put his head on his shoulder and the next time I looked at him, he was passed out.

I kept pressure on the leg and felt panic build inside. I left him to find my phone. It was still working, but now had two new cracks in the screen. After dialing nine and then one, I hesitated.

It didn't occur to me that people had to make decisions about their health based on their bank account. My parents had great coverage and all of us kids took advantage of it, whether we were seeing therapists or getting broken bones fixed.

I certainly didn't want this dude dying on the floor. He was tragically beautiful in a broken doll kind of way and full of angst. He was the kind of person that just made the wrong choice over and over. And hell if I wasn't drawn to the mess of it all.

I set down the phone and began a vigil. I'd monitor his pulse, his color, and his bleeding. If anything got worse in that regard, I'd call.

Now, after walking into the empty living room, I noted the old, worn stain from that very night on my area rug. I'd scrubbed it more times than I could count, but the stain stayed despite all my attempts.

Just like Endgame. He'd made it through the night. In the morning he quietly thanked me for not calling the cops or an ambulance. It felt like I had helped him do something I shouldn't. And my gut had been right. Endgame had double-crossed two dealers that night, and the fact he was walking around with a flesh wound was a testament to his luck. He could weasel out of anything it seemed.

He hid in my apartment for a week. And then hiding turned into living. And then living turned into loving. And now he was out, God knows where, pouting because he perceived me as moving on.

He thought Taylor was my next person. My girlfriend. And continuing with the farce of it was another one of those decisions that was making my gut give me the side-eye. I was telling myself I was helping her, but I also wondered if I wasn't just trying to put an obstacle between Endgame and me so I wouldn't fall back into my old ways. Into his old games.

I hated that I couldn't trust myself to stick to my guns around him. The danger mixed with the drama was heady.

Breaking up almost killed us both, but I had to make sure that he and I were done. And having him still living here was not making the situation any easier. Because I was worried. I was worried he wasn't here. I was picturing what would have happened if Endgame hadn't made it to my apartment that night. If I hadn't kept pressure on his leg and monitored him all night? Would he have been in an alley? Would he have made it at all?

I didn't think so. And if he was in a similar situation tonight, he'd never come to my window. He would die out of spite, just to give me the final middle finger. I needed him to move on. I needed to move on.

What I should've done was pack up his stuff and put it on the curb. Instead, I texted a number that made me feel slimy for just knowing it. Endgame's boss—Julian. The guy that ran all the dealers in the city.

ME: Have you seen him?

The response was instant.

JULIAN: Yeah, want me to film his last words?

Shit.

14

I ran my answers through spell check and then sent them to my professor. My back cracked when I stretched my arms above my head. I walked over to my bag as I listened to Axel snore. He was so content to be dead center in Austin's bed.

As I put away a few of the things I hadn't worn this weekend, Austin came into the bedroom. He was pale and scared.

"What's up?" I left the closet and sat on his bed.

"I've got to go get him." He ran his hands through his hair.

"Endgame?" I already knew.

"Yeah. He's in trouble."

I didn't bring up that I thought Endgame was probably in trouble more than he was out of it.

"What's the plan?" I stood up and paced with Austin.

"I'm not sure. I can't leave him. I know where he is, but I have no idea if they will let me in to get him again." Austin began gnawing on his fingernail.

"Where is he?" I had visited the city quite a few times with the Burathons, but I didn't know my way around.

"It's mostly a brothel."

"What are we—in an old timey movie?" I knew my face was showing disbelief.

"I wish. Things would be easier than getting to him now. If I could talk to his boss, Julian, I could maybe make arrangements. But I don't know how to get in." He paced again.

"What if you had a lady? That you were bringing in?" I wasn't sure, but most brothels had women.

"No. No way. Sorry, pretty, it's not a place where you can be." He put his hands in his hair and leaned over.

"Hey, if you can be there, I can be there." I touched his back and rubbed. "You helped me so much with Axel and Brutus. I owe you." I waited to see what Austin needed. Whatever it was, I'd figure it out.

"I just need to get in and talk to him." Austin looked at me as if he was considering my offer.

"Is this life or death?" I was going to ask the hard questions.

"For Endgame? Pretty much." Austin's color drained and his jaw tensed.

"If you think talking to the people at the brothel will work, then let's dress me up and get you in there." I headed to the closet. I was going to need his help picking out what would make sense.

The only thing I knew about brothels was what I read in history class.

"I can't have you do that." Austin ran his hands down his face.

"I don't know how many choices we have." I pulled a black bodycon dress off the hanger. I normally paired this with a blazer and sneakers. Instead, I dug out a push-up bra and a pair of my highest heels.

Austin stopped protesting and waited until I was dressed before helping me pull my hair into an updo. I stayed still with my eyes closed as he quickly applied my makeup.

While I got my shoes on, he hustled into a suit and pulled his hair back. He still had on black nail polish, but it was worn away. When we were done, Austin pulled a shoebox off the shelf. Under a pair of heels, he had a wad of cash.

"Hopefully, this will be enough." He tucked the bills into the inside pocket of his suit jacket.

I grabbed my purse and observed Axel. He was happily snoring away. "How far away is this place?"

"Just a few blocks west. The city has secrets and rough sides of town close to ritzy places. I have so many reservations about you going with me. I'll just go in and see what they say." He tapped his pocket.

"We go together. I'm not letting you go by yourself to whatever screwy ass place Endgame wound up in because he was high out of his mind and doing business where he shouldn't. I owe watching your back to Teddi. And I take that very seriously." I turned and studied my reflection in his full-length mirror.

"You look fuck hot." Austin skimmed his lips on my bare shoulder and I forgot to breathe.

Teddi would kill us both for heading to a brothel to save a drug dealer from a mafia boss. Or whoever Endgame owed so much that they were willing to kill him. This was big time, big city problems.

Axel didn't stir as Austin and I walked into the hall. Austin set the alarm from his phone and locked the door. He ordered a car service to pick us up. Someone passing by would think we were going to a party. And as I palmed the pepper spray in my wrap, I silently wished they were right.

The car ride was as short as Austin had predicted. Austin held out his elbow as we headed toward a warehouse with a nondescript door.

"You sure we're at the right place?" I felt like I was going to be looking at the insides of a place that made paint cans or something. Instead, a man stood impassively guarding the door.

"Hey, I'm here to see Julian." Austin stood still as a statue as the man assessed us.

"You giving him her? 'Cause he's not taking visitors tonight." He looked me up and down.

Austin lifted his chin but didn't agree to anything.

"He'd make time for her. Shit. She's amazing. He loves those long legs." He dragged his gaze from my heels to my chest.

I got the willies marching up and down my spine. As the man let us in the building, I got a very serious sensation that we were out of our depth. I flashed to Austin. He smiled at me, but it didn't reach his eyes.

We were escorted through the warehouse by another man. I tried to keep my eyes down, not wanting to see too much. This wasn't good. I felt like I had snakes in my chest.

I squeezed Austin's hand hard. He pulled me closer and put his arm around my waist. "It'll be okay."

When we were finally shown into Julian's room, I was shocked to see that it had a huge round bed, a bar, and a desk all in the same space. It was the very embodiment of a multipurpose room.

Julian was wearing a light blue silk robe and a pair of boxers. I'd never been around hard drugs, but the color of Julian's eyes had to be bad. He was curling his upper lip a ton and doing a weird sniffing thing like he was part bloodhound.

Austin recoiled a step and then proceeded forward. "Where is he?"

Julian moved slowly but had great flourish with his hands. "No small talk? Aren't you famous on TikTok now or some shit? Like, let's talk. Let's party."

"You threatened to kill him, so maybe we just talk numbers." Austin had a steely gaze and his shoulders back. He was either confident or doing a great job acting like he was.

"Well, he doesn't pay back his loans. Then I give him more time. Then he makes a ton and what does he do? Fucking gambles it all." Julian walked closer to us and Austin moved a bit so he could put his body in front of mine.

"What's the number, Julian?" Austin tilted his head like he was losing patience.

"You know, you don't get to come in here and tell me about my business and how to do it. You're some sort of social media freak." Julian staggered a little and then grabbed the back of the velvet chair in the sitting area to steady himself.

"It's a long night. No ill will. Just trying to get you what you need and get him out of your hair. That's it." Austin held up one hand, palm out.

"How many times are you going to bail him out? This has to be like the fourth time." Julian moved around the chair and slid into it.

"It's five. And this is the last time." Austin started to snake his hand into his jacket.

"You said that last time, I'm pretty sure." Julian tapped his temple with his index finger.

"I probably did." Austin shook his head and pulled out a thick yellow envelope.

"You only work to bail his ass out?" Julian held out his hand and Austin set the envelope in it.

"Maybe, Julian. There'll be more there than you need—for interest." Austin stepped back as Julian opened the envelope.

"Yeah, today I'm going to need a bit more." He looked me directly in the face.

"This is what you get. This is what you always get." Austin's tone got darker.

"You saying you didn't bring this girl by for a sample?" Julian put his index finger between his teeth.

"No, you said you wanted to look at something pretty. Just no. We're leaving. And she's my girlfriend, so no." Austin pulled me even closer.

"You into girls now? I thought you and he were married?" Julian pointed in the direction of the big round bed. It was then I noticed that there was a foot sticking out from underneath.

Austin pulled me with him and we both studied the floor. Endgame was passed out, his shirt pulled up to reveal his stomach. Austin stooped low so he could cover him. It was a tender motion. A caring gesture.

Endgame had to have been at the losing end of a fight. His black and white face ink had more color where bruises had formed. One of his eyes was swollen shut.

I kneeled down and took his pulse, a trick I learned over and over at my first aid classes for my lifeguarding job. He was alive. I felt relief but also more concern. He was very much unconscious, and I had no idea how Austin and I'd get him out of here—if we were allowed to leave. Julian had the money and we had nothing to show for it really.

Austin brushed Endgame's hair off his forehead.

I whispered to him, "Will they let us call an ambulance?"

He gave me a short shake of his head. Of course not. No ambulance would be let in here.

"You sure this is the last time?" Julian was over my shoulder now.

"It's the last time," Austin confirmed. There was a finality in his statement that seemed to have a ring of truth to it.

"Seriously. I mean, I know I've said this before, but that guy is a piece of shit. No one cares about him. You need to get rid of the dead weight in your life." Julian lit up a hand rolled cigarette.

"When you write that self-help book, I'm going to need a copy." Austin tried pulling on Endgame to get him to sit up.

I didn't bother warning him that Endgame could have a head or neck injury. It seemed like we were in suspended animation where normal concerns were tossed aside.

Another man appeared in the door with a wheelchair. Julian exhaled and pointed to the place right at Endgame's feet. "You knew he'd come and save this fuck-up, huh?"

The man nodded once as he positioned the chair. He set the lock on the wheels. Austin and the wheelchair pusher went to either side of Endgame. I moved backward so they could maneuver him.

Julian stepped close to me and blew his smoke over my shoulder and toward my cleavage. "Is your money situation good? Because I have jobs for you, pretty one."

After Endgame was positioned slumped in the chair, I noticed that it had handcuffs on each of the four points where limbs would touch. This chair wasn't just used for moving people that needed assistance. They had done weird crap with the chair.

Austin lifted the lock on the chair's wheels and waited as I took my place next to him.

"Okay, baby. Let's see if you really mean it this time. Great doing business with you. Tell that asshole he doesn't work for me anymore." Julian pursed his lips toward me and made a kissing noise. I swallowed my revulsion and stayed close to Austin.

We wheeled Endgame out the way we had come in. When we got outside, the same Uber driver was waiting for us. He didn't look too surprised at our new unconscious guest.

He even hopped out to help Austin transfer Endgame. I sat up front while Austin sat in the back with Endgame. I peeked over my shoulder a few times, and in the light that illuminated Austin's face when we passed under street lights I saw his pain.

This was a low point. Another boundary that Austin was

crossing for Endgame, and had crossed before. It wasn't a sign of strength at all.

On the way home, I got chills twice more. I had the feeling that there were a few outcomes for this evening that we somehow avoided. Like we were meant to run into far more trouble than we did. I also got the sense that the trouble was just waiting for another opportunity to pounce.

15

Austin

I had a few things on Julian. Not a ton, but knowing people who knew people was a way to ensure that Endgame could get out of situations. It was a risk because it wasn't like Julian was an upstanding citizen or anything.

As Taylor slid under Endgame's arm to help me help him stagger up to the apartment, I had regret. She wasn't ready for this. For what I let myself be involved in because of him. As we waited for the elevator, she leaned forward so she could look at my face.

She was total support for me. I saw it then. Her unwavering belief in me. She would march right into hell if I asked her. And I felt like I had done just that. Her blue eyes connected with mine as the elevator doors opened.

I made sure to slide most of his weight onto me as we maneuvered him inside. "So, is Endgame his given name?"

I think she was trying to use his name to keep Endgame from falling completely unconscious again.

"No. Torin Rulle. But hell if anyone uses it."

"That's a cool name." She checked Endgame over as we waited in the elevator as much as she could while still making sure to hold up her end.

"Yeah. It kind of is." The elevator stopped and we got him out. We had a slippery moment when I was unlocking the door.

Endgame was slipping into a more boneless state. Taylor took the keys from me and I had to full-on bear hug Endgame to keep him upright.

Once we were inside, Axel came bull running at us. I had totally forgotten that we had a new pet guest.

Taylor put out her hand and tried to stop Axel, but he was a freight train. His tongue was everywhere, like it was a helicopter blade. I watched as his eyes showed more white than usual as his back legs tucked under him. Despite Taylor's blocking hand, Axel's face connected with Endgame's crotch.

"Shit!" Endgame came alive with pain. He folded like a lawn chair. Taylor switched from helping Endgame to scooping up her huge dog.

It was like he manufactured four extra legs, and they were everywhere. "So sorry. Oh gosh. Super sorry."

Axel whined and struggled to get to Endgame and me. Taylor wrestled him back into my room.

"You trying to kill me after I'm already dead?" His voice was husky and strained.

"You're the only one that effectively tries to get you killed." Now that he was awake, he was able to help me help him walk, albeit with one of his hands covering his dick.

All he did was groan as I got him to his bed. After depositing him onto his bare mattress, I propped up some pillows.

"So what hurts? I know you don't want to go to the hospital, but what's the worst thing you have going on?" I found his blanket on the floor and shook it out before draping it over him.

"Headache. Nut ache. Possibly a dislocated shoulder and a few cracked ribs." He rolled his hips and hissed with pain.

I felt overwhelmed as I tried to guess what the best course of action was. "I never planned on being a doctor, you know."

"That's because I'm your only patient." He covered his one swollen eye with his hand. "Oh, this is fucking killing me. I think they popped my damn eyeball." He winced and touched the skin gently.

Taylor peeked in, stepping just past the doorway. "Can I get anything?"

I turned and looked at her. She had swapped to pajamas, but still had on the makeup and fancy hairstyle.

I shrugged and held up my hands.

"Let me get some warm towels, some ice, and some antibacterial cream for starters." She ducked out to the kitchen.

"Tell her to get me whiskey and a fucking pistol so I can end this shit right now."

Ah, the self-harm ploy. An old Endgame favorite. How many times did he convince me I was the only thing keeping him alive? Too many.

The worst time flooded my memory.

I was at a club with Tinsley and Parker when I got the video call from Endgame.

"Don't answer it." Tinsley tried to block me from touching my screen to pick up the call.

I brushed her away and stood from the table we had been using as a home base that night. It was littered with empty cocktail glasses.

I glanced at the screen as it connected. Dark. The screen was dark and having trouble picking up the subject in the video. I saw speckles of stars behind him and had to find a place to hear him. The bathroom sufficed. I picked a stall and closed the door.

"Where are you?" I turned up the volume as I tried to make out his location.

"Gone. Remember? You kicked me out." He'd turned a bit and I finally made out where he was. The rooftop of our building.

"I told you that you couldn't deal drugs out of my apartment. That you would've to move a few fucking feet away from the building. I mean, you get that, right? That I don't want to be kicked out when the landlord starts getting complaints." The angle Endgame had the camera at was confusing. It almost looked like he was on the opposite side of the safety fence on the roof.

"You know, sometimes, just sometimes, I like to pretend that you care about me. That you care if I'm alive or dead. Not tonight, though. You want me gone, and there's only one way I can think to go." The camera whirled around, and I could see so many colors. The street below my building. Fifteen stories down. He had the tips of his sneakers in the frame, right on the ledge.

"What the hell are you doing? Do you even know?" I clutched the phone hard.

"I'm feeling the things you want me to feel. This is what you want." The view was tipsy and turvy.

"Well, I'm feeling like I really want you to step back on the roof." My stomach fell to my feet.

"There are only two ways off this. That way..." And then he did his best impression of Singing in the Rain, twirling on a safety pole, making my mouth drop open. "Or in your arms." And then he ended the call.

The Uber ride to my place was fraught with worry and self-doubt. Should I call the cops? Would they be able to save him? He was so wary of cops, I could see him jumping just to make a statement.

I ran up the steps as fast as I could, and when I banged the *rooftop door open, he was still there. Still fine. Sitting on the edge, feet kicking like he was a schoolkid on a swing instead of a grown man being dangerous as hell.*

I slowed my steps, no sudden moves, and put my phone into my back pocket. As I got closer, I saw he had an almost empty liquor bottle, a spoon and a tourniquet.

"So fast for a guy you couldn't fucking care less about." He took a swig, draining the last of the bottle.

I snaked my arms around him. He was a mess. A mess of a person, a horrible owner of my heart. He leaned his head back and I kissed his temple.

"Does it always have to be this hard?" I asked against his inked skin.

"It wasn't this hard until you showed up."

He meant his whole life. Taking these dangerous risks for my attention. The toxic turnaround because it worked. He took my hand and moved it lower until I was able to thread my fingers into his pants. Endgame's sigh of relief and excitement was not okay.

But it happened anyway. I was drunk and he was high. And instead of bringing him in from the ledge, I gave him the most insane hand job in the existence of the world. And when he came, it was a fountain of cum from the top of a fifteen-story building. It wasn't until after he was over the fence and kneeling in front of me that I saw if his emissions had intervened on anyone below. Luckily, the alley below was empty. But Endgame's mouth wasn't. He put my erection there. I threaded my hands in Endgame's hair as he took me deeply. He swallowed my passion with only the stars as our witnesses.

We'd laughed later, hard and with tears in our eyes, thinking about his long distance jizzing. Imagining a poor bastard just walking along and getting an epic, unexpected rain shower.

Taylor came back into the room, her arms filled with supplies. She went to the end of the bed and dumped them out. We worked together now, both wearing gloves as we disinfected his wounds and bandaged him up as much as possible.

At one point I watched as Endgame glowered at her. I had a thought right then. Axel began barking in my room, and Taylor excused herself to leave.

Once I was sure that Endgame had ice and warmth in all the right places, I sat on the edge of his bed. "Did you do it on purpose?"

Endgame had his eyes closed. "What?"

"Did you take a bad bet from Julian so they would kick your ass and then I'd have to come get you?" It was the ledge all over again. Endgame's go-to move. Threaten his own life so I'd keep him in mine.

Instead of answering, Endgame snorted.

I didn't need confirmation. It was the truth. He was trying to force my hand, always was. Making me prove that I'd drop everything for him. That I could never place my attention anywhere but on him.

And it masqueraded as love. It was desperate. It was immediate. But it rang hollow now. It seemed sad now. That he was willing to constantly take chances with his own safety. Used that recklessness as a weapon.

"I'll be back to check on you in a few." I got up, straightened his blanket, and then went to my room.

Taylor was on the bed, rubbing Axel's belly. "Are you okay?"

I crawled onto the bed and started petting Axel's big head. "Yeah, I'm good. I think he'll rest for a little while, then I'll check on him and make sure he's still doing well."

Taylor timed it so that her belly rub worked its way to Axel's neck and there we held hands. I felt tension release as she worked on him.

"He's just a freight train, you know? But you heard how Julian talked about him? It's just hard to know he feels so harsh on himself, too. It gets me in the feels. In my empathy to know that he values his life so little." I was dumping on her, forcing her to be my therapist.

"It's super sad and very scary." Empathy softened her pretty eyes.

"Yeah." I felt like it was an excuse. I was making it so that I was the only one that could fix Endgame. Even he didn't hold a candle to how much I'd do to make sure he was safe.

"I can't pretend to know what this is like for you. He's not the devil, I'm sure of it. But it's hard to see his good points right now. I feel like he took chances and you paid the price." She stretched out her legs.

Axel looked from her face to mine and back again. "He's hilarious. He's part seal, part cartoon character."

"He totally is a giant dingbat. I love him so much. I hope he didn't hurt Endgame too badly." She held her own hands.

"Yeah. He's okay. Been hit in the nuts plenty over the years." I pushed myself off the bed and shed parts of my suit. "I'm going to get into something comfortable, then I probably have to stay in his room with him to make sure he doesn't have any issues. I mean, they for sure hit his head a few times. I'll google head injury protocol."

"Okay, good luck." She gave me a sad smile. I appreciated that she didn't give me grief about going to help Endgame. Tinsley and Parker would've been busting my balls left and right.

Taylor was a good human being, and I had put her freaking through it.

16

I watched as Austin gathered his phone charger and a water bottle. I knew he was just monitoring a friend, but I was jealous.

I kind of understood why Endgame was a pain in the ass. Having Austin's attention on you was addicting. A rush. I didn't want to share it for a moment, and part of my schoolgirl heart crashed at the thought of losing a night with Austin in his bed.

Instead, I had my farting dog. A big nutball. I noticed that Austin locked the bedroom door on his way out. I knew he had trust issues with Endgame. And if tonight was any indication, it was a very valid opinion with lots of supporting incidents.

I wasn't sure how long it took me to get to sleep, but in the morning, I was nose-to-nose with Axel and his drooling mouth.

I slapped my hands over my face as he sneezed. "Ugh. Gross, dude."

Axel licked my face over and over as soon as I peered through my hands at him. He had no shame. I scrambled to get out from under him and to find clothes to walk him in.

After I put on a thick hoodie, I clipped his leash on his collar. He started bouncing and jumping so high that his eyes were even with mine as we waited for the elevator. Axel dragged me to the dog walk area and then got intensely interested in a leaf in a hyacinth plant.

I cuddled my chest in the chill of the morning. I could have tossed my winter jacket on top of the hoodie. Axel stood sniffing the air like he was trying to decipher the Dead Sea Scrolls. "Bud, let's get busy."

I used the command that in theory would get the process of Axel going to the bathroom started, when in reality it was just me sounding really hopeful that my dog would move his process along.

After he was done and I neatened his mess up, we headed back inside. I was surprised to see Austin up and sipping from a coffee mug. As I unclipped Axel, Austin grabbed me a coffee mug and then held it out to me.

"How's he doing?" I took off my hoodie and wrapped it around my waist. Austin started pouring me a coffee.

"Better. Has a big headache and quite a few injuries that I think should have him in the ER. He's got his color back and seems ready to start to cause problems again."

"Have you had the conversation about Axel yet?" I added fresh water to his bowl.

"Not yet. I'm not even sure he remembers his nut encounter last night." I watched as Axel inhaled his water like he was mad at it.

"That might be a mercy. It was quite the nose check." I ran my hand down Axel's back.

"It sure was. I thought Endgame was going to be a soprano." Austin tilted his head to one side.

"I'm sure Axel can arrange that. All Endgame has to do is eat a hot dog and Axel will risk it all to snag a bit of a leftover." Axel flapped his ears, spewing water onto our legs.

I grabbed a hand towel and wiped myself down. I tossed the towel to Austin who did the same.

"This is a sloppy dog." He gave Axel a soft smile and a side rub down.

"Hey, you must be exhausted. What's your day look like?" Mornings were new here, with Austin. Sunday was sort of a free flow day for me. I had to make sure to keep up with my college work, but I had some leeway.

"I am. I have a shoot this evening. I have rented out a space at the rooftop gardens downtown. But Tinsley has been in my messages telling me she can't be my model." He walked over to his camera bag and started rifling through it. "I thought I had another model's contact info in here. She was handing out magnets at a meet and greet last year." He stopped and switched his weight from one foot to the other.

Axel hopped up onto the velvet chair Austin had in his bedroom sitting area.

After I followed my dog, I sat on the edge of the chair. When I looked back at Austin, he was tilting his head, looking hard at my face. "Can I see something?"

"Sure." I held still while he pulled out his phone and took a few pictures of my face. When he scrolled back through to review them, he went quiet. He was quiet for so long, I had to remind him that I still didn't know what the hell he was thinking about. "Penny for your thoughts?"

"Well, this brand I'm working with really liked Tinsley's style for their lip balm campaign, but I think you could work. If you were willing. It would really, really help me."

I already knew I'd say yes. This man could ask me to jump a mountain and I'd try.

"Is Tinsley okay? You didn't mention why she can't do it."

Austin took a deep breath before answering. "She knows that I went to help Endgame last night and she's mad."

"Oh. Okay. Will she be mad at me if I do this for you?" That would suck because Tinsley was cool and I really liked the vibe we had together when we had hung out.

"No. She makes sure to hold the grudge with whomever it truly belongs to." He took a few more shots and I started to feel my skin heat up with his scrutiny.

"She wants you to leave him there? With Julian?" That seemed like a horrible idea considering how much of a beating he took.

"Tinsley wants me to let him experience the consequences of his own actions." Austin set his phone down and motioned for me to follow him into his huge closet.

"She has a point." I waited in the center of the small room as Austin pulled dresses and hung them on the garment rack.

"I know she just wants what's best for me. I get that. But in the heat of the moment, when I knew his safety was in jeopardy, it really was hard to draw a line in the sand." He pulled out a white off-the-shoulder outfit with see-through cut-outs in the legs.

I took it from him and he turned his back. *Oh.* He wanted me to change right here. And my privacy would be his turned head. I contemplated my choices.

I quickly changed into the outfit. Once I had it adjusted and my breasts covered, I offered, "You can turn around now."

He spun and then smiled. "The way you wear clothes is such a gift."

Again with the effortless compliments. This was why I was ruined for other guys. This quick, effervescent approval.

He adjusted the sleeves and then ran the back of his hand down my cheek. "Light makeup. They have an image they want me to paint your face for the shoot. We can work on that now because time will get away from us."

He took my hand until I was seated in his bathroom at the vanity.

Austin fastened a drape around my shoulders and clipped it so my clothes would stay makeup-free. I waited while he set up his makeup workspace. It wasn't out of the ordinary for Austin to help us with our makeup for cheer or dances. It was different that it was just he and I. He was alarmingly close to my face, stroking my skin with a sponge to get my foundation in place. Then eye makeup and lashes. Next, he did my cheeks and lips. He had transformed my face. He highlighted my cheekbones.

After applying an expensive curling wand to every chunk of hair I had, my big beachy waves were set with spray.

Just when I thought we were done, I remembered about his client's specific requests. Austin pulled a large, colorful, fake tattoo flower out of an overnight mailer. He mumble read the directions before prepping my skin with a light bit of alcohol.

Before I knew it, he had smoothed the design over the side of my face and held a warm, wet cloth over it. We waited a few beats before he carefully pulled it off.

I had no intentions of getting a face tattoo, but if I had to get one, this would be it. Austin secured a magnetic nose ring and a few ear cuffs for me before stepping back and helping me up. After removing the drape cloth, I had a look in the full-length mirror.

He put his hands on my shoulders. "Perfection."

I went from his eyes in the mirror to mine. I gave myself a look over. I didn't look different. Just edgy. The face tattoo highlighted my eye color and his makeup and the hair style made the blonde pop. The softness of the outfit was a great dichotomy. I smiled back at him.

"Your beauty raced past me and now it's all I can see. I can't believe you look like this." He bit his lower lip and the constant simmer I was on for him flipped straight to boiling. I swallowed and was about to tell him that I was all his. No matter what. But then he added, "My client is very, very lucky. You're going to sell a million bracelets." And I felt the words on the tip of my tongue mist into regrets.

"Okay, let's go. Can we bring Axel?" I leaned down and petted his head.

"He is going to get hair all over you." Austin gathered his camera and tossed in a few things from a desk drawer into a messenger bag. I thought about leaving Axel here with Endgame, not knowing how the man would treat a dog. When he turned, Austin lifted the bag over his shoulder. "But yeah, we are going to bring him. They allow dogs and he's our special problem child."

I grabbed Axel's leash and he started with his giant jump, looked me in the eyes, and then commenced with his tippy taps dance. And then repeated it. I had to put a hand on his back to steady him so I could clip his leash on him.

"He's part kangaroo. That's great." Austin held out a hand for the leash. "I'll walk him so maybe he can get his hair on me instead."

I caught a glance of us in the mirror. Austin in his dark jeans and navy blazer and me in all white. Almost like a wedding. Almost like a dream come true. So close. So far. I followed him out the bedroom door to do my first ever modeling shoot.

After stuffing Axel in the back and holding open the door for Taylor, I headed to Window Corner Gardens. I met them through Endgame, which was sort of funny, sort of not. He'd been using the Gardens to sell drugs to high-end clients. He was banned, but the manager was willing to let me use the location as needed after closing hours. It helped to be charming and ballsy. And I had both of those things going for me. I glanced at Taylor at the red light. She was beautiful while we were growing up, but soon her features had become just a hallmark for who she was. Dressing her and highlighting her made me see her differently. She was graceful and somehow a little klutzy. She loved Axel so much, but her jaw clenched with the responsibility of him. The way she looked at me lit something inside me.

She couldn't be anymore off-limits if I tried. First, my ex was living with us. Second, and more importantly, Teddi was Taylor's long-time best friend. If she and I did something, and it went haywire, and I had to face the fact my relationships had the danger of taking that turn, I wouldn't be able to look my sister in the eye. Taylor had to feel comfortable coming to our place. Especially after seeing her house. She needed the escape of the Burathon family manor. It made sense now. I wondered if my parents knew about Taylor's home life. I got the sense that there was a lot of love there, just something else that had to be dealt with. She was neat as a pin to live with. Always wiping things down and setting them back in their place.

I pulled into the garage for the Gardens and grabbed a ticket. I had a card in my wallet that I waved to allow free parking. The garage was almost empty, so I parked right by the elevator.

Taylor got to work on securing Axel and seemed to be making an effort to keep him away from her white outfit. He was doing his damnedest to body slam her. I heaved my two bags and raced around the car so I could take him from her.

Taylor hopped back just as he lunged. She was frustrated by him, but still soft for him. I let my gaze fall. I had to stop finding things about her that called to me. I was a doomed case. Look at Endgame. I literally had to pull him in off of ledges. I could not try to charm my way into her pants. She was different and very, very special. Now I was off to stare at her through my lens for an hour or so. I was sure that would be fine.

Austin used his key card to open the elevator and hit the top floor button. Axel sat waiting like he had all the manners in the world. It was weird.

I met Austin's gaze.

"What's gotten into him?" He noticed the same thing I had.

"I don't know. Calm before the storm? Hold tight to that leash." I pointed to the leather strap.

When the elevator opened, I gasped.

"Gorgeous, right?" He stepped off the elevator. The whole roof was another world. There were trees, gorgeous ferns, and flowers. "We'll have to come back in the spring. Are you cold?"

I shook my head. I wasn't cold yet, but there was a nip in the air. Austin put his bags down and Axel tugged to be allowed to go on a sniffing spree. I took the leash. Axel took me on a forced, high speed tour of the garden, zooming us through the cobblestone printed path.

On my way around, I found that there was a rooftop pool, and judging from the steam coming off of it, it was heated. When I got back to Austin, he was already snapping pictures.

"That dog brings out the most stunning smile on you. I'm so glad we brought him." he bit his bottom lip.

Having Austin look at me like this, like highlighting things that he liked about me, was a heady feeling. "He brings out a lot of feelings in me."

"The company we're working with is called Stars Unlimited, and their jewelry is all-star themed. I'll give you a choice or two to pick from and we'll work from there." He gestured to the bench next to him.

Axel began sniffing the jewelry as I perused it. I chose a silver necklace with a glittery star and a crown. I draped a necklace over Axel's head. He seemed very pleased that he was being included. I added a bracelet to my arm as well.

Austin switched his demeanor and I got to watch him become the professional that he was. He was quieter and moved more carefully. I pulled Axel along with me. We made the entire circle of the path edging the perimeter.

When we got to the pool, I pointed it out. "This glass sided pool, I think I recognize it from the street. Is this the one you can see from 80th Street?"

Austin moved toward the pool and ran a hand through it. "One and the same. I have to move the water because I wanna show the lack of stillness."

Axel must've thought that Austin was getting ready to play. I was a little off balance, and when he moved, I panicked. Axel jumped into the water and I tilted in next to him. I came up sputtering. The pool had a safety railing, but I was concerned that the dog would be able to get around it. Of course, his Labrador retriever nature took over and he wanted nothing more than to swim and splash.

I flipped my hair back away from my face. Austin was taking pictures the entire time.

He broke his concentration to ask, "Are you okay?"

I answered, "I'm okay, just wet." I covered my boobs. The white outfit was now almost completely see-through.

Austin seemed focused on the task at hand. "The way the water is working with the jewelry and your face is just everything I could ask for." He leaned even closer and Axel did his best to try to lick Austin's face from inside the pool. I was grateful that the pool was heated and the steam coming up around me. I could feel it messing with my makeup.

I touched my face. "Is this all ruined now? I'm so sorry."

Austin smiled. "No, kitten, you look like an angel that fell straight into this pool from heaven. Just keep posing for me, that's all I ask."

I knew I'd be really cold when I finally got out of this pool, and to stay warm I had to keep my shoulders under the water.

The pool was pretty shallow, and although Axel preferred to swim he could also stand. After he had exhausted himself, Austin jogged back to his bag and brought out another crown.

He placed it on top of Axel's head. "The only thing I need to add is flowers for the crowns." Austin went and picked a few beautiful stunning red flowers off the ground where they had fallen from the plant and threaded them into the crowns that my dog and I were wearing.

I laughed when he said we looked perfect. "I feel like if I described this whole experience to someone they would think I was having a fever dream."

I could barely see Austin's handsome face around the camera. "That's kind of the feeling I'm going for. I want a surreal dream feel and we're nailing it."

Our photo shoot lasted for a little while longer, but when I had to keep dipping my head underwater to keep myself warm, he insisted I get out. Austin put away his camera as I lifted my dog. Austin made sure to hang on to his leash because his relaxing in the pool had brought out the wild man in Axel. I stepped out and Austin held out his jacket to me as I shivered. He wound his arm around my shoulders and then just stayed that way. His nose was inches from my forehead and I focused on his full lips.

"When I'm with you, everything quiets inside me. You remind me so much of home, happiness." He took a deep breath like he was gearing up for something big.

"That's me–an old keepsake from home." The romantic setting and the fact my entire outfit was pretty much see-through crashed down around me.

I was just his sister's best friend.

"You're way more than that." Our gaze caught. He looked from my lips to my eyes and back again. "I feel like you're a mistake I'm trying not to make."

I swallowed hard and nodded. That was me—his mistake and something that was never going to happen. I tried to avoid him while still staying in his arms. Axel chose then to shake his fur dry.

Austin let out a slow curse. "Fuck."

I stepped back and grabbed the leash. "I'm already wet, so I'll take all his dog showers."

I was doing my best to hide that this conversation was affecting me, arousing me.

Austin entered my personal space. "It's beautiful out here tonight."

I tried to swing into the shift in conversation and looked up at the stars.

I held his jacket closed over my chest. "Yeah, it's great out here, but I think I have to go somewhere with actual heat so I don't get sick."

He wasn't moving. "I mean, it's beautiful out here with you. I just don't wanna make anybody mad, but I'm pretty sure I need to taste your lips."

He ran his thumb over my bottom lip and I held my breath. I didn't want to break whatever spell this was because we weren't acting right now. We had nobody to convince that we were together, that we were a couple. I felt hope expand in my heart. In my dreams Austin was always my soul mate. And to hope that he might kiss me was just... I mean, I had kissed him before, but this? This kiss would be just for me.

"Breathe, Taylor. Take a breath."

I did just that and I heard the intake of my breath sound like inflating all my hopes.

"Will that be okay with you? Can I make this happen? Can I take this chance? I never want to change how much you need my family in your life and we need you." He leaned closer.

Everything inside of me wanted to kiss him, but I waited. If he was going to make this happen, if it was going to be real, I needed him to kiss me. I felt my lips part.

He was waiting for my consent, so I gave him that. "I'd like it very much."

And then Austin leaned down and kissed my lips specifically because he wanted to. If there was something equivalent to fireworks that went off in someone's chest, that's exactly what happened to me. My brain was screaming in delight. And then it occurred to me to kiss him back. I had Axel's leash wrapped around my wrist so I could only use one hand to cup the back of Austin's neck. He unleashed passion on me that I had only imagined existed between us.

His words misted over my skin. "You're beautiful, you're amazing, you taste so good." He was nipping my jawline and running his hands up and down my back, underneath his jacket. The chills he gave me combined with the goosebumps I had from the cool air. "Taylor, I don't wanna make this complicated, but this is the most exquisite kiss in the world."

I nodded slightly and returned my lips to his jaw. He smelled delicious. In the gentle lighting of the garden, his profile was something I never intended on forgetting. "This is beautiful." I was wearing a flower crown and surrounded by intoxicating foliage. Again, I pictured a secret wedding just between Austin and me.

Leave it to me to make things complicated. Well, even more complicated. I just couldn't leave this girl unkissed in this setting. She deserved to feel endlessly wanted. Spectacularly beautiful. Because she was just that. I knew she was cold and we had to remedy that situation. And Axel needed a nice warm blanket as well.

"Let's go. I have a blanket in my trunk." I grabbed up my bags and she kept Axel's leash. I hugged her to me once we were in the elevator, trying to give her some of my body heat.

Axel started kangaroo hopping until he could look us dead in the eyes. "He's a really weird dog, right?"

Taylor laughed and buried her face in my chest. She was like holding a freshly bloomed rose. So easy to crumple, but sculpted with beauty. I had to be careful. When we made it to the parking garage, Taylor was chattering so much that her teeth were clicking together.

I ran to the trunk and pulled out the soft blanket I had in there for photo shoots and this exact type of moment. I required models to do some wild crap, and more often than not, they needed a way to warm up between shoots.

I wrapped the blanket around her and cuddled her into the passenger seat. I was able to dry Axel off with a real towel and then he was happy to jump in behind my seat. When I got in the car, I started it up and flipped the setting to heat. I pointed the vents in her direction.

"I'm sorry this will be chilly until the car warms up." I touched her shoulder and stared into her eyes. "You really saved my ass tonight. Thank you."

"Anytime." She slumped down in the seat and I leaned over to grab her seatbelt. So close to her face, I had to give her another kiss. She leaned forward and moaned.

"Oh shit. Taylor, don't moan. You'll make it worse." I put the car in reverse.

"Make what worse?" Her innocent blue eyes were wide.

I shook my head and ran one hand over my face. "The things I want to do to you."

I watched as she wiggled in her seat. Teddi was going to kill me. Hell, my parents might kill me.

As I drove us home, I knew the consequences of kissing Taylor for real would come. But tonight, I just wanted to be with her.

When we were in front of my apartment door with all of our stuff and Axel, I was about to go digging for my keys when the door swung open. Endgame stepped back and let us in with a sweeping gesture. Music pumped through the air.

"Uh. Thanks," Taylor murmured and then struggled to keep Axel from giving Endgame a nut check.

"Hey, I hate that dog." Endgame pointed at Axel and then took a swig of vodka straight from the bottle.

I stepped between him and Taylor. "Yeah, I just bought your ass from Julian, so let's just call it a fair trade." I stared down my nose at him.

I wondered if he felt the shift. The things that were happening in me because of Taylor. I wanted that safe feeling. Living with your ex-boyfriend got harder and harder to do. I was learning that the difficult way. I saw a flash in his eyes. He did know. And just like every time in the past, he wasn't going to make things easy.

"You should've let Julian keep me. He'd be using me as an ottoman right now and my asshole as a drink holder. That would serve me right, right?" Endgame sneered at me.

I rolled my eyes and swallowed my smile. He was funny, I had to give him that. He lifted his chin in my direction before taking another pull.

I walked over and turned down the music. "You know you shouldn't be drinking."

"Alcohol fixes pain on the inside and the outside." He gave me the finger.

"Goodnight, Endgame." I watched him slam the door as I followed Taylor and Axel back into my bedroom.

I snuck into the bathroom with my change of clothes and my phone while Austin gave Axel a treat. I stared in the mirror and touched my lips. He'd kissed me. He'd hugged me. He was turned on by me? Austin Burathon of my wildest dreams and numerous daydreams. I did a little jumpy dance in a circle. I sent a text to Peaches.

ME: KISSED ME
PEACHES: SHUT UP
ME: ON THE MOUTH
PEACHES: SHUT UP
ME: MORE THAN ONCE
PEACHES: I DIE
ME: SAME HERE
PEACHES: Oh, girl, you are in so much trouble. Teddi is going to wear you like a hat.
ME: I know. But still. I mean, what was I supposed to say? No? No, don't kiss me, fuckhot Austin, who the entire world has a crush on?
PEACHES: I would have let him kiss me at any moment at any time in our lives.
ME: Don't tell me that now.
PEACHES: It's the truth. You want me to lie to you? YOU WANT ME TO LIE?
ME: No. You're right. We all want him. OMG! I have to sleep next to him. Will we kiss again?
PEACHES: WILL YOU SMACK BUSINESS ENDS TOGETHER? WEAR A CONDOM!

I sent her a picture of my face with wide eyes. I had no more words. And I really, really needed a warm shower to stop this shivering. After I had used the "HELL" temperature setting for fifteen minutes, I was pretty sure I was back to normal human body heat.

I had just pulled a baggy t-shirt and a set of boy shorts for my pajamas. And now I wished I had something more sophisticated. I had the fancy underwear, that was a rite of passage for all girls, but it hadn't occurred to me to bring them in. All I could make sure of was that I was freshly smooth and smelled really good.

When I came out of the bathroom with a towel wrapped around my hair, Austin was waiting in his desk chair. He had a mug of steaming something. He hit me with those infamous bedroom eyes and I felt my knees go weak for a brief moment.

I crossed the room to him and he held out the mug.

"Thank you."

Axel was curled up on the end of the bed. He always started as the smallest version of himself, then by the end of the evening, he would be stretched out as far as he could be. He was an expander.

I sat on the bed and sipped my drink.

"Do we want to talk about anything?" He templed his fingertips and put his elbows on his knees.

No. I didn't want to hash this out. I didn't want to analyze motivations and consequences. "How about we do that in the morning?" I offered.

"That's the best idea I've ever heard." He stood up and went to his dresser, pulling out clothes before he went into the bathroom next.

His hair was wrapped in a towel when he came out, and I set my now empty mug onto the coffee table in the sitting area of his bedroom.

Austin whipped back the sheets on his bed and I climbed in the opposite side.

"No pressure tonight. Just let me cuddle you, kitten." He held open his arms.

I crawled into his chest that was still slightly damp from his shower. He hugged me close. After cuddling for a bit, he reached over and pulled his phone off the charger. "Want to see the pics?"

He unlocked the phone with Face ID and navigated to an app. "This will have the unedited images."

He made the screen bigger. He flipped through picture after picture of Axel and me. I had no idea how many he had taken— they seemed limitless. He would sometimes pause on a picture and make it bigger or adjust the properties of the image to play with it a bit. This was truly his art. He had transformed me into a winter princess, a warrior goddess with just the camera and some water.

"These are incredible. Wow." I put my hand on the center of his chest.

"Right? The pool was fire. I really think I can design a hell of a campaign for them from this. It's just great material. Check this out."

He showed me the picture of Axel and me in matching crowns with our noses almost touching.

"I love how carefree this one is. And the fussiness of the crowns mixed with the flowers just says everything I needed it to."

He wasn't wrong. The steam from the pool was making a natural hazy filter. "I have a few video clips of this moment, too, which I think we can work with. Great set of assets." He tilted his torso enough so that he could put the phone back on its charger and then he wrapped his arms around me.

I looked up at his face. I wanted more kissing. All the kissing. And unlike my previous relationship, Austin had no goal he was trying to reach. We kissed for maybe an hour, before he started to stroke my hair. "Sleep, Taylor. Let's just do sleep tonight."

So I got to be in his arms when I dreamed of him. It was something I would love to be used to.

IN THE MORNING I woke to Austin tapping on his laptop at his desk. I was awake for a few minutes regarding him when he finally turned around to smile at me.

"Morning, pumpkin. These pictures from last night are straight fire. Come look." He held out a hand to me. I shuffled out of bed and wrapped the blanket around my shoulders.

Austin pulled me to sit on his lap. "We have so many first choices. The camera loves you so much, it's fantastic."

He started clicking through the offerings. It was another level looking at them on his huge computer monitor. One after another, I had pictures that had me smiling at Axel, looking him eye to eye. Our crowns were adorable. The focus of the pictures was just slightly different than I'd expect. And the changes allowed for the negative space and greenery to be highlighted.

"You do great work. Wow."

"Yeah, well, I had a great subject." He leaned forward and pulled down my blanket, kissing me on the shoulder.

I leaned back against him. I was glad he was still feeling romantic. Whether or not I still got to kiss him was the only question I wanted answered this morning.

His phone vibrated. "Oh, great. This is the CEO. She's thrilled and I have to take this."

I stood as he did. "Yes, Beth, I know. Thank you so much for all the kind words."

After gathering my clothes for the day, I went to the bathroom to get ready. Sunday was a hard focus on school day for me, and I needed to spend significant time on some of my assignments.

I still freshened up and brushed my teeth and hair. My cheeks seemed to already have a rosy glow, and I blamed that on thinking about Austin. When I came out of the bathroom, Austin was just finishing up his phone call. The bedroom door was open and Endgame was leaning on the frame. Axel was busy getting pets from him.

I stilled halfway across the room.

Austin focused from Endgame to me and back again. "I thought you were allergic."

"I am. This one has a pretty short coat, so it's not choking me up too bad." He gave Axel a final pat and he padded over to me.

"What are you doing today?" Endgame sipped from a steaming mug. Like we were all friends. As if he hadn't needed to be bought like a souvenir to save his life at all.

"I have work." I sat near my bag and took out my laptop. I had a five-page paper and a few discussion questions.

"Good for you. Can't always rely on what's between your legs to pay the bills. I mean, look at me? Now what the hell am I going to do? You guys need me to move out, right? Isn't that the conversation we're doomed to have?" He lit a cigarette. It smelled like weed.

"Yeah, man. You're going to have to go. Where are you going to stay?" Austin lifted the edge of his shirt a little and I saw a peek of skin.

"Act like you care. That's the best. I love to think you'll be really worried if I'm out in the rain or not." Endgame took a long pull and then exhaled his smoke.

"You're not supposed to smoke inside. You know that." Austin folded his arms over his chest.

"Like I do what you tell me. Shit. Have you been paying attention at all?" Endgame turned and left the room.

I looked to Austin, who in turn stared at the ceiling. "He's a hard one to care about."

It was confusing. This whole situation was a problem. No one in their right mind would get involved with a guy that still lived with his ex. I opened up my computer and tried to focus on the text. I read the same question three times and barely had an idea what my answer was going to be.

I loved Austin. Always had. But if Endgame came with this deal, that was going to be a very difficult situation to navigate.

Austin came over and kissed my cheek before returning to his computer. We would have to discuss this, but today, right now was not the moment.

O ur Sunday was low-key. When it was time for dinner, we ordered in. Endgame was out or very, very quiet in his room for the night.

By Monday I had finished all my work and was ready to start the week, even if it got going way too early.

When I got to my economics class, I saw a very unwelcome

sight. Roberta. She cruised by my desk and seemed to relish in the fact that we would be seeing each other a few times a week.

"Hey, Taylor, so great to see you here. I love that this professor lets anyone sit in on the class. So open-minded. I bet you brought my money. You're prepared like that, right?" She sat in the seat two rows away.

"I don't owe you money. The damage you claim I did is either made up or manufactured." I started setting up my notes, writing the date and the chapter for our lecture.

"I had a feeling you would say that. Which is another problem I had with you—you were predictable."

Roberta had lost her freaking grip on reality. Or maybe she never had it there to start with.

I chose silence accompanied by a deep breath as a response. I knew people could be like this—unreasonable and liars—but it was upsetting to have this girl I was forced to live with be such a devout practitioner of the style.

"You can act all high and mighty, but you know and I know that you destroyed my bed frame, my contact lenses, and a number of outfits. Expensive ones."

I knew she had a habit of leaving her contacts out and never closing the lids on things. Both these tendencies most likely led to her contacts lack of moisture. But blaming me was way easier than changing behavior.

I looked past Roberta and focused on the professor who was setting up his display.

Roberta shoved her phone's screen in my face before angrily swiping through her photos.

"This is you. This is you." The pictures were blurry and too close for me to make out. I was pretty sure that some of them were her bathing suit parts. Or her boyfriends. "More you. Do you need more proof? I'll get you more proof."

The professor started the lecture and Roberta eventually found a seat a few aisles away toward the front. I pretended to be focusing, but my mind was reeling with her bizarre accusations. I was out of her precious single dorm room, so she needed to move on. Anytime I glanced in her direction, she seemed to know and shoot me a horrible look. I realized she had her phone propped so that she could see me from her camera. She was either using the camera feature to see me or straight-up just recording me the entire time.

As the class ended and I put my stuff away, Roberta was back in my face. I did my best to not look at her.

"So you're dating a famous influencer, huh? I found that out. He gets paid advertisements and everything. So tell him about your bills. Suck that dick so hard money comes out." She tapped her index finger hard on the back of my chair.

I turned my back and slung my bag over my shoulder. All of a sudden she screamed and dropped to the floor. "Oh, shit! She hit me in the eye. It was on purpose. She hit me."

A guy behind us started laughing. "Give it up. She wasn't anywhere near you."

Roberta was recording herself on the floor. The guy shook his head and it must have thrown off her dramatic recording because she shut it down. As I took off after class, I heard the remnants of Roberta's fight with my defender.

"She *could* have hit me, though. She's careless. Careless..."

I had put enough distance between her and me that I couldn't hear her voice. I was going to have to thank that guy in the next class. How she found out I was dating Austin, or well, pretend dating, but actually may be real dating, I didn't know. But this was escalating in a way I was not comfortable with. I didn't want to be chased out of school just because I had an unfortunate roommate. I had met a lot of people in my life, and none of them had been as unstable as Roberta. I was able to step onto the city bus to get home quicker.

When I got back to the apartment, I looked around before going inside. I didn't see anyone, but didn't love the idea that I was possibly being followed from time to time. She was making me paranoid and creating issues that weren't even problems yet.

After saying hello to Barker, the doorman, I took the elevator up to our floor. Earlier I asked Austin about the tipping situation and he said that the maintenance fees of the apartment building took care of that. We only had to make sure to give nice gifts at the holidays.

When I got inside, both Axel and Austin were gone. I pulled out my phone and saw a text that had been sent on my walk back to the apartment.

AUSTIN: Took puppy for a walk. Endgame won't be home.

The text was followed by a kiss emoji. I locked the door behind me and stood in the apartment alone. I had to handle Roberta somehow. She seemed to be escalating and getting more dramatic at the same time. It was a problem.

20

Tinsley and Parker met me to walk Axel. He was a huge hit with them both. I was trying to work on his crotch slamming habit, but he was stubborn and quick. I warned them both to stay prepared to guard their loins. Once we all established a rhythm, we set out to stretch Axel's legs.

"So Stars Unlimited was okay with Taylor?" Tinsley looped her arm in mine. I had always appreciated her for her directness.

"Yeah. They loved the pictures." I shrugged. All I could see of her reaction was my own reflection in her sunglasses.

"That's good. Really good."

I heard Parker snort. "You sound genuine, Tin."

She shot him the middle finger. "You know how much I love Austin, so shut it."

I pressed her arm with my bicep. "I know, sweetheart. I know."

"And you would totally teach me the same lesson if the heels were on the other foot." She tapped her right foot one beat extra while we walked.

Parker looped his arm in mine as well. "Did you learn your lesson then? Are you going to kick out your danger pony with the giant dick and all his baggage yet?"

I shook my head. "Man. I wish I knew. I mean, he has to go. It just makes sense. But it kills me to know that I'd be tossing him out on the streets."

Axel was leading the pack of us, tossing his head over his shoulder to look at us with a dangling tongue.

"You care too much about a guy that would burn your whole world down because he was bored for two minutes." Tinsley let go of my arm to maneuver around a grate and then resumed her position.

Parker let go, as the grates were coming in a regular pattern, so Tinsley could still hang on.

"I know how you feel about it." She had told me in a joking manner and a dead serious manner how an outsider viewed Endgame's effect on my everyday life.

"It's from a place of concern and love, I promise you."

I leaned over and kissed her cheek. "I know."

Parker held out his hand for Axel's leash and I let him take the lead. "You know it's not just you in that place anymore. Taylor's a nice girl. Mind if I take Axel for a little jog?"

I nodded my approval and he took off. Axel was thrilled to go faster, hopping up and looking Parker in the eyes before galloping along.

Tinsley and I now had just each other to talk to while we walked. "So how's it going with Taylor, really?"

I thought back to our kisses and how we fell asleep last night. "Dangerous."

"How do you mean?" Tinsley slowed down our pace a bit.

"Last night got pretty real for me." We paused where we were walking and she led me to window shop at the shoe store. She lifted her eyebrows over her sunglasses. "She felt right in my arms. Like the energy coming from her was so beautiful and pure." I let out a sigh.

"Oh my gosh. Really? Really?" Tinsley tilted her head to one side and then the other. "Are you falling for her for real?"

I rubbed my forehead. "I mean, who wouldn't? She's gorgeous. But, like my little sister's best friend. I can't imagine what that looks like. Or the amount of beatings all my brothers would dole out. She grew up in our house. And I'm living with my ex."

"You kissed her? Did you guys have sex?" Tinsley pulled her sunglasses down on her face.

"No. Sweet craps, no. I didn't take it that far." I pulled her along so we could resume walking.

"But you wanted to..." She trailed her fingers up my arm.

"I may have started something that I should've stopped instead." I was finding it really hard to regret the night Taylor was in my arms. Her peaceful sleep was a delight. She kept finding reasons to touch me with her hands and feet. Every once in a while she would open her eyes and check to see that I was still there, then wiggle her butt like a happy kitten. It was calm and beautiful.

"You know Endgame has done some damage, right?" She pushed her sunglasses on her head.

"To the apartment? Yeah, I know. Hell, I wouldn't even leave him alone with Taylor this morning. He's got a meeting with his parole officer." I stepped us to the side as a guy on a skateboard whizzed by.

"To you, babe. He did damage to you." Tinsley had empathy in her eyes.

"What do you mean?" I never really had to worry about Endgame's effect on other people, I was the only one in his crossfire.

"He emotionally abuses and manipulates you. Like the whole reason I wouldn't do the shoot with you. You had to pay for him to be alive again, right?" She and I waited as Parker and Axel jogged past us. Parker gave us the motion with his finger that he was going to go around the block again.

"Yeah. Same old, same old." I narrowed my eyes as the previous times flitted through my head.

"You know he does it just because he needs to be the center of your universe." She pat my chest.

I covered her hand. "For a long time, I thought that was love."

"That makes sense. Shit, you've the most stable homelife I've ever witnessed, so the rush of the danger and dysfunction with Endgame probably felt a lot like love. But putting you in danger, putting himself in danger isn't an adventure. It's hostile and chips away at your soul."

"You're going to be a great relationship therapist someday soon. How's school?" I slid my sunglasses over my eyes.

"School is exhausting. Stop trying to change the subject." Tinsley slid her sunglasses back on as well.

"I get it. I know. I have to figure it out with him." I felt my stomach twist at the thought. Conversations were always arguments with Endgame being defensive and aggressive at the same time. He was super smart. Part of the reason he kept me on my toes.

I led us away from the shop and to the intersection.

"If you care about Taylor, do it soon. Hell, if you need privacy, she can stay with me." She and I waited for the crosswalk light.

"I'll think about it, babycakes. First, I have to deal with this campaign. And they've asked for something." Now I had to see how angry she really was. "They want you and Taylor together for the next one."

"Oh, do they? That's interesting." She smirked.

"What do I have to do to get you to participate?" Now we could negotiate.

"Just be good to yourself. Realize that your well-being matters just as much as everyone else's." She went to her tip toes and kissed my cheek. "Even more to some of us."

Parker and Axel came up next to us just in time for a water break—well, at least for Axel. The local bakery had a huge water bowl set out for dogs that passed by.

I thought Parker looked thirsty enough to take a few licks himself. I popped into the bakery and grabbed three waters for us and a cookie for Taylor and a dog cookie for Axel. Parker huffed and praised the Lord when I handed him his bottle. Then he thanked me with a clap on the back while he gulped.

Tinsley rubbed Axel's head but addressed me, "Yeah. I'll do it."

"I'll get back to you with the details." I gave her a wink. I appreciated her concern. And she wasn't wrong. We headed back to the apartment, and before we got to my door, Parker and Tinsley said goodbye.

I had about another hour before Endgame was home from his meeting with his parole officer, at the earliest. I wanted to be sure I was home if he was home. When I got upstairs with Axel, Taylor had wide eyes.

"What's wrong?"

Austin looked all over the apartment before coming to my side on the couch.

"It's not Endgame." I guessed what his concerns were and saw the relief flood his handsome features.

"What happened? Are you okay?" He put his arm around me and took my face in his hand and kissed the tip of my nose.

"Stupid Roberta. She's in my economics class and started giving me the business."

"Oh, for fuck's sake. She's like a tick. Can't let go of anything. Sucks, too, and has diseases, I bet." He pulled me against his chest and I took comfort from being in his arms.

I laughed at his analogy.

"She's as annoying as a nest of ticks, I hate to tell you. She brought you up and social media stuff." I felt my stomach turn at the thought of him being affected by her stupidity.

"That's alarming. That means you're being stalked." He hugged me harder.

"I'm sorry." I offered to his chin.

"Please. For what? I'm so grateful you're here and not living with her anymore. We need to make sure to be careful, and maybe investigate a restraining order."

I nodded against his chest.

"Hey. I have an idea. I have a friend that has a house out on the beach. This weekend, let's go there. I bet Parker and Tinsley would love to watch Axel for us. We can reset." He kissed my forehead and I twirled the ring on his thumb.

"That sounds awesome, Tinsley isn't angry anymore?" I sat forward so I could see his reaction.

"Oh, no, she's still angry. But me going away with you will make her happy. And I'm pretty sure Parker will turn Axel into a marathon runner by the time we get back." Austin leaned down and kissed my lips. He was so, so good at it.

"I'll go anywhere with you." I couldn't believe this was my life now. I was this lucky.

Later that evening, I texted Peaches while Austin edited pictures of me on his computer.

ME: WE ARE GOING TO A BEACH HOUSE.
ME: ALONE.

Peach responded right away.

PEACHES: Holy crap. This is real. Real. Like you will know what color everything is. And what it tastes like. I bet it tastes like cake and mangos.
ME: That's my hope. That he's made of part unicorn and I have all human scents.
PEACHES: Don't let me make you nervous. You are a snack. With a six pack. Paddy whack.
ME: Are you drunk? It's Monday for crap's sake.
PEACHES: I'm not drunk. I'm just me.
ME: I apologize. I know you have a weirdness in you that needs to come out.
PEACHES: Thank you.
PEACHES: I'm so excited about the beach house. Give me the address and I will be waiting in the driveway.
ME: Absolutely not.
PEACHES: It was a worth a try. But you owe me a blow-by-blow. I

want to know how minds get blown. Penises get blown. I want to know it all.

ME: I feel like I owe you a tasteful summary.

PEACHES: Emphasis on taste.

I sent an emoji with the tongue sticking out.

ME: Seriously. I have to pack for the weekend. I mean, I have time, but I think I need new everything.

PEACHES: Definitely. Don't bring the grandma drawers.

ME: Stop remembering that happened.

PEACHES: I can't. Sometimes I see it in my nightmares. You and I getting changed at my house and me spotting you in the same Hanes Her Way as my grandmother.

I sent her the middle finger emoji.

PEACHES: I'm so happy for you. Honestly. Get it. Get it good. I'm glad one of us is going to know what Austin is like in bed. I hope you stretch and like, eat protein. There's an old rumor that pineapples make the boom box taste like heaven.

ME: I heard the same. I think it's an urban legend. But I'll swallow a few for science.

Peaches sent back an emoji with the tongue sticking out.

PEACHES: Swallow, baby. Sometimes it's worth it.

I told her good night and headed into the shower. Austin was busy enhancing a drop of water on my crown.

THIS WAS GOING to be a long week. And a short one. It made perfect sense to go to a beach house with Austin. I was an adult. I was able to do these things on a whim. It'd be great to put some distance between me and my concerns about Roberta and Endgame. I did a deep condition and took off my nail polish.

When I came out in my pajamas, Austin took the nail polish remover and took off his remnants of polish.

"I do you, you do me?" He gave me a wink that somehow let me into his world even more.

21

Austin set up his friends to pick me to and from class every day. Some I had met before; some were new to me. He knew a lot of people. He seemed to be selecting the beefiest of his man friends to do the work. He was in deep with planning the campaign with Stars Unlimited and was also taking calls from a place in France that was interested in working with him.

Judging from the four packages he received that were stuffed full of free products, Roberta wasn't wrong about Austin being sort of famous. Hell, I saw him manufacture an obscene amount of cash to save Endgame.

Speaking of Endgame, he came and went with a grumble, though I saw him more than once sneak a pet on Axel's head. Plus, he came into the apartment covering his crotch. Well, that was a habit everyone had. It was low-key hilarious to watch back the video footage of the front door that Austin had because everyone was ready for the attack.

I was going to have to work on that. I checked in with Raven and she was happy to have a break from Axel, but I sent her a few videos anyway.

The undiscussed situation was Dad, but she was doing okay. I had planned on going home for the long weekend, but now that Austin and I were going to the beach, I didn't bring it up. I felt guilty leaving my sister without me, but I knew I had to go. It was Austin. And he'd asked me.

I spent time at a few stores with some of my escorts. I was able to get a few new night clothes and things to take with me. It would be cold, most likely, though the weather forecast called for sun.

On Friday evening, after Parker and Tinsley picked up Axel, Austin held open the door for me and I got into his car. To go with Austin. To a beach house and have sex with him. At least that was my intention.

Once we were on the road, I pulled up the weather app on my phone. "Looks like sun this weekend. I've never been to this beach before."

How was he even cool at driving? He was smooth. Didn't react quickly to anything. "This song okay?"

He put on a band I'd never heard of, but liked the sound of. "Yes. So tell me about these people. They just give you keys to their places?"

He laughed and slid on his sunglasses. "Well, a bunch of us have kind of come up on social media together. We sort of have a code. We help each other when we can. These ladies are amazing organizers and life coaches. And I've styled them a billion times. They always want me to take them up on their offer." He scratched the tip of his nose.

"Which was?" I turned my shoulders toward him.

"To bring a beautiful person up to the house and make sweet, sweet love to them." He bit his lip.

I knew he was being funny, but I still felt it between my legs. "Oh."

We pulled up to the beach house, which didn't look like much, but I could hear the ocean almost immediately.

I met Austin by the trunk of his car and we kissed for a few minutes. Eventually, he tilted his head up. "I'll have you right here. We need to stop."

I was delighted to see he was affected by me. He grabbed our suitcase and I grabbed our tote bag. After Austin had plugged in the key code, we were inside. The money was invested on the inside. The house seemed like it was three-fourths glass.

"Oh. Wow."

Austin chuckled. "Just you wait." He walked over to a touch-screen on the wall and held his phone near it. After popping in a few codes, his phone was now a remote. "Check this out."

The windows to the outside engaged and rolled open. The lights in the house dimmed. We had an entire section of the beach to ourselves. I walked out on the deck and it spilled down to wide steps, ending buried in the sand.

The moon was gorgeous and lit the beach and crashing waves as if it was filming a private movie.

I turned to face him. "You wishing you took them up on this every weekend now?"

He laughed. "Yeah. It's too gorgeous. Like you."

I saw a spiral staircase that went to a deck even higher.

"Let's go. There's a bedroom I want to introduce you to."

He let me proceed first, holding my hips as I walked.

The bedroom had its windows/walls open as well. "We're

going to sleep so well in here. This is a real-life white noise machine."

He pulled me into the bedroom. The walls had beautiful low-light sconces. It was romantic and inviting.

"Let me get our stuff. I'll be right back." Austin gave me a little bow and left.

When he returned, he placed the suitcase on a table and unzipped it with flourish.

I snagged my things out of the suitcase, then kissed his cheek. He gave me a low growl.

I freshened up in the bathroom, I was working with a classic —black panties, black bra, and thigh highs.

When I was ready, I was ready. I checked the mirror and my eyes flashed. I was thankful that I had been staying with Austin for as long as I had been because he didn't stun me stupid with his good looks. I was used to him—mostly.

I stepped out of the bathroom and let my eyes adjust to the candlelight. The sconces had some help from a scattered few decorative candles.

He was sitting in the plush lounge chair, the wall of glass doors the bedroom had were pushed open. I could hear the surf just beyond and the breeze kicked up. He was silhouetted, slumped low in the chair with a glass of some liquor in his hand. Music was playing softly, coming out of everywhere it seemed.

Austin stood up and set his glass down, holding his hand out to me. "Beautiful Taylor."

I walked to him. "Beautiful Austin."

His smile made me return it. "Are you okay with this? Can I touch you?"

"Yes. Please. Otherwise I just wore a really awkward outfit to hang out with you." I took his hand and placed it in the center of my chest.

His laugh was deep in his chest. "I want to have an interview with you first. I need to find out what you like, how you like it."

The way he was looking at me. Like he would teach me things I never knew about my body gave me a chill.

He wasn't ridiculously older than me, but his life experiences had been exceptional. It was in how he walked. How he knew to do so many things in the real world. It was heady. He was a dream come true, but I had a feeling my imagination hadn't been good enough as far as he was concerned.

"I should ask you the same things then." Was I whispering? I think I was whispering.

"I can answer those easily. I want you. I want to see what it's like when you forget to be you, when you only feel so good all you can do is growl and scream." He ran a finger down my jaw and then tucked some hair behind my ear. He leaned close to my ear and gently licked the shell of it.

"You expect to have a conversation? After that?" I put my hands on his biceps. He was wearing just lounge pants, his hair down. He still had his layers of necklaces and stacks of rings.

"Absolutely. Come with me. Sit with me." He grabbed my hand.

When I was sitting on his lap, I felt that conversation wasn't the only thing on his mind, but he acted cool.

"I want to find out how you handle this kind of stuff. Does anything make you uncomfortable? Has anything ever happened that we need to talk through?" He rubbed his thumb on my hand.

I felt the unexpected prick of tears.

"What is it? Just know, being here with you, it can be whatever you need. No matter what you're wearing, no matter what expectations you think I have. Your safety is the most important thing to me. What you want is sacred to me." Then Austin sat back with the most understanding look on his face.

"I've just never had a conversation like this. I mean, in the past it was pretty much trying to get things done." I wiped my stupid tear away.

"Yeah, but it's you. So this is important." He nodded slowly. "No pressure, ever."

"You're something else, Austin Burathon." I leaned forward and kissed his lips. "Are you okay with me touching you?"

He was being so thoughtful with consent, I made sure I was giving him the same treatment.

"I say yes. Whatever you want—you can try it, feel it. Whatever you need." He held his arms out to either side.

I felt his chest while I spoke to him. "I like romantic talk and press right here." I took his hand and placed it between my legs, through the lace, and we applied pressure to my clit. "I really like that."

His eyes hooded. "Noted. External stimulation is a necessity. Have you ever come before, sweetheart?"

I squirmed a bit, his hand between my legs caused my heart to start pounding. "I think so."

"If that's something you want, we can make that happen. There won't be any thinking about it. It's natural." He didn't move his hand at all, but maintained the contact I'd asked for.

"That is what I'd like. I want you to treat me like you think I'd enjoy." I leaned closer to him.

He had a soft scent of musk and something floral. His profile could have been on a classic Roman statue. Being looked at with his eyes underlined with eyeliner made it ten times hotter than it had any right to be.

"Okay. But remember, at any time you are safe and we can stop." Austin leaned forward and touched his forehead to mine.

It was different from sweaty moments with Brutus. He was obsessed with boob, boob, pussy, and pumping his way to victory.

"What's your safe word?" He waited as I started to squirm. I was addicted to these powerful new feelings he'd made me experience.

"Pickles," I offered.

Not sure where it came from, but Austin grinned. "Got it. Pickles."

Austin started with my face, kissing my cheeks, my lips, even my eyelids. "Beautiful Taylor. Your skin's like silk." He ran his hands from my hips to my back. "Can I move you to the bed?"

"Please." He stood then, easily lifting me.

He nuzzled my neck and I tilted my head to give him access.

He placed me on the bed carefully and climbed next to me. This part with past boyfriends was awkward. The first roll in the hay. But with Austin, it was the comfort of dreams come true. I'd imagined it so many times, that having it happen was like déjà vu.

I acclimated to his weight next to me and he gently moved my hair from my forehead. "So, I want to start small and work up to your big finale, okay?"

I nodded and took him in. He got off the bed and returned from our bags with a velvet bag of his own. He showed me while he unveiled what was inside. A vibrator, a bottle of lube, and a few other small orbs and a ring. We took a few minutes to unwrap and unpackaged the new items.

"I've never used anything like that before, so I'm not sure what to do." I pointed at the small pile.

"You just have to feel. Tell me what you like and let sensations wash over you." He grabbed his long, brown hair and then threaded a hair tie through it to keep it from falling in front of his face. His bicep and the veins moved with his motions.

He was between my legs now. "Men are the worst, right? In a porn, there can be ten of them in a room and not a single one touches the clit. Like, it's right there. And it's full of sensations. Would you want to have sex if the lady only touched your balls? Hell no. It's about slow pressure. I can have an orgasm any day, any second with my hand, but you ladies have to earn it. And I'm here for the heavy lifting."

"Heavy lifting?" I felt my eyebrow raise.

"Metaphorically." He held the band of my panties with his fingertips. "Can these come off?"

My legs were on either side of his hips. He would have the perfect access to me, and also the view of everything I was worth.

"Yes. Please," I responded.

Slowly, carefully he took them off of me. Pausing to rub my thigh, kiss my ankle. He took a deep breath. "Heaven." He leaned over me and I felt his erection push against my thigh. He retrieved a small pillow from the bed. "Lift your hips for me, angel."

I did as I was asked and tried not to think about how the motion would affect his view. He propped up my hips.

"There. Now, I have somewhere to do my work." He gave me a wicked smile. Austin slid his pants off with a soft look on his face. I left on my bra. He took a second to roll on a condom.

The small pile he had on the bed was dragged closer. After all the mouth love, I was ready for all the things he promised. He picked up the first vibrator and flicked it on. Then, with a squirt of lube, he started massaging me. The outside, my labia, with deep, knowledgeable movements. Every once in a while, he hit the spot on my body that sent an electric-like zap through me and made my nipples ache.

"I'm going to be using both hands, but feel free to pinch those for me." He bit his bottom lip.

I listened and did as he asked, another wave of lust causing me to arch my back. Deep inside, I was getting a weight, a pent-up something going on. I rolled my ankles and curled my toes.

"That's it, precious. Start feeling it."

I heard the low hum of the vibrator. He moved it around, close to where I was feeling a pull. Then he swiped the spot again and I spasmed under the touch.

"There we are. That's the spot that's mine." He touched it again. "When you need to be full, tell me."

"Okay," I breathed.

Something was going to happen. My body was reacting to a drumbeat that I didn't know it heard.

He set the vibrator directly on my clit and held it there with a firm hand. It took me past where I'd ever been sexually before. Like it had felt good, I had fun, but I was meeting a part of myself with Austin that was otherworldly.

I moaned and squirmed. The way he had me anchored and

propped, there was no getting away. I was addicted to the buzz but scared of what was welling inside me. I tried to grind against the vibrator.

"Oh, are you ready for more?" Austin kept the vibrator in one spot.

I heard the crinkle of the lube packet again and the buzz of the vibrator disappeared, but was quickly replaced by Austin's strong sure fingers. And then I felt the delicious hum of vibrations moving lower as he eased the toy inside me. Rocking gently, giving it to me inch by slow, euphoric inch. Now I could grind on something while whatever my body had planned built up. Austin's fingers strumming my clit. I was coming. That's what it was. In the past the small chances at pleasure had visited me.

Now it was going to hit like a revelation.

Austin encouraged me, "Just ride it out. Feel it. I can tell you're coming. You're pulsing. I'm going to slide my dick in. It's happening. Please touch your nipples, it'll feel amazing."

He was inside now, the fullness brimming me. I pushed aside the lace of my bra and shamelessly pinched my nipples. At the same second, he swirled his hips while pulling in and out. The buzzing was still there, still present. Something was marching up me. This lust, this animal passion. My throat was hurting, and I realized it was because I was guttural moaning his name and cursing.

"Here you go. God, you're so fucking hot. Come. Come on my cock. Let me feel you feel it."

I felt the pursuit he was talking about. Deep in my belly, I had an ache, and in a rush, it was happening. I heard the moisture I was generating hiss against his dick.

"Oh yes. Like that. Shit. Shit." Austin started pumping like crazy. He was hitting something deep inside me that tipped me over yet another edge. I was falling off a roller coaster and hollering his name.

His whole body tensed and his abs clenched as he came to his ending.

I was panting so loud, and so fast, it felt like there wasn't enough air in the room. I felt Austin gently wrap his fingers around my throat. "Breathe, pretty Taylor. Take a breath or you'll burst blood vessels around your eyes."

He was panting, too. I moved my legs and felt the wetness there. He was still wearing his condom, I was pretty sure. I sat up. "What happened?"

"You had bliss. And this is what happens when it's handled correctly. You came." He winked at me.

I started laughing. Laughing so hard. I was naked and laughing and Austin joined in.

"Oh my God, what?" He cuddled me to his chest.

It took me a minute to speak. "I didn't know any of it did that." I pointed between my legs.

"Women should have access to a handbook. You deal with so much because of the baby-making side of things, getting to the pleasure part should be easier." Austin locked his fingers with mine.

I felt a surge of love for him. Maybe it was post-orgasm endorphins, but I felt closer to him than I ever had with anyone right this second.

"I've wanted you for so many years. You were my first crush. Honestly, the only crush that mattered. I'm pretty sure you just taught my vagina to write your name in cursive."

He burst out laughing then retorted, "By the end of the weekend she'll be writing it in calligraphy."

I touched his cheek and turned toward him on my side, feeling the wetness again. "I need to clean this up."

"Give it a second, kitten. I want to hear what you have to say. And I made you make a mess, I'll help you clean." He turned on his side as well, a touch more somber.

Looking in his eyes forced my smile. "Was that okay for you? I mean, I know that you've been with models and stuff."

"That was incredible for me, but again, more importantly,

you learned what you need to expect from a lover." He ran his other hand from my ribcage to my hip.

I felt my throat close. He was talking like this was just a stopover in our lifetime. An experience gainer. Not a step in a relationship. That I'd have more lovers in my life.

I closed my eyes to try to stop the fear from reflecting there. "Yeah. Sure."

"Hey. Hey, I'm sorry. Was that crass? To talk of the future like that?"

I felt his hand go from my hip to my cheek.

"It's okay. It's totally fine." I opened my eyes and shook my head briskly, pushing the rush of emotions I had for him aside as best as I could.

"Say the next thing." He tipped his head so we touched our foreheads.

"What?" I was getting desperate to put some panties on. Put some distance between us.

"After you said, 'It's totally fine,' there was something else. Because I've said that exact line before. And there was a quiet part in my mind as well." He narrowed his eyes.

In the past, I'd have pushed through the feelings. Made myself feel something else besides the disappointment.

"I guess, I know you've lived this whole life ahead of me and experienced a ton of things. Just being Taylor couldn't be enough to keep you to myself—like I want." Holy crap, I just dumped the truth out between us. And it felt like watching a full glass water pitcher hit a tile floor. No fixing it, only dealing with it.

"Oh, baby." He pulled me against his chest for a hug.

"It's true, though, right?" I pulled the lace over my breasts.

"No. Not true at all." He rolled off the bed and held out his hand to me. His flaccid dick was still impressive.

I took his hand and let him help me out of the bed. It felt freeing to walk with a naked him anywhere. He took me to the full-length mirror in the bedroom.

We stood side-by-side and he waited patiently until I made eye contact with him in the mirror. We'd just had sex, but I felt the zap between my legs all over again, just from his gaze.

One hand covered the lace on left breast. He touched my bare hip with the other hand.

"See this curve right here?" He let his fingertips paint the touch sensation on my skin. "It's worth a lifetime." Then he took my hands and stepped behind me. He wasn't a head taller than me, so he leaned a bit so he could see around my messy bed hair. "These dimples right here?" He put his thumbs over the two indentations in my lower back. "A war to get to put my hands here and know I can enter you."

He pulled my hair away from my neck and tilted my body into his. "This throat? The beautiful things you say to me? Create a universe I want to fall into." He twisted me so I was chest-to-chest with him. "This gorgeous face? This profile?" He used his index finger to trace from my forehead to my nose to my lips. I kissed his finger. "You are the very epitome of a gift to this world. You are a luxury and a pilgrimage. Remember these words. Take them into your soul, my incredible, beautiful Taylor. Please promise me you'll do that. You'll hear me say that when the voice in your mind isn't playing nice?"

I knew then that my heart was right. And if my heart could write a man into existence, I wasn't sure she could come up with someone this good. My soul recognized in him this beauty before I knew what it meant.

"How can you just say these things? And all of a sudden I believe them?" I put his face in my hands, running my thumbs along his high cheekbones.

His eyes sparkled. "Because I'm right, it's true and I've never lied to you."

This was happiness. This was forever. This weekend had to be the beginning of the best love story I could have ever imagined between Austin and me.

IT WAS AMAZING. The beautiful house had marble and soothing beige colors and pops of blues as well.

"You want something to eat, kitten?" Austin was wearing just a scarf around his neck and I had on only a tank top.

"I'm hungry. I could definitely eat." I kicked my feet up onto the white ottoman.

Austin pulled out his phone. "I got you. How's an elaborate fruit arrangement, sushi, and a gourmet cake sound?"

I let out a laugh. "Impossible?"

He shook his head slowly. "Oh, baby. The things I can make happen. The people who owe me favors? You'll learn." He gave me a bow and then started pressing the screen on his phone.

"You like pineapples?" He peered over the screen.

"Mmmhmm." I licked my lips.

"Awesome. Okay. We should've everything in about half an hour. Want another orgasm while we wait?" He took his scarf off and came close to me.

"If you're offering..." I sat forward and he looped the scarf around my back.

"I think I am." Before I knew what was happening, Austin had wound the material around my wrists and pulled them above my head.

He tightened the scarf and I lay back on the couch. At first I was thinking about being outside the bedroom with my legs spread, but then Austin had his mouth on my inner thigh and I stopped caring where I was and focused on what he was doing.

His tongue felt like a wave of sensations. He began sucking on my clit. That electric feeling was boiling again. It sizzled through my inhibitions and then through my decency.

When Austin added fingers to sensations, it became pure decadence. The orgasm he expertly guided me to made me scream his name. My tank top was pushed up under my chin and I was heaving to breathe.

"That's it, Taylor. That's it." His breath was on my stomach, and then the sensations were back. It had to be the second one in a row.

When I finally had my wits about me, I realized my head was hanging off the edge of the couch. Austin's self-satisfied smolder looked handsome even from the weird angle I was in. He freed my hands.

He helped pull me up, and I faced his erection. I wrapped my hands around it, with every intention of repaying the favor, but his cell phone had an alert. "Food is almost here. Get out of here. I don't want to share any of this with the delivery guys."

He ran his hand from my left breast to my hip. He helped me up, and then he led me to the staircase. I turned and gave him a kiss.

He was such an amazing kisser. He knew just when to add tongue and when to nip at my bottom lip. Nothing was sexier than this man.

The doorbell sounded and Austin took off. I peeked around the wall to see how he handled his nudity. He was wearing a trench coat he must have found in the front closet.

He thanked the first delivery person, and then the second. He turned and set a huge fruit bouquet onto the coffee table and then a brown bag next to it.

The doorbell sounded through the house one more time, and then we had a cake and flower delivery.

When all was clear and the delivery people were gone, I inched back into the room.

"No kidding. You get shit done."

I opened the brown bag and saw the artistic looking sushi packaged with chopsticks.

He indicated the beautiful flowers. "For you. To celebrate orgasms."

I touched the irises and the azaleas. They were a stunning arrangement of ombre colors.

"Thank you. For the flowers and for everything else."

We carried the food and the flowers upstairs and opened up the balcony doors. We could hear the ocean and the huge, full moon provided the light.

Austin pulled the comforter from the bed and spread it on the hardwood in the bedroom.

We both laid out all the things we had to munch on now. We started with the sushi, and then moved on to samples of everything else. When we were overfull, Austin and I stood and stretched.

This was the perfect getaway. The perfect weekend. We cleaned up our mess, him naked and me mostly so, and then we crawled back into bed. I laid my head on his chest as we both pulled out our phones for a scroll.

Austin tensed first, and I got a message that caused the same reaction in me.

The cracks started. Perfect was only perfect for a little while.

22

Well, shit. This was not what I had in mind. I had an email from Stars Unlimited, that their ad campaign featuring Taylor was doing great. The one problem they had was a very effective spam account that kept commenting that Taylor was dating a "lady man." The offender(s) were emailing, calling, and even had somehow figured out how to send fax messages to the main office, all while constantly responding on Twitter. I felt Taylor tense next to me.

"Teddi is messaging me. Apparently, the "lady man" thing is going sort of viral."

I gave her an eye roll. "What do you think this is about? Do you think this is Endgame? That wouldn't make any sense, I don't think. But he does bizarre stuff when he's hurting."

Taylor shook her head. "I don't know. It seems like it's personal, right? They always say that with murderers that, like, if there's sixty stab wounds, that it's personal. But I think this is sort of the internet version of a personal attack. I feel like it has Roberta written all over it.

"Teddi, of course, still thinks that you and I are friends pretending to be dating. And I feel like it makes sense to hold that line." Taylor's phone lit up and the word "dad" was highlighted. "I have to take this."

She got out of the bed and I missed her immediately. She wrapped her arms around her waist and answered the phone. I tried not to eavesdrop, but things were echoey in the big house. I heard her end of the conversation.

"Hey, Dad. I'm glad you like the pictures. And yes, you know the photographer. It's Austin Burathon. He's Teddi's brother." She listened to the other end of the phone, but she was far enough away that I could not hear the other side. "Well, actually, he and I are not really dating. I needed a cover for someone that was giving me the business and he's a friend. But no matter what, whomever I'm involved with is my business."

Her voice was slightly higher, and I could tell she was gearing up for a fight. I knew Taylor was not as close with her father as I was with my family, and the chaos at their house highlighted the fact that things could be difficult. I truly believed that the state of their house was an obvious call for help. I couldn't imagine that communication was fantastic between the two. My phone rang and Tinsley was on the other line. I knew it was serious because she was actually calling. My eavesdropping session on Taylor's conversation ended when I picked up my phone.

"Who the hell is after you?"

I took a deep breath. "I'm not sure. I haven't even seen what's been going on. Stars Unlimited is going to send me screenshots of things before they turned off the comments. They are rightly concerned that there seems to be somebody with a vendetta against Taylor and me. The good news is, they are completely understanding of the fact my outfit choices tend to be outside the 'normal'."

Parker spoke up from the background, "Oh, these assholes need a new asshole. I'm happy to kick one in for them." I stifled a chuckle knowing my friends accepted who I was and how I dressed.

Tinsley seemed to walk away from the angry Parker because his voice faded. "How is Taylor doing?"

"She's talking to Mr. Boland right now and the conversation isn't going smoothly."

I heard a door close and I figured it was to put some more distance between Taylor and me while she had her conversation and I had mine. The next phone call I had was Teddi.

"Tinsley, I'm gonna have to call you back. My sister is on the phone," I said.

She told me good luck as I switched over to answer Teddi.

Teddi immediately started in, "Whoever is doing it is a problem, and I have Gaze and Pixie, Ruffian and Milt on the phone right now."

I loved my family, and I loved that they immediately began circling to defend me. Of most importance, possibly, on the line was Milt, who had a background in computers that I probably would have called first had I not been fielding phone calls from my concerned friends and family. "Hey, Milt, what can you tell me so far?"

Milt's end of the conversation came through. "Well, I got my guys on it and the IP address has been run through a VPN, so we're having slight difficulty locating it. But I'll have it for you within an hour." Milt's voice was hard. "I'll have everything this person has ever done on the internet and their entire life. Their social security number, their dog's name, everything you could ever want on them."

My brother, Hamilton, and his friends were adorable with their cosplay party company. I forgot that they could do so much with computers, including building them.

"Thanks, Milt. I appreciate that." I felt a shiver thinking about what they would find about Endgame. Hell, even the fact he was still living with me might be a surprise. Though I knew that they knew. I was secretly hoping that Roberta was the problem. Taylor knew some of what I got involved in with Endgame, but not all of it. I felt like I had a bunch of warriors on my side, but I wasn't sure this was a fight I wanted them to get involved in.

My beautiful weekend with Taylor was ending on a crushing blow. We would have to go back and handle whatever this was. Tinsley began sending me text messages that she wanted to do the photo shoot with Taylor as soon as possible.

TINSLEY: We will be supporting you and we will be giving the middle finger to anyone who dares to give us the business.

I texted back while listening to Gaze and Pixie ask me how things were going. I heard a soft sniffle and looked up to see Taylor with her eyes filled with tears. "Hey, guys, I have to go. Thank you and I'll be in touch with anything that we figure out."

I didn't have a chance to tell Milt privately that I wanted to make sure that some of my stuff stayed my stuff.

"What's wrong, beautiful?"

"I was just so happy, and this isn't what I wanted our weekend to look like. I hate that me stepping in as a model for you brought you pain and frustration."

I held out my hand to her. "Sweetheart, this isn't pain and

frustration. This is just stupid. We'll handle it together. What did your father say?"

I knew it would've been something she maybe didn't want to deal with. "Oh, he had a lot to say, and I kind of got into it with him. I was saying in a way maybe you don't get an opinion when you've checked out on my sister and me all these years. And I spoke about the unspoken elephant in the room, which is all the crap at my house. So he wants to meet you and he wants me to come home and not in that order. What did Tinsley have to say?"

"I'm sorry that you're in this because of me." I pulled her into a hug.

"Don't get it twisted. You don't get to take the blame for this because, if you remember correctly, you did me a favor first because I'm not kicking Endgame out. I get that made Tinsley mad and she's not wrong. And you didn't ruin this weekend. It is probably the singularly most beautiful weekend I've ever had."

She burrowed her face into my chest. "That's a good thing at least because I feel the same way. It's my favorite weekend. I feel bad for all the other weekends in the past that had to compete. And I hate that we have to leave, and I honestly don't even know what I'm going to tell my dad. Because he doesn't know that I'm not in the dorms anymore. I didn't wanna get into it, I know he'd just tell me to come home instead of sticking it out." She took a deep breath. "He never liked the idea of me going to college, so coming home would be his favorite. Which is kind of hilarious because he gets home and pretty much hides from my sister and me." She put her fingers to her forehead and rubbed as if trying to smooth out memories there.

"Okay, so we need to figure out what you want to tell him. What you're comfortable with telling him and then we will handle that. Milton should be able to tell us who's behind this in about an hour. He and his friends are working on it."

Taylor's eyes went wide. "They're gonna be able to figure out everything anyone's ever done. That's like using a firework for a birthday candle. A lot of power."

I felt my jaw tense. I didn't want to convey my concern to her. She had enough to think about.

"Let's get back and we can organize on the drive. How long until your father gets to town?" I asked.

"Oh, well, he has to get my sister back from her friend's house, so we've maybe got like three hours," She responded.

"We can make that work. Let's do it." I looked around the room, assessing.

Working together, we picked up all of our things and neatened the house for my friends. Taylor and I kissed a few more times, but I could tell that we both had a lot on our mind when we got back into my car. I sent a text message to my friends to let them know we were leaving the house early. They responded by saying that they were setting the alarm remotely.

Halfway home, Taylor started to cry. I didn't know what to do or where to go.

"I've got it. How about The Coffee Shop? That seems reasonable? Right?" I waited to see if that would work for her.

"That could work. Do you think Tinsley could keep Axel? Because I had Raven tell Dad Axel ran away." She looked bashful about the fib.

"For sure. I think we'll be lucky to get Axel back. Parker wants to run a marathon with him." I wiped the tears from her cheeks.

"Thanks, that'll be good. I think a coffee place will be good. But what do I tell him? He'll never understand why we are pretending to date."

I took a breath. "How about it's not a lie? How about we really are dating? I'll be happy to meet your dad. I mean, unless you don't want me to."

"I'll cut anyone out of my life that doesn't want to meet you and accept you for being the amazing guy I'm getting the honor of being with."

It meant something that she was willing to be so all in. "Thank you so much."

I put the car in gear. I guess I was meeting Taylor's dad

tonight and that was quicker than I anticipated, but it was going to happen.

I still felt like I was flying blind. I really wanted to see what was going on online. Dad insisting on meeting me pretty much immediately after finding out about this scandal was throwing me for a loop. I could never tell from looking at Austin. He had a calm smile and would squeeze my hands from time to time. He couldn't check his phone while we were driving, but he assured me that we could look at the screenshots as soon as he had them. The drive home was tense for me, and I texted back-and-forth with Peaches.

ME: You'll never guess where I'm going.
PEACHES: To run far, far away from Teddi when she realizes you guys are going out for real?
ME: Oh no, I actually would prefer that. I'm taking Austin to meet my dad. We literally just got together for real this weekend, and I'm pretty sure I haven't brushed my hair yet from our last romp. And I'm gonna have to explain to my dad that he's gonna have to be okay with Austin.
PEACHES: How do you think he's gonna take it? Like, what are his issues?
ME: I haven't honestly spent a lot of time talking to him one-on-one. I don't know what his opinions are on men wearing dresses

and nail polish. I've told Austin that it's non-negotiable for me. Anyone that doesn't accept Austin will get cut out of my life.

Peaches gave me a surprised face emoji.

PEACHES: That doesn't surprise me but, man, this is getting deep quick.

I sent a shrugging emoji.

ME: I guess all of this is happening way faster than I thought it would. Don't get me wrong, I'm thrilled. Austin is a dream come true. But I wanted to finish this weekend and have conversations with him, and now it seems like we have to run a gauntlet, and we're not even sure who we're running from.

Peaches texted me back a computer emoji.

My phone rang. It was my father. I answered, "Hey, Dad."

"Hey, Taylor, where am I meeting you? The dorm?"

"No, let's meet at The Coffee Shop. It's open and it's got delicious coffee that you would like. Plus, a full menu for dinner if you're hungry."

"Am I going to meet Austin?"

"Yes, you are. He's coming with me and we're very excited for you to get to know him. I'll text you the directions. Do you have Raven with you?"

"No, I left her at home. I feel like this is a discussion we need to have in private." I shot a look at Austin. "Well, privacy is at a premium in college, so The Coffee Shop is as good as we're gonna get with that."

He grumbled on the other end of the line before agreeing, "I'll see you there in about a half an hour."

I ended the call, set my phone in my lap, and put my hands in my hair. "I wish this wasn't an emergency meeting with my dad. I wanted to savor you in this relationship for a few hours."

Austin checked his rearview mirror. "Yeah, you sound like you think it might be the end of our relationship with this meeting. Is that what you're thinking?"

I shook my head no. "I'm in if you're in. My dad will see sense. I mean, we're going to have an interesting conversation. But I'm the one that's paying for my college. He doesn't have any say anymore." Austin put his blinker on, and before we knew it, we were parking in The Coffee Shop's lot.

I took a minute to fix my hair and my makeup, and Austin pulled his hair back. He looked at his nails, which were painted black. I grabbed his hand and kissed his fingertips.

"This is okay. Don't feel self-conscious about it. Promise me this meeting with my dad won't do damage to you because I don't think I could live with myself if anybody in my family hurt you after all your family has done for me."

Austin smiled. "Don't worry. I've had to prove myself time and time again. And it hasn't changed who I am."

"I'm counting on that." I leaned over and gave him a kiss.

Then Austin and I got out of the car and headed for The Coffee Shop. As far as I could tell, my dad's car was not in the lot, so Austin and I ordered some food and drinks for all of us. After we had coffees in hand we picked out a table by the fire. I couldn't stop tapping my foot, and Austin put his hand on my knee so I wouldn't spill the coffee with my anxiety. I heard the jingle of the bell on the door and looked up to see my father glowering back at me. Austin stood up, and then I stood up. I came around the table and gave my father a hug and then indicated to Austin.

"This is Austin."

Austin held his hand out for a shake. "Sir, it's a pleasure to see you again. Of course, I've known Taylor for a long time."

My dad lifted his eyebrows.

"Young man." He gave him a man nod.

I waited as the tension trilled between us. "Hey, let's sit down before the coffee gets cold."

He touched one chair, and then Austin pulled out my chair.

My dad commented, "A gentleman. That's nice to see."

I hadn't told Austin how much my father disliked Brutus, although they had only met a few times at football games. Austin didn't respond but gave a soft smile. My father started the inquisition.

"So what do you do for a living? And you're Teddi's older brother? How much older?"

I wanted to be swallowed up into the floor. He just never had that kind of interest in any of the boys I dated before.

I started answering for Austin. "Only four years and how come you haven't started by telling him what *you* do for a living?"

Austin reached over and touched my hand. He told me without saying anything that he wanted to answer the questions and he was okay.

"Currently, I work with brands on social media promoting their products and helping them with their online presence, along with taking pictures of merchandise to help them sell their brand. It's sort of a new field, and I really enjoy how every day is different than the last. It lets me enjoy my creativity."

I loved how Austin was gentle with my father. He wasn't trying to talk down to him, even though he was resistant to a lot of new technology. Austin could have used more complicated words and tried to seem like he was gatekeeping the information he knew. Instead, he framed it in a way that my dad would understand.

Dad cleared his throat and nodded. The Coffee Shop employee approached and shuffled the plates and drinks on his tray. The tray of mini bagel appetizers and cold drinks were placed on the table with precision. We each got soft drinks in addition to the hot coffee we already had. The cluttered table held our attention for a few beats and gave me a moment to collect my thoughts. I was curious about why we were here and how my father had become interested in who Austin was.

"Can I ask you what brought this situation of Austin and me

dating to your attention, as I have not formally announced it anywhere?"

I didn't think my father would be searching hashtags on obscure social media. It wasn't his style.

He pushed back in his chair a little. "Funny enough, I actually got a phone call from an old friend of yours who told me she was concerned."

I shot Austin a look. None of my friends would be concerned about me dating Austin. Literally, all of my friends would be high-fiving me for spending time with this insanely hot guy.

"Did she say her name?" Austin asked.

My father looked at the ceiling for a few beats before answering, "I'm sure she said it. I just don't remember what it was. She was just really concerned that he'd be taking my daughter to an alternative lifestyle. And she had a point."

At least he said it out loud. I knew that's why we were here. The alternative lifestyle was something my father had an opinion about or a prejudice toward. I stood up and put my hands on the table.

"No, you don't get to call what I do alternative, or who I do it with alternative. I am not alternative. I'm just myself. Who I am with and who I'm attracted to is one hundred percent my business. Your job as my father is to get to know the person that I'm interested in and provide support. That's all I need, and to be honest, I don't actually need that. I just would like it. But you notice I'm not the one that told you about this? Just an anonymous person that called you to give me shit."

My father's eyes went wide. All these years, we'd shuffled around who I was as a person. It was about maintaining the distance we needed to ignore what was going on in our house and to ignore the problem that deep down my mother leaving gave him. He had confidence issues, and the way he insisted we kept our home was a way he could keep people away from our family. It kept us in and it kept others out. My leaving would make him uncomfortable.

I was outside the walls of his house now, but I wasn't going to let him saddle me with his issues. And as I stood in the restaurant glowering at him, I realized I had to do this and stand up to him so that my sister wouldn't have to have the same scene in a restaurant years from now.

Austin stood up next to me and put a hand on my shoulder. "What do you want to do? Do you want to go home?"

I sat back down and Austin did, too.

"Yeah, I just want to figure out what is going on in this world right now." I addressed my father, "Did it even occur to you that someone called you out of the blue to talk crap about me? Do you have any concerns about that at all? Do we think about that? I know this seems like I'm being disrespectful, but I'm really not enjoying dealing with this whole smear campaign from someone who has a vendetta against me for no good reason." I watched as understanding reached my father's eyes.

"Wow, I didn't know that we had a whole campaign we were dealing with." Concern made his forehead wrinkle.

I put my forehead in my hands. "Yeah, Austin is dealing with some stuff at work, and I'm dealing with stuff all because someone's decided to be a jackass to me. And the thing they are highlighting is not something I consider a problem. It's something I'm attracted to. Instead of furthering their agenda by pitting you against me, I'd rather we acted like a family where you put me first. Or at the very least not last when it comes to accusations." I crumpled a napkin in my hand. "I don't mind us continuing dinner if your goal is to understand and meet my friend, Austin. If it's anything other than that? I'm leaving."

My father studied his empty cup. "Okay, I definitely see that this is upsetting you, and I don't think you're wrong about being upset. Is this something you need me to call the school about?"

"No, thank you. I don't think they would talk to you. I'm the adult of record for my college degree, so no. But I'd appreciate you not listening to anonymous phone callers. And maybe monitor who's calling you."

"Did you check the caller ID?" Austin interjected.

My father tented his fingers. "No, well, it was an unknown caller, which I thought was weird. But I always like to answer anything that might be about you or your sister."

The vulnerability in his face made me take a moment to have empathy. I had to understand that people had to adjust and sometimes reteach their brains how to think in a way that was useful for society today. The older generations had to be open to change, or at least that was what I'd hope for them.

My father looked across the table at Austin. "I hope I didn't say anything offensive here. It really comes from a place of wanting to make sure that my daughter is okay."

Austin gave my father a slight smile. "I think we both have that in common. Taylor is exceptional. And being around her is a gift."

We had a few moments of silence before starting some small talk about cameras and pictures was comfortingly non-confrontational. When we got up to leave, Austin reached for the bill, but my dad insisted on paying.

"Thank you for coming on short notice. It's been great to meet you." My dad's eyes lingered on Austin's nail polish. He shook his head like he had a question, but he didn't ask it.

I gave my father a hug and Austin held my hand as we went back to the car.

"Well, that was something." I buckled my seatbelt, as he did the same.

"I actually think he adjusted pretty well. I have to say, I'm impressed how you stood up to him." His cheekbones were highlighted by the streetlights in the parking lot.

"I'd fight anybody for you." It seemed outlandish that I'd be offering this up to him. He was taller than me, stronger than me, but still, I meant it.

He nodded. "And it's really nice to have that. It's been a few years since someone was fighting for me instead of just fighting me."

I knew we were talking about Endgame then. The damage that relationship had done was not going to be fixed by one weekend in a fancy house. I hoped we had enough of a foundation to make it through whatever was ahead of us. I didn't want to think I was someone Austin was settling for. I certainly wasn't as exciting as Endgame. I started to think about what we had in front of us.

"So, I'm guessing it was Roberta that called my dad. Which is concerning and escalating at a rapid pace. I'm not sure what to do next about her."

Austin put the car in gear. "I feel like we're getting close to restraining order type behavior here. I don't know what she thinks she's going to get out of this."

I looked out the window and saw my face reflecting there. I didn't know either. I wish I knew.

23

Austin

When Taylor and I returned to the apartment, it was not empty. The music was pumping, and all the windows were wide open. The place was littered with empty alcohol bottles and beer cans. For some reason, the whole place smelled like salsa. I happened in on the scene of three guys attempting to break into my room. The door had a padlock on it, but that seemed to just be slowing them down slightly. I held Taylor's hand and stepped through so I could stand in front of them after pushing them out of the way.

"Hey, this isn't your place. This isn't your bedroom. Where's Endgame?"

The guys attempted to argue with me briefly.

"Where is who? I don't even know who you're talking about, man."

The shortest one looked Taylor up and down.

"Everybody leave." I went over to the speaker and unplugged it. A slew of groans greeted me.

I spoke to Taylor, "Hey, do you wanna go in our room while I clean this place out?"

She gave me an indignant stare. "No, we're going to do this together. Obviously."

After letting go of my hand, she went and found a trash bag in the kitchen. The empties clinked together as she started collecting them.

As the people left—some belligerent—Taylor plucked full drinks from peoples' hands. She motioned with them to encourage everyone to leave. Some of the interlopers took the hint and wanted to keep their drinks, so they hustled out the door clutching them.

When I finally made it over to Endgame's room, I opened the door, and he was passed out on the bed. Wearing a pink tank top. Not a great sign. People had been in his room as well because there were more bottles here and some drug paraphernalia. He needed to go. It was that simple. No matter what he told me about his intentions after he left my apartment, or what he would do to self-sabotage, it was time to set boundaries. As soon as he was coherent, it was happening.

Taylor rubbed between my shoulder blades. "Come on, let's go to bed. We'll deal with this another time." She was great. We didn't have the emotional bandwidth to deal with this right now. We had too much on our plates.

As Taylor picked up a few stray bottles, she froze. I came over to see what she was looking at. "This is Roberta's. Roberta has been here."

"Are you sure?" I bent down to grab the lanyard with pins all over it.

"Yup. She used to lose it all the time when I lived with her. The clip here cuts loose because she has all these pins on it. It's too heavy." She grabbed a spoon off of Endgame's chair and used it to lift the lanyard.

The way she was treating it made me reconsider picking it up.

"The upper part had her dorm key so she will still be able to get in tonight. If she had been a friend, I would've gotten her a better lanyard." She let the lanyard swing back and set the spoon down.

"I hate to do this. Let's sweep this place, make sure everyone's out, and then I need some time with him."

Taylor leaned over to me and kissed my cheek. "I got it. No worries. You just let me know if you need help."

After making sure every closet and room was clear, Taylor and I were relieved to find out no one had gotten into our room.

I tried to let my heart harden before I went into Endgame's room. It was time.

His hands were behind his head. "Were you awake the whole time we were here? Was it all an act?" I leaned against his doorframe.

"You know I felt the shift this weekend. That you're done with me." He licked his teeth like the words needed moisture.

"Hence the pink, I'm assuming." I nodded at his shirt.

It would start now—the mind games. He was fantastic at them. And maybe I was a sucker for them as well.

"Yeah, it wasn't just this weekend, though. So you know, I mean, you're in a separate bedroom and it's been this way for a while. I've been trying to put up boundaries and somehow you always break them down." I pushed the clothes off the chair in his room and sat down. "You and I both know that this was never gonna last forever."

Endgame scoffed. "I never said forever. Listen, you were a mark. You were a safe house while I let my reputation cool. That's all you've ever been."

"You can... you can say that. You're allowed to say whatever you want, but it's time. I can't come home to an entire apartment filled with people I don't know doing things that could get me tossed in jail. I can't trust you. I've never been able to trust you. All I've done is love you. And look where it got me with you."

Endgame sat up in bed and leveled to stare at me. "Yeah. It's true. It hurts, though, you know. I didn't want to care what you thought, and now that you've ended that, I feel the pain." Maybe it was just right now, but he seemed like he was being more real than he'd ever been before. "When do you want me gone?"

I held up Roberta's lanyard.

"First, we talk about this. How are you and Roberta involved?" I stood and stepped closer to toss the lanyard onto his bed.

"I don't know what the fuck that is." He looked at it like it was a snake.

"You know I'll find out down the line. Just tell me." I crossed my arms over my chest.

Endgame got off the bed in a rush, moving with jerky purpose. He grabbed up a duffle bag, then he began tossing things into it. "You want me gone? I'm gone. Fuck you. And fuck her. You all straight now? Time to make Mommy and Daddy proud?"

He was launching his worst, being as hurtful as he wanted to be. I wouldn't let his insults goad me into the response he wanted. I was sure of who I was. My parents were as proud of me standing next to anyone that made me happy, or even standing on my own.

"And when I'm homeless as a fuck outside? You happy to just step over me? Or will you step right on me?" He tossed his bag over his shoulder. My empathy reared up again. How he got me in the past would not be how he got me now. He came close to my face and I didn't flinch. "You feel nothing now? Her magic pussy made you forget how I touched you?"

I let the hard exterior I was trying to maintain slip a little. "I never did anything to hurt you."

"Yeah. Except give the fuck up on me." We were inches apart.

I was a bit taller, but he had a broader chest. I knew where every tattoo was on his body. I knew he had a soft spot for Harry Styles' songs and Lucky Charms. I knew his mom would leave him in an empty apartment for days at a time, until she didn't come back at all. All the things I knew ganged up on me. I watched hope flicker in his eyes before crashing closed.

The silence said it all. I wasn't swinging into the old habits. I wasn't taking ownership of his pain anymore.

"Give the fuck up on me then, Austin Burathon."

It was the first time I ever remember him using my full name. It was a struggle, but I didn't try to smooth things over, make things better.

Endgame, the biggest blowhard I had ever known, slumped his shoulders then. The fight was out of him. It was over for us. For me.

I expected slamming doors. Things getting thrown. Instead, Endgame walked out of his bedroom and then out the front door, not closing either of them.

The backdraft of emotions and worry hit me. Where would he go? What would happen to him if I wasn't there to pick up his pieces?

I went to the door and closed and locked it. Sadness and relief. Keeping him together was a huge responsibility, and I was setting it down and walking away.

I sat on my couch, which smelled like beer and had a cigarette burn in it now. It would need to be cleaned. The whole place was going to have to get scrubbed down.

When it had been a while, our bedroom door opened and Taylor stepped into the living room. I held out a hand to her and she crossed the space between us.

"Are you okay?" Her beautiful face was etched with concern.

"It doesn't feel fair to make you deal with this." Dealing with Endgame was my cross to bear.

Taylor moved my hair from my face. "How about we don't worry about keeping score and we just take care of each other?"

"How do you always know the right thing to say?" I put my hand on her chest as she smiled.

"I learned by watching you. I was paying attention all those years. Did he give you any indication about whether or not Roberta did anything here?" She glanced around the room and seemed to be looking for ghosts.

"He said he didn't recognize the lanyard. He was lying. It's what he does—he lies." I rubbed her back.

"I'm sorry." She rested her head on my chest.

"It's a ball of crap we have to deal with here," I mumbled into her hair looking at the destruction around us.

"Yeah, but we can make sure we're okay and stay near each other. I think that's our best bet." She slipped her hand under my shirt and rubbed her fingertips above my navel.

I wrapped her hair around my fist lightly. "You ready for bed?"

She lifted her head and looked in my eyes. "Always."

In the morning, we had a fresh hell of stuff to deal with. Whoever was working with Roberta was relentless. The school website and a few of the club websites had a splash page featuring

Austin in a white dress and me in my white dress from the Stars Unlimited advertisement. Austin turned his laptop so I could see the screen.

Two brides!
No one wears the pants in this family.

I was furious.

Austin lifted one eyebrow. "She's not even clever. Who goes through all of that and then delivers that limp line?"

"She does. She'd totally do that. All gas, no brakes. No forethought. I mean, she literally spent all her time naked when I lived with her. I could have taken a million pictures and videos of her, but I never did and never would, but, like, that's your choice of torture? It could backfire on you." I stomped over to the kitchen and got out a spray cleaner and a roll of paper towels. I would rage clean. He remained on the stained couch and turned his laptop to face him again.

"Yeah, she's not working with a full crew. I'll text Milt. I wonder if they can pinpoint where she's based out of? Then maybe follow that activity?" Austin pulled out his phone and started sharing the websites that were an issue.

He looked tired today. Being with me right now had to be a heaping pile of annoyance. Then the man kicked out his ex-boyfriend last night, and I knew that was a difficult scene. He would, I was sure, enjoy having a day where his balls weren't being busted by my ex-dorm mate.

I called Peaches and she picked right up. "The bitch you were living with has such a boner for you. What's up with that?"

"I don't know. I'm out of her dorm. The only thing I think she's still obsessed with is some belief that Austin is a celebrity, which he is not." I set down the cleaner and started filling the dishwasher while we spoke.

"Well, he's hella more famous than I am, that's for sure, and screw Roberta. Both of you wearing white at your wedding is a great damn idea. You both look hot in that color."

I left the dishwasher open and stepped into the bathroom near Endgame's room. "Seriously, he and I just spent the weekend together, like talk about putting pressure on right at the beginning of a relationship." The bathroom might need to be set on fire instead of cleaned. The amount of toothpaste all over the sink was alarming. There was a buzz from the intercom. My first thought was Endgame was coming back. "Hey, let me get this."

Austin and I were both by the front door when he hit the app to get to the camera for the entrance to show on his phone. It was Teddi and Peaches, beaming into the screen with her arms full of clothes.

"Open up, sunshine." Peaches wiggled her phone.

Austin opened the door and behind the girls were Gaze, Ruffian, Milt, and Pixie Rae. They all trudged past. I gave Austin a side-eye and he seemed to have no idea what this was about either. I ended the call with Peaches as she hopped by me.

They all had piles of white lace and taffeta. Teddi hefted hers in my direction.

In no time we had what was basically a full-on wedding thrift store in the living room. Teddi was already organizing. She and Pixie were noting the sizes inside the dresses.

"Care to explain?" Austin picked at the hem of a nineties era dream bride gown.

"Oh, yeah. We saw the bullshit that was on Taylor's college website, and we've had enough." Teddi picked up one gown and started sizing it on Gaze's broad back. "This one will work for you, but I don't think you'll be able to zip it."

Gaze took the gown and started stepping into it. Pixie hopped over the coffee table. "Let me help."

Ruffian came up next to Austin. "If we're all brides, then nobody can say anything. You guys are just trendsetters is all." Ruffian squeezed Austin's shoulder.

"What?" Austin was amused but still confused.

"We're having a flash bride-ing." Teddi unzipped another garment bag. "I've contacted everyone I can think of, and we're all going to show up on Main Street as brides. Today. In four hours."

Austin shook his head. "That's my sister. Why ignore something when we can make a party out of it?"

"Listen, no one gives my brother shit. I'll end this chick and anyone that works with her. Milt is going on a deep dive of anyone that's ever dealt with her. He will have the entire picture." She pointed to Milt. All his friends had laptops open while Pixie, Gaze, and Teddi sized the gowns to the shoulders.

Austin stepped in. "If they can fit the waist around their necks, the dress should fit. Insider info just for you, Teddi Bear."

I stepped in and started helping size the boys to the gowns. Just as we had found something for nearly everyone, another intercom buzz caused Austin to pull up the app on his phone. We had Tinsley and Parker, Axel, and a host of other people now.

The hugging and laughing evolved naturally. Austin and I went from wondering how to handle this to being supported by every damn person we'd ever met and then some.

Social media had picked up on Everyone's a Damn Bride Day, and the hashtag was trending. Leave it to Teddi to organize something this massive in a matter of hours.

"You better get dressed if you guys are coming." Somehow Teddi had found time to wrangle herself into a huge princess-style gown. "Mom and Dad are coming. I have to meet them downstairs."

Austin snagged my hand and pulled me into our room. "Do you want to do this?"

His sexy eyes searched mine.

"Yeah? I think so? It seems like the best way to ever make a stand. I mean, it's sudden, but cool." I felt my smile get wider.

"Okay. Let me think then, because if we're going? We have to be the best dressed." He leaned forward and gave me a lingering kiss.

When he pulled back, I reminded him, "Teddi still thinks this is all an act, so be careful. You can start my motor, if you know what I mean." I shook my shoulders for him.

He laughed and covered my breasts for a few seconds before letting them go. Austin disappeared into his huge closet, and when I followed him in, he had a small step ladder set up. The topmost box was his goal, and when he went on his tiptoes, he knocked it toward him.

The box flopped off the shelf and spilled out. I was covered in tulle. I parted the gauzy fabric and Austin helped me untangle myself from it.

"That'll be the bottom."

I started to try to make sense of the yards, folding them like an endless accordion.

The next set of boxes had white tuxedos inside.

He held out his hand and I stepped onto the low coffee table he had in the closet. The way he looked at my body now was different from how he had not even twelve hours earlier. It reminded me of the demeanor he had when we did our photo shoot.

He worked with the material he had, draping it around me. "Okay, this will work. Are you comfortable ditching your jeans?"

When I nodded in agreement, his devilish smile came out. He did the honors, unfastening them and sliding them down my legs.

He paused to linger a kiss on my thigh. "Beautiful."

Then he was back to business. When he was done, I was wearing a modified tuxedo bodice and tulle wrapped to form a beautiful skirt. Austin pulled together a matching ensemble. The difference was mostly in our shoes. I had heels; he had white combat boots. We both went into the bathroom and rushed to get some makeup on.

When we were done, I took a second to link my arm with his. "How cute are we?"

"So cute. Let's get out there before they leave without us." Austin grabbed his bag and packed a camera.

When we walked back to the living room, everyone there was dressed as a bride.

Teddi had two cell phones, but paused when we stepped out. "You two are the sexiest people on the planet. Let's go give a giant middle finger to any dickbags that think they get to bully you. But first? Group shot."

Austin placed his camera on a collapsible tripod. It took longer than Teddi wanted, but we eventually had a few poses that made us laugh.

"Let's roll out." Ruffian held open the front door.

Pixie Rae had to keep reminding Gaze to keep his skirt down. Someone had fashioned a bridal veil on Axel, who was so excited to join us all for a walk.

And it was a walk. Main Street was six blocks away, and three blocks in, Austin offered to carry me piggyback style. I took him up on his offer. Teddi gave me a few side-eyes that had me wondering if she and I would have a more detailed conversation after this makeshift display of solidarity.

When we got to the meeting spot, we were by far the only brides there. People were tossing toilet paper streamers and some of the apartments that lined the road had wedding music blasting. There was the wedding march, the Bruno Mars number, and a few country songs that merged with one another.

Brides were everywhere. Some guys inverted their white t-shirts into veils on their heads. Older women were coming out and walking in their actual dresses they had in storage. Restaurants were throwing handfuls of rice and the cars honking was wild.

Austin leaned down to me. "Did Teddi accidentally make us a holiday?"

"I think so. And I bet she's going to have it worldwide within ten years. She's a beast." I knew my friend well.

His eyes crinkled as he smiled.

A lot of brides held their phones up, streaming the celebration. We were ending the march at the pretty movie theater near 5th and Vine.

Teddi, Peaches, and Tinsley were making a TikTok dance, and Milt, Gaze, Ruffian, and Austin had their arms draped around each other's shoulders.

It was good. It was really good. I was taking it in, when a bride off to the side and down an alley caught my attention. He had a lit cigarette, the veil splitting his smoke like a sieve. His shirt a light pink, he almost blended in.

Endgame. He and I locked eyes. He looked left, then right before curling his index finger at me.

In the swamps of brides, I lost track of my people. Endgame seemed urgent.

I walked closer to him. "What do you need?"

I couldn't place where Austin was as I scanned the sea of white.

"Just forgot to do some stuff. And I have a few of Austin's things. Could you take them to him? I just don't want to hurt him anymore."

He was on something. Or drunk. "We walked here, so I can't really carry anything big."

"It's his grandmother's necklace. I took it by accident. Can you carry that?"

He was slurring slightly. He dropped his cigarette and stepped on it. "It's just back here, but no pressure if you don't wanna get it for him."

I stepped into the skinny alley behind Endgame. He walked with a bit of a tipsy gait.

When we came out the other side, he motioned me over to a white van. All of a sudden I felt very far away from my friends. Very far away from Austin.

"It's right in here."

I stayed at least a car length away from him. He could get the necklace and bring it to me. His half-assed veil tumbled off his head as he rooted around in the van and landed in a dirty puddle by his feet.

Run.

There was a voice in my head that knew stuff. It was the way my body verbalized gut feelings and everything about this was off. I turned to do just that and slammed right into a man's chest. My phone clattered to the ground. I watched as the man stepped on it.

While I was trying to apologize, I realized there were three people behind me now. The wall of a guy, Roberta's boyfriend, and Roberta.

Shit.

I started to fight, but they had me in the back of the van in no time. Before I could scream, Roberta slapped duct tape over my mouth. I felt my wrists getting bound in a tight tie.

I was shaking, and I couldn't stop it. This was bad. Super horrible.

It had tipped over the edge. I should've figured something was amiss when I found her lanyard in Austin's apartment. I should've gotten the restraining order. Endgame was here with me, slumped over in the back of the van. Possibly no help at all.

Roberta snapped a few pictures of me. "Your boyfriend? He's got lots of money, right? He can pay what you owe me. Plus interest."

Peter snorted. "A lot of interest. You broke so much of her shit."

I couldn't tell her she was wrong; my mouth was taped. Claustrophobia mixed with my panic, and I felt like I wasn't getting a good breath. I needed my mouth. Roberta had put the tape on in such a way, one of my nostrils was blocked.

Things got fuzzier. With my arms behind my back, I couldn't help myself. Everything turned black.

24

T aylor was gone. Just poof. I'd been talking with my brothers when my parents showed up—both in wedding gowns. They were supposed to meet at our apartment but had gotten caught in traffic. We all hugged and laughed at Dad's version of a bride. He had a beekeeping veil with some silk flowers hot-glued on it.

When Mom asked to say hi to Taylor, I knew. I knew something was very, very wrong.

We came together. We would leave together.

"Maybe she needed to use the restroom?" Tinsley offered.

I pulled out my phone and sent her a text message, and then called. Straight to voicemail.

It was absurd to go from overjoyed and feeling my friends' and family's support to having my stomach drop. I found Milt and his buddies.

"Taylor's missing. Can you find her?" I pointed at the ATM on the sidewalk. I knew there were cameras in there, but I had no idea what it took to see what was on them.

Milt and his friends found a curb and all started to work. In seconds I was looking at footage with them, all of us scouring the faces. So much white, so many veils. It wasn't Taylor I found first, but Endgame with a veil on. My heart thumped, thinking of how amazing it was for him to support Taylor and me, but all of those feelings washed away as Milt's buddy showed me footage from a different angle.

Taylor was being put into a van and Endgame helped. They had taken her. She'd fought them.

"Call 911. Shit, call 911." I looked from my parents' faces to Teddi and then to Gaze. "They took her."

Taylor

I woke up to an argument. Endgame and Roberta. They were inches from each other, yelling.

"You said we were just going to spook some money out of him. And now she's unconscious. I want to take her to the hospital." Endgame was spitting mad.

"She's weak. That's not my fault. And you were supposed to handle the tape, but you forgot, you drunk asshole."

A moan came out of my mouth, and I realized I could take a deep breath. No more tape. My eyes focused. We were in some sort of warehouse, with parts of cars all over it.

Endgame heard me and rushed over. I was on a couch, my hands still bound, but they were in front of me now.

"Shit. I'm so sorry. Are you okay? Shit." Endgame pushed my hair away from my face.

"What happened? What's happening?" I was fuzzy.

There were four more guys that I didn't recognize, and Peter and Roberta were still here, too. I was reclining on an ugly mustard couch with huge flowers on it.

"You passed out. Thunder farts over there blocked your airway." He pointed at Roberta.

"Shut your mouth, coloring book face." She took a step in Endgame's direction.

"Are you kidnapping me?" My head hurt.

It was like his whole body cringed. "I did this stupid thing. I was being vindictive. I was being heartbroken. And your old roommate stopped by my party and we got to talking. She had, like, so much weed. Did you know she sold weed? Well, her boyfriend's brother sells it. So crazy."

He took out a cigarette and lit it. "Want a pull?"

I shook my head no, then felt the pressure in my temples from the movement.

"Okay. Yeah. Maybe not because you were having trouble breathing. I just wanted him to worry a little. I wasn't going to take it this fucking far." He glowered at Roberta.

Roberta, to her credit, appeared a bit sheepish.

"Just call your boyfriend and tell him to bring the money to pay for the shit you broke and we can let you go home with him. It's not a kidnapping, it's just paying your bills, you know?"

The guy that had a wall for a chest cleared his throat.

"I'm calling the shots, bitch. You wanted to borrow my guys? Fine. But I'm not doing this for free. I get to keep her. That's fair." He walked closer to me.

Endgame scooted so my hip and his hip were touching. "No, dude. I'm sorry, but I can't let you do that. She's, like, a good person."

The wall chest guy's eyebrows pulled together. "I don't give four flying fucks if she's a saint. She'll work for me. And I'll like it. A lot."

I looked from Endgame to Roberta and back again. No one knew what to say.

"Bullsen, I thought you owed Peter's brother a favor?" Roberta shifted from one foot to another.

He stormed over to her. "I owe nothing to no-fucking-body. That's it. Get out. Get out right fucking now."

The veins in his neck flexed. Roberta bit her lip like she might say more then thought better of it. She met my eyes, and I saw fear and regret there.

These two assholes had delivered me to a monster for no good reason.

A distant door slammed.

"I never did anything to her crap. She broke some of my stuff and stole my closet." I tried to make a case for myself.

Bullsen whirled in my direction. "I'll tell you when to speak. And fucking you," he pointed at Endgame, "you're bad fucking luck. You need to get the hell out of here, too. I don't owe you shit either."

Bullsen was yelling at Endgame, but staring at me. It was unnerving. He seemed like a butcher sizing up what parts of my body would make the best dinner.

Endgame stood up. I tried to grab his shirt. I didn't want him to leave. Then I would know no one.

"Nah, man. You gotta let me get outta here with her. This was a mistake. A big, hairy mistake. That chick, Roberta was bad news. You don't want the kind of heat she'll generate on you." Endgame stepped in front of me, putting his body between Bullsen and me.

"You little ass pimple. I'm not taking orders or suggestions from you. Get out. Now. Last warning." Bullsen was towering over Endgame.

I knew I should be paying attention, looking for exits, but the tone in Bullsen's voice brought tears to my eyes. This was a different type of human than I was used to dealing with. He was scary.

"Yeah. I'm not leaving her. That's not happening." I saw Endgame straighten his spine.

I reached and touched the leg of his pants.

He turned a little bit so I could see his profile.

"Go. Just go. He's going to hurt you," I whispered.

Endgame gave me a small head shake. "Nah. My mistake. I'm paying for it, not you." He faced Bullsen again. "You gotta do what you gotta do, but if you want her, you gotta go through me."

It was a ludicrous suggestion. Endgame was outnumbered five to one. And that was just the people I could see from here. I had no idea how many more people were around this building.

Bullsen was almost nose-to-nose with him. "Get out of my way. Last chance." He was so angry, spittle was spewing from his lips.

Endgame shook his head slowly. "I'm good, my dude. I'm good."

It almost looked like a hug or a handshake. There weren't any telling noises except a forceful exhale from Endgame.

Bullsen let go of the embrace and Endgame fell to his knees. I moved forward without thinking, kneeling behind him. He fell back against my chest and then rolled to the floor. His light pink shirt was now stained a deep, murky red. Bullsen had a knife in his hand, and it was marked with blood.

Endgame's eyes were rolling in the back of his head.

"Endgame? Endgame!" I tried his real name. "Torin!" I was concerned he had hurt his head when he hit the cement floor, but the pool of blood forming under his torso was growing quickly and clearly the most pressing issue.

I put my hands on where I thought the wound was and tried to apply pressure. I wasn't entirely sure if I was helping at all. I couldn't get the range of motion I needed with the zip tie on my wrists.

Bullsen bent over at the waist. "That won't help. I know right where to slide the blade. Remember that when you're working for me."

Sirens. I could hear sirens in the distance.

"They won't know where we are, right? What the fuck?" Bullsen stormed off, Endgame's fate falling in his list of priorities.

Endgame coughed and then groaned.

"Hey, the police are coming, and they'll have ambulances. Just hang in there."

"I'm sorry." His lips made a flat line.

"Now's not the time to worry about blame." I glanced up to see Bullsen and his men darting around the building. They were either getting rid of evidence or gathering things together to leave.

The police sirens were getting louder and seemed to be multiplying.

"He's gonna hate me so much." Endgame's cheeks filled with air before he exhaled.

I knew who he was talking about. And I couldn't offer any condolences. Because Austin would be wildly angry, if we ever got to see him again.

"Can you tell him?" There were a few seconds where Endgame coughed and sputtered. He seemed to fortify himself to keep talking. "Tell him I ain't never loved anyone, but right now?"

Endgame's eyes filled with tears and his bottom lip quivered. "All I can see is his face."

My tears that had started with Bullsen doubled. Endgame's eyes focus on something behind me, then slid out of focus.

I had nothing to offer him, except half-assed pressure on his wound and a little bit of solace by saying, "I'll tell him."

The next few breaths were horrible, and I felt the wound under my hands bubbling with air. His lung—that was my guess. Bullsen's knife had pierced his lung.

I tried to make myself small, in a bid to be forgotten by the men running around.

I reached for Endgame's throat and tried to get a pulse. Nothing.

In the interim, between the cops coming in and Bullsen's crew evacuating, I set myself up to do chest compressions. The zip tie bit into my skin as I tried to replicate the position I knew my hands needed to be in. I pressed down and the air expelled from the wound again. I looked at Endgame's face, and I knew I'd do what I could, but he was gone. The soul inside of him was gone. The cops came in. I heard them in my periphery. They were shouting at me, and I couldn't make sense past the chest compressions. I'd taken the CPR class so many times, but at no point did we discuss that you might be surrounded by cops with their guns drawn.

Paramedics came in next, and they pushed past the guns and took over.

"Hey, do you know what happened?"

The one nearest me carefully took over the compressions, his rhythm faster than mine had been.

"A knife. A guy named Bullsen stabbed him because he wouldn't leave me."

I sat back on my heels, studying my hands. My palms were covered in blood. The cops had put away their guns and a female officer came close to me.

"Hey, can we move over here while they work?" She guided me to my feet.

I staggered a little, and she was quick to support me. She must be used to people in shock. And this was shock. Time was going fast and slow. The female cop's words slurred in my brain. She touched my bound wrists and then waved another paramedic over. I could see all the lights in the driveaway. At least two ambulances.

"What's your name, hun?" The burly man was a hulk with a high voice.

"Taylor. And his name is Torin." My voice sounded too quiet in all this chaos.

"Okay, listen, I want to evaluate you and I think we're going to at the very least need some bandages on these wrists." He was a force, this EMT. He had the warmth of a grandma and the sass of a best friend. He helped me out to the ambulance.

As I sat on the steps of the ambulance, he pulled out the things he needed from the back.

The first was a pair of long scissors, and he was careful, but I still flinched when he snipped the binding.

He handled my wrists like they were made of glass. My fingers felt like they were kindling in a fire.

"That's the blood flowing back into your fingers, and I'm not going to shit you—it'll hurt." His eyes crinkled.

I looked over my left shoulder. All pain could be was pain. I was alive.

The other two paramedics had Endgame on a gurney and were wheeling him to the back of the ambulance. There was a slump in their shoulders that told me what I already knew.

"He a friend of yours?" I slid my focus back to the EMT that was wiping a cool cloth that smelled like alcohol on my hands. His name tag read Nick. With Endgame's blood gone with his actual body being wheeled away, I could see the abrasions on me that the confusion and adrenaline kept me from feeling.

"Maybe." I had mixed feelings about Endgame. Tonight, with

my head muddled with fear and shock, was not the night I'd be able to define that man.

"I know the police are looking for you, so I think it will be happy news for your loved ones that you're still with us."

"Can I borrow your phone?" I held out my right hand that was now fully bandaged.

"Yeah, sure." He took off one of his gloves and dug a bright green iPhone out of his jacket pocket. He unlocked it and handed it to me.

I didn't know Austin's number. I couldn't think of any numbers. Hell, my old house number where my father or sister would answer? Couldn't even bring it to mind.

"Do you have Tikgram?"

"Yeah?"

"Can I send a message from that?" I knew Austin's handle and punched in a request for a private message. I knew those pinged on his phone.

It's Taylor. Call me at this number.

Nick must have been reading over my shoulder because he rattled off his phone number.

In a second, the phone was vibrating. I stared at the phone, trying to decide how to answer it. Nick used his pinkie to press the button.

"Hey, it's me. It's me." I was crying now. His voice connecting me to the reality that I'd been kidnapped.

I heard Austin gasp on the other end. "Holy shit. It's her. It's her! Are you okay?"

I thought of my answer, watching the paramedics in no real rush to get Endgame to the hospital.

"Yeah. I'm okay. It's just..." I had no idea where I was. What this place was.

"Where are you?" Austin's voice was a low grumble.

I stared at Nick.

"Tell him to meet you at the Birdville Hospital emergency room. We have to go now." Nick slipped a steading hand under my armpit.

I relayed the information to Austin, and then when I readjusted the phone, it hung up. I handed the phone to Nick and crawled into the ambulance. He had me hop up onto the gurney. I was clipped in and propped up.

Nick was all business now, getting my vitals and starting an IV right there in the bouncing emergency vehicle.

"I didn't want to tell him on the phone." I said it like Nick might understand how complicated the whole situation was without any surrounding details.

Nick gave me a deep hum. "That was good. Let's worry about you right now. Bad news can wait. I'm going to get some saline in you."

I stared at my feet popping out from under the blanket.

I heard him amend, "And maybe a few painkillers. 'Cause I know those fingers are throbbing right now."

The anxiety of it all dulled and blurred. I closed my eyes as the painkillers hit my veins. I could still feel the vehicle moving, but I was crashing now. My hands were throbbing. I let the road noise mix with the siren and tried to imagine a world where I wasn't going to have to tell Austin that Endgame had died.

25

Austin

The level of distress I was in—we all were in—could not be quantified. I was dressed as a bride. Hell, everyone was. And instead of fun social media pictures, we'd been trying to coordinate where Taylor was and what happened to her.

My parents were rocks, as usual, but when I saw my mom give my dad sneaky big eyes, I knew they were concerned.

Thank God Milt and his friends could hack the living shit out of the surrounding technology. They were able to ping Endgame's phone and the hope was that he and Taylor were together. We were able to give the cops the coordinates of the location. We had been driving to that location as well when Taylor had messaged me on my social media.

Speaking to Taylor was a huge relief but hearing how altered and distressed she sounded added a layer of concern.

As we sped to the hospital in my parents' minivan, Teddi was sending out for social media prayers. My dad had a friend in the police department, and he had an update that Taylor was okay, just like she'd said on the phone, as far as he knew.

When my father pulled into the emergency bay, I hopped out, as did my mom. At the information desk, I informed them that my wife was admitted. We were directed to a room that was mostly curtains. I peeked inside and Taylor was looking back at me. She was still in the same outfit as I was, except hers had brownish red stains on it. Her wrists were bandaged and she had an IV.

"Sweet hell. Holy shit." I caught my balance on the footboard of her hospital bed. She appeared a little buzzed. A nurse pushed past Mom and me.

"Hey there, family members. I'm Nurse Mayborn. Once you all get to say hi, only one of you can stay in here at a time." The nurse had jet-black hair and elaborate eye wings. Normally, I'd note the talent it took to do that. Not now, though.

I came next to Taylor and rested my head on hers.

"Are you okay?" I put my arms around her gently.

She turned her face toward mine. "I'm okay. They say it's mostly the wrist stuff."

I touched her thick bandages. "What happened?"

I saw a flash of emotions on her face. Fear, anger, and sadness. She informed me, "A zip tie. It wasn't great for moving around."

It felt like an actual zip tie cinched around my heart. I tilted my head backward and looked at the ceiling.

My mother rubbed my shoulder. "Once Taylor's dad gets here, I'll send him up. I'll text you as well. You okay?"

I grabbed my mom's hand. I wished she could stay—just having her here felt important. Like this whole situation would be easier to stomach with her support.

"Thanks. We'll be good." I kissed her cheek and then turned my attention back to Taylor. Her eyes were closed.

The nurse got some readings and checked Taylor's temperature. "You need anything, sweetheart?"

Taylor mouthed, "No, thank you." Then the nurse and my mother were gone. I closed the curtain even though it did very little to grant us privacy.

Taylor met my eyes and then she had tears.

I felt a surge of guilt. "I'm so sorry. This is all my fault."

She touched my face and the bulky bandage grazed my chin. "Listen, I have to tell you something, and I wish I didn't have to be the one to tell you."

I pulled back so I could look in her eyes. "What's up?"

My mind reeled with what she could have encountered that would have to have her reading me like this. All of it was terrifying.

"Endgame—he didn't make it. A guy stabbed him. I'm so sorry."

It was like her words didn't make sense. Like she was talking in another language at high speed.

"Didn't make what?" I was not putting it together. I mean, I guess my heart and my brain were on different frequencies.

"He died. He tried to help me and he got stabbed." I fell into the hard plastic chair next to her bed.

"Were you stabbed?" This was a nightmare. An actual, horror movie style nightmare.

"No. I wasn't. It was him. He was stabbed because he wouldn't leave me there. He told them to go through him to get to me, and they did."

I didn't know who "they" were.

"Taylor, what the hell happened? Please, start from the beginning."

She took a deep breath. She seemed exhausted, but I had to know. I needed to know.

"When I was at the event with you, I saw Endgame. He had on a veil and said he had something important to give you." She paused before continuing. "Maybe I shouldn't tell you this? Is it bad to tell you what Endgame did?" She placed her injured wrists on her lap.

"Please tell me." My voice was demanding, but soft.

"I went with him because I felt bad for him and thought he might have something important of yours—he mentioned your grandmother's necklace. I thought he was supporting you because of the veil. And Roberta and her stupid boyfriend were there, too." She rested her head back against the pillow, the motion causing a few tears to track down her cheeks.

"And then they tied me up and taped my mouth and some of my nose, so I passed out." I covered my mouth. The horror of it all. The lack of safety.

"And when I came to, we were at Peter's brother's crime boss' place. He wanted to keep me. Endgame said he wanted to make a point to you. But then when the crime guy, Bullsen, made it clear that he wanted to keep me, Endgame wouldn't leave. Even dumb Roberta seemed like she didn't want to leave me. Endgame stood up for me, and for that he was stabbed." She wiped her cheeks and rubbed her nose. "I gave him the best CPR I could with my hands tied up. And we lost him. Right in front of me while I was doing CPR. Maybe before. The Bullsen guy said he knew where to stab people, and I believe him." She looked at my chest and held out her damaged hand.

It's funny to get the news that you were always dreading. Not ha-ha funny, but a prediction coming true and the universe doing what it does kind of funny.

I gently took her hand. I saw it in her—the pain I was feeling. She was connected to me so deeply. So non-judgmental. She was exceptional. She was alive. Thank God she was alive. I scooted close to her and put my hands on her face.

"Kitten." I rubbed my thumb down her cheek.

"I'm so sorry. I tried to save him." Taylor sounded tired.

"I know." I cradled her head.

I had tried to save him, too. Maybe I always knew I'd be destined to fail, but I had not expected it this soon. This real.

Taylor's dad stepped into the room. "Baby."

I got out of the way so he could hug his daughter. The nurse had followed him in and motioned me out.

I didn't have a chance to say goodbye or that I'd see her later. Nothing. I was just in an elevator down to the lobby with nothing but my thoughts.

WHEN THE ELEVATOR OPENED, Gaze was there waiting for me.

"Brother." He gave me a huge hug.

I unloaded on him. "Man, I've made so many mistakes. So many. That beautiful girl is in the hospital. Endgame is dead. Like, dead."

Gaze gave me a shocked look. "He's dead? What happened?"

I covered my eyes and dragged my fingers down my face before answering. "He helped Taylor's unhinged roommate kidnap her. And then when the guy in charge wanted to keep Taylor, Endgame refused to leave. Told them they had to go through him to get to her, and they did. They just fucking did."

"Is Taylor okay?" Gaze put his hands on my shoulders.

"She's okay. I mean, what the hell? She was kidnapped and fucking did CPR on Endgame. Holy shit. I think I'm going to be sick." I felt my stomach roll.

Gaze dragged me to the restroom and I made it to the toilet to throw up.

"I never wanted to hurt anyone. Instead, I managed to hurt both Taylor and Endgame." My voice echoed in the bathroom.

Gaze held my hair and rubbed my back. "I'm sure it's not like that."

It was. It was exactly like that. I felt my whole world swirling with the bowl as I flushed it.

26

Taylor

My father kept his hands on my hospital bed. It was like he wanted me in arm's reach. Every time I looked at him, he was looking at me. At least I had been moved into a private room, at least Dad a soft chair to sit in.

The doctor was in and out and the nurses and nurse techs were pretty constant foot traffic. My worst injury was my wrists, and they would take a while to heal. I was sore. The doctor wanted to keep me overnight for observation and monitoring because I had lost consciousness.

Two cops came to visit as well, and Dad didn't have to leave for that. I didn't think he would have anyway. He was clearly dealing with some deep feelings, and leaving my side was not on his agenda.

"So, just to sum it up, this Roberta girl has been stalking you and demanding you pay for stuff? And this guy, Torin, was a friend of your friend, Austin? And he was involved somehow in leading you to the van?" All the information was tapped into a laptop.

"Yes. That's correct." I felt like filling out paperwork was a waste of time. Endgame had died in front of me. In my arms.

Before the tall policeman with the bushy eyebrows could ask any more questions, Nurse Mayborn was back in the room.

"That's enough for now. She's exhausted and needs rest."

The cops handed me a business card and said they would be in touch.

My father resumed his spot while Nurse Mayborn went over my vitals for what felt like the millionth time.

"So who is Raven with?" I patted his big hand.

"She's at Valerie's." Dad looked at his phone.

"You probably have to get home to get her," I recommended.

Nurse Mayborn added, "And visiting hours are almost over."

Dad shook his head. "Here, take my cell phone. I'll use Raven's until we can get you a new one. That way, if you need anything, you can get to us." He handed me his phone. I unlocked it with my sister's birth year. The font was huge and he had four apps. The battery was at eighty-eight percent.

"Thanks. I'll keep you posted. Can you get Austin this number? So he and I can text?" I set the phone on my chest.

"If he's still downstairs." Dad stood and shifted his weight between his feet.

"What's wrong?" I smoothed out my blanket with my hand and dad's phone.

"I don't like him. I don't like Austin, and I'm not afraid to say it." He folded his arms over his chest.

This was the version of my father that I was used to, not the wide-eyed awestruck version I had been dealing with for the last few hours.

"Okay. I don't have any fight in me now, Dad. I'm just exhausted." I closed my eyes.

He wasn't done. "I've never been more scared than I was earlier today, not knowing where you were and then finding out you had been taken. His friends were involved, that roommate was involved. You should've stayed home, gone to online school, and helped with your sister. That's where you should've been."

I opened one eye.

Nurse Mayborn stepped next to my father. "That sounds like a ball of fun for a twenty-year-old girl." She touched his elbow. "All right, Dad, let's save this for a different day. Tell her you love her and get home safe. That's what she needs right now."

My father stared at the nurse and then nodded. She had a commanding way about her. Maybe she was part therapist or something because that was exactly what my dad did.

Nurse Mayborn closed the hospital door behind Dad and turned to me. "Honey. Rest. I see this kind of thing all the time—with trauma, people wanting to retain control so the scary part can stop being so scary. He'll come around. You didn't do anything wrong. This isn't your fault, and living in the past with decisions you didn't make changes nothing for anyone."

She pulled the covers up as if she was a mother tucking in a child.

"Tonight, we thank God and all the things that happened to get you here. You're safe and I'm going to see you stay that way tonight, okay?"

I didn't even get to thank her for her kind words—I was asleep.

IN THE MORNING, the sunlight brought me fully awake. I had spent the night getting woken up for vitals every few hours. But it was still a safe sleep, just like Nurse Mayborn had promised. At seven in the morning, she introduced me to the next nurse on shift, Nurse Quay. She was much younger, but still on the ball.

"Hey, pretty! Great news. I bet we get you out of here today." She took my vitals again. "Everything is fine. How are the hands?"

"Sore." I carefully rolled my wrists.

"I bet. They said you did CPR with your hands bound, so soreness is going to linger for a while." She checked my bandages, too.

The whole scene flooded back, clear and brutal. Endgame's last breaths. The terror of waking in a warehouse.

Nurse Quay frowned a bit and came closer. "It's going to take time. And healing—of more than just your wrists."

I was guessing a lot of nurses did this: their job with emotional support sandwiched in. After turning on my TV, she clicked to the menu channel.

"Just order what you'd like from here, and that'll be up in about an hour. Your doctor has a few surgeries today, but she wants to stop in before then to do her rounds. Sorry to get you rocking and rolling so early."

"Thank you. You guys are kick-ass." I used the TV remote to pick a light breakfast. After that was settled, I texted Austin. I was betting he was still asleep.

ME: How was your night?
AUSTIN: It hasn't ended yet. How was yours?
ME: Exhausting. They poke you so much here. They are super nice. I'm worried about you.
AUSTIN: Says the lady in the damn hospital.

ME: Are you in your apartment?

I hated the thought of having to go back and clear out Endgame's things. It had to be horrible if he was there alone.

AUSTIN: No, I went to Tinsley and Parker's place.

A picture beeped through of Axel, tongue lolling out between Austin's legs.

ME: My big baby. They are so sweet for taking care of him.

I set my phone down. Texting was doing a number on my hands.

AUSTIN: Parker is obsessed. He wants to buy Axel buttons so he can communicate better.

I pressed the microphone so I could use voice to text on the phone.

ME: He will ask for food one hundred percent of the time. And maybe to play fetch a couple of million times.
AUSTIN: Parker thinks Axel is a genius that hides his intelligence so he can get more out of us.

I smiled for what felt like the first time in a billion years. I touched the microphone icon again.

ME: I miss you.
AUSTIN: Same here. I'll be back in the hospital as soon as you tell me I can be there. I know it is only one at a time and your dad wants to be with you.
ME: I'll let you know. They say I'm getting out soon, and I have no idea where to go.

AUSTIN: Do you want to go home with your dad?
ME: No. Not at all. I need to finish classes. Are we not going to go back to your place?
I was getting a feeling that Austin was avoiding that particular thing.
AUSTIN: Just getting a few things together. We can stay in a hotel for a few days, if you want.
ME: Sounds good.

My heart clenched. We had to figure this out. How to go forward when everything that had transpired had been so devastating.

My father was back at my bedside by the time the doctor checked me over. I was cleared for release.

"Remember, though, some pain is on the inside. Be kind to yourself. Give yourself time." The doctor pat the bed.

Dad stepped outside when it was time for me to get dressed. I had no purse, and I didn't have my phone. It felt weird getting rolled out in my pajamas that my father had brought.

When we got to the main entrance, Nurse Mayborn was back on duty and she was doing the honors of pushing my wheelchair while Dad went to get the car.

"You know where you're going?" She helped me stand up from the wheelchair.

"Not yet." I shook my head.

Nurse Mayborn leaned close. "Is there anyone in your life that makes you uncomfortable or injures you? This is a safe space and I have ways to protect you."

I looked at her earnest face. "You really do, don't you?"

"Oh, hell yeah. Just say the word." She gave me a wink.

"You're so badass. I'm grateful we got to meet." I smiled at her.

My brief stint in the hospital had really highlighted how amazing nurses were at their jobs.

Dad's car was even with my wheelchair now. I answered her

question, "I'm good. Thank you for asking. Thank you for being willing to step in and step up if that wasn't the case."

I slid into my dad's passenger seat and Nurse Mayborn closed my door.

My father's jaw was set. "Coming home?"

"I'll go as soon as I get a break from school."

Dad rubbed his scalp. "Okay. Okay. I'm going to have to be up here a lot then, I guess."

"I'm going to be okay, Dad."

We pulled into traffic. "You're going to have to bear with me for a little bit. I promised your sister that she would get to see you."

I used my father's phone to text Austin.

ME: Hey. Dad wants to take me home to see my sister. Is that okay? Axel is okay?

The response came back quickly.

AUSTIN: No problem. I'll miss you, but I understand. And we're doing great with the pup.
ME: Are you sure? I know you are healing and I don't want you to be alone.
AUSTIN: You're too much. You're healing from actual, physical wounds. And I'm staying with Parker and Tinsley until you get back.

I sent him a heart emoji. Dad wasn't wrong. I was craving home, even the home that it was. I wanted to see the place I was in before this whole scene.

I set my head back on the seat rest and closed my eyes. I saw Endgame's last breath over and over again before it faded into an ombre blackness.

27

Austin

I was petting the dog after I texted with Taylor. Tinsley was across from me, crocheting a sweater for Axel.

"She okay?" She twirled her wrist and made a knot slip through a loop.

"I wish I could've seen her, but it's better for her to see her sister. Everyone was worried." I flopped one of Axel's ears over his eye.

"You okay?" She paused her crocheting to stare at me.

In response, I glanced at my feet. "I don't know. No. Not okay. It's a lot of guilt. A huge patch of guilt."

Tinsley set her project down and crossed over to Axel and me. She folded herself next to me and hugged my non-petting arm.

"You should say it," I offered.

Her eyebrows wrinkled. "Say what?"

"That you told me so. That Endgame was bad news." I made Axel's fur go in the wrong direction and then sooth again.

"You already knew that. The reason we're friends is that you found the good in him. And guess what? I know the whole situation was fucked up and we can smear blame around, but he did the right thing in the end."

"Helped Roberta kidnap Taylor?" I turned a bit and Axel huffed when I stopped petting him.

"He refused to leave and always put himself first. I think he did the right thing at the very end because he knew that you would never forgive him if Taylor was gone forever." She rubbed my shoulder and then rested her head on it.

"How do I look at Taylor's father in the face again? What do I say to Taylor? That I'm so broken inside right now? No one deserves this half-assed human that I am." I rested my head on top of hers.

"That you need to process. You need some you time where you can focus on centering yourself. Heal from the damage that this death and the change of your reality brings to you." She crossed her arm over my lap so she could pet Axel. "This isn't your forever. This is now. You always look out for everyone else, but I know Taylor a little bit now. She'll always be okay. And she loves you. She'll wait."

"That's the thing, though. What if I never get over this? What if I'm just drained of any confidence in my decision-making?" I felt like my heart was barely holding on, clinging to quicksand as it fell into a sinkhole.

She lifted her head and turned to me. "Hey, you changed

Endgame. Remember that. The guy that set you up with his drug supply just stood up and did the right thing. Before you? I'd bet that he would've never, ever thought about Taylor in that same situation. Maybe that was the saving of him you were supposed to do."

"Thanks, Tin. You're one of the good ones. Can I crash on this couch tonight? If I have to go home to that place without him or her there..." I didn't finish the sentence.

"Of course. This knucklehead might want to share, though." She pet Axel again.

"That'd be great. Petting him will give me something to do." We still had plenty of time in the day. How did it seem like forever since we found Taylor and everything else, and it had only been fifteen hours?

Tinsley pulled her yarn out of her bag. She powered up the TV and surfed the options until she found a mundane gameshow. It was the perfect thing to stare at while thinking of everything else.

When we got home, Dad gently shook my shoulder. I had to wipe my eyes to get my lids to open, but before I could get out of my car, Raven was smothering me.

"I love you!"

I held her. "I love you, too, small pants."

I glanced at my father who shrugged. "It's been a long wait."

He got out of the car to speak to the mom. They chatted quietly while I struggled to get out of the car with my sister hanging on my front like a wild animal baby.

"Look at your giant Band-Aids!" She touched my wrist and squirmed down my body.

"Yeah. They are way bigger than these cuts need. Lots of overdoing it at the hospital." I fluffed the back of my sister's hair out from under her shirt collar. It was an unconscious habit that I was guessing was going undone while I was gone.

"Look. Have you looked?" Raven leaned towards the house.

All of a sudden I realized that Raven's friend Valerie's mom was in the driveway. Chatting with my dad, just like normal families do. All the crap was gone from in front of the house. Sure, the grass was dead in giant appliance—shaped crop circles, but the first thing you noticed was the house.

I whirled to look at Raven. "What happened?"

She was absolutely glowing. "You have to see inside. It's not done but..."

As we rounded to the front door, I saw a giant garbage dumpster parked a little bit behind the house.

I followed Raven up the steps. The steps were really wide. Normally, we had an uneven footpath to navigate. The deck had parts that didn't look sturdy, but I could see all of it.

After following her inside, it was clear they had been working on this place nonstop since I left.

"We still have to do Dad's room and the garage, but check it out." She flung her hands around like she was presenting a PowerPoint.

"This place is so much bigger. There's even an echo. A freaking echo!"

Raven twirled in a circle. "We were going to have it done by the time you got home, but then you were kidnapped and now you get to see it too early."

The front door closed behind me and I faced my father. He had a proud bloom when he met my gaze.

"What brought this on?" I touched the cushion of the couch that had not been fit to sit on in a long time. Sure, there were stains, but it was actually a couch.

He shuffled into the kitchen where Raven went from drawer to drawer flinging them open. "We hired a service for a few days to help us get started. It was long overdue."

Overdue was an understatement. But I didn't want to make him feel anything but proud. "It's fantastic. Looks great. So calming."

I walked over to my dad and gave him a congratulatory hug, Raven joined to turn it into a double whammy. Dad hugged back so hard, it was obvious he needed the contact.

"Proud of you, Dad. I know this wasn't easy." I let him see my smile.

"Yeah. It was a lot. I started small, and Raven's helped me every step of the way. Once we had a pile taller than her," Dad lifted his chin in Raven's direction, "then it was time to rent the dumpster."

"I cleaned out so much stuff, and Dad and I had to wear masks sometimes. But we're doing good." I saw Raven smile at Dad and I had a rush of happiness for her. A normal-looking home would help her so much. I lost a lot of confidence because there was no way I could ever offer to do things at my place. And I felt like I made up so many lies to get people to drop me off at the end of the driveway. Maybe they felt I wasn't genuine? I wasn't sure that was the case, now that I was older, but young Taylor put a lot of thought into the very thing.

"I feel like this is going to help me heal. Thank you both so much." When we broke the hug, Dad started talking about grilling burgers. Raven got out a bag of frozen broccoli and a few potatoes. Nothing gourmet, but we had plates and we had a table to eat on. I helped my sister set the table, and before I knew it, we were having a good, old-fashioned family dinner.

Raven and Dad wouldn't let me help clean up. Instead, they

encouraged me to sit while they loaded up the dishwasher. When it turned on, I jumped. It was loud. Really loud.

Dad frowned at it. "It's just getting used to working, that's all."

Raven grimaced at the old thing as it started to make a high-pitched whine. "It doesn't like doing its job."

We moved to the back deck, another place I hadn't set foot on in a long time. I could see the almost full dumpster clearly now. It probably seemed like a big pile of crap to anyone else, but I knew it was a huge move for Dad. Everything was tied to a memory he had been trying to recreate, even though that was always impossible.

The lawn was cut and the weeds had been whacked. We sat down in mismatched lawn chairs, but I appreciated that we could look at the view and not feel a pit in our stomachs of the undone chores that seemed to be in an unconquerable pile.

"Listen, I'm going to run to the store and get Taylor a phone so I can have mine back. You guys stay here, okay?" He pushed up from his chair and both he and it groaned.

Raven nodded. "Yeah, she and I have a ton to talk about. I'll watch her."

After Dad had closed the screen door, she leaned closer to me. "Dad's been talking to a woman."

Oh. Now it made sense.

I mean, I'd have loved it if self-realization had brought on the changes, but his being serious about a lady for the first time since Mom left was great news.

"Valerie's mom?" I took a guess on the new woman. And how do you feel about that?" I rested my wrists on my knees. It would be time for a painkiller soon. I didn't want the pain to gang up on me as the medicine wore off.

"No, not Valerie's mom. She has a husband. Willa is the lady Dad's been seeing. She's nice. I don't love her hair, but she has chickens." She pulled out her phone and found a chicken that resembled the one the lady had.

"They're cute. Does she eat them?" I tried to hold a serious face.

Raven stuck out her tongue. "Ew, no. Just the eggs. They all have names and personalities. God, it would be horrible to eat them."

"That makes sense, small pants." I looked at her legs.

"I'm getting as tall as you—that's what Dad said the other day." She tapped her feet like she could will them to be farther from her hips. "He took me to get dinner, and the other day I got a pedicure with Willa." She toed off her sneakers and pulled off her socks. She had a little French manicure with hearts painted on them.

"Those are stinkin' adorable. Do you think I'll meet Willa while I'm here?" I wondered how they met.

"Yes. She has no children, but her pug dog is like a toddler. He screams all the time and wears clothes and everything." She nodded at me like her analysis made perfect sense.

"Those dogs look like aliens," I offered.

"I want ten of them." She smiled at me and pushed on her nose and made her eyes buggy.

"That sounds reasonable." I wanted to reach out and grab her hand, but my wrists were starting to hurt. "Let's go back inside so the mosquitoes don't carry us away."

My sister and I relocated to the couch. She sat next to me and we looked at funny videos on the internet. I tried to stay focused on her, but my mind drifted to Austin, and then as if it was a requirement... Endgame. It was messy. *What was next? Did he have a family that needed to be notified? Was there to be a funeral?*

"You're not watching." My sister put her phone back in her lap.

"I'm sorry. I have to take my pain meds and I drift a little." I stood up and found the tote bag Dad had brought home from the hospital. I carefully read the labels and took two large white pills with a gulp of tap water.

My dad came in the front door and I met them in the living

room. It was weird to have a really family-like interaction in our house. I was thrilled for Raven.

Dad handed Raven the new phone box and she took it upon herself to open the package and peel off all the stickers so that it could be used. It had half a charge from the manufacturer.

"I'm going to call some friends and Austin. Give them an update."

Dad and Raven went their own ways, but I had a feeling I'd see Raven later in the night.

I got to my room, which had remained untouched. I wanted to grab a quick shower, but it would require some Ziplocs and rubber bands to make sure my wrists stayed dry. I only had those limitations for about twenty-four hours. I changed my clothes and got on my bed. It took me a few beats, but I programmed Austin's number into my phone and sent him a text, letting him know that this was my new number.

I had a video call almost immediately.

"Hey, kitten. How are you feeling?"

"I'm good. I miss you, but I feel good." I fanned my hair out behind me. He imitated my pose.

"You look tired." He pouted a little.

"So do you. And your eyes are red." I touched the side of the phone like it was his face.

"When are you coming back?" He moved the phone so I could see Axel. His long pink tongue hanging out of his mouth made me chuckle.

"That dog could tie off boats with that licker." I shuffled my legs so I would be under the covers.

Austin gave Axel rubs on his chest.

"So?" He wasn't letting me forget the question.

"After I get my wrist bandages off. Then I have to head back for schoolwork." I didn't like something. Austin was off a bit. Just a tiny bit. If someone hadn't known him for years, they wouldn't notice.

But I did.

He changed the subject. "I'm not sure if you're ready to look, but there are tons of pictures of Bride Day. They're hilarious and touching. If you feel okay, you can look at them." He sat up and I could hear him tapping on his computer.

Soon, I had a link in my text messages so I clicked through.

It was amazing. So many hairy, hairy man legs sticking out under the bride's gowns. Some guys had pillowcases on their heads, but the effort was there. They wanted to support Austin and anyone like Austin.

Gaze's whole ass basketball team had shown up, and they were fantastic. I clicked through a few more pictures. There was a link to the day's hashtag.

I tapped on Austin's social media page and saw he had a stack of pictures of us in our matching outfits front and center.

We spoke about each one as I perused. Then I saw a blurry image of Endgame in the background of one picture. I heard Austin take in a sharp breath.

I went back to the video feed in time to see him shaking his head. "It still doesn't feel real."

It felt like there were evil holograms inserted in the happy memory. "Yeah. We had no idea how much would change that night."

"Hey, I have to walk Axel. I'll call you in the morning—or wait, maybe you should call me so I don't wake you." He blew me a kiss and ended the call.

Dread filled me. Austin hadn't said as much, but I'd bet a considerable stash of money on the idea that the next time I saw him, he was going to break up with me.

I tucked my new phone under my pillow and started to cry.

Austin

I did, in fact, walk the dog. It was dark and the city always felt alive to me. I couldn't see the stars, but I knew they were out there, doing their best.

Tonight, I saw Endgame's face in memories that danced on the sidewalks like ghosts of hope.

I had to break up with Taylor. And that was another heartbreak. It wasn't fair to her that she was kidnapped. My decision making had done that. I knew Endgame was bad news the minute he'd hid his stash in my camera bag.

But the part of him that stood up for Taylor—that wouldn't leave her—that was the part I'd loved.

He was broken. He didn't process his emotions correctly, and he didn't know how to handle a heart, least of all mine.

I just had to deal with the guilt of it. I was selfish to start with Taylor before I was done with Endgame. It wasn't cool. I had talked myself into the belief that I was helping her, but I was the one that benefited most. I had a beautiful girl to taunt Endgame with. It wasn't the right way to start a relationship. Especially one that turned out to mean so much to me.

She was easy to let in. She was so devoted. Hell, I knew she was head over heels for me long before she went to college.

And now I'd break her heart. And my own. But she could not be around me while I processed whatever this was going to do to me.

She deserved a guy that would focus on her. Focus on taking her on dates, making her happy. Not the guy that had baggage that almost got her killed.

The guilt was huge. I would not let myself hurt her more. And ending things with her would ensure that she had a future. She wouldn't be single long.

While I was checking my email, I saw a message from Stars Unlimited.

Dear Austin,

We are so pleased with the recent campaign with Taylor and look forward to future collaborations. We are onboarding a small French company and would love for you to consult on setting up the vibe for Stars Unlimited FRANCE. We would like it consistent with your most recent work. We will provide transportation cost and housing for the duration of your employment.
Please let us know if any of this sounds like it would work for you.

Sincerely,

John Bartson

Maybe the universe was offering me a way to wipe the slate clean. Get out of the country and give Taylor space. Give me space. From the pain. From the guilt.

28

The next morning, Raven helped me put the bags on my hands and pre-opened all the body products in my bathroom before I took my shower.

I must have spent a half hour just standing under the hot water. Raven came knocking twice, checking on me because I was taking so long.

When I got out, she insisted on helping me do my hair. I

didn't have the strength to do anything other than let it drip dry, but Raven braided it into a style.

She picked out a soft sundress and shrug, along with leggings and slippers. When I came out of the bathroom after dressing, she was wearing something similar.

I had a pang of regret. My sister needed more of me. The condition of our house had kept me on edge. She deserved a more relaxed older sister. I went to her and gave her a hug.

She rubbed my back. "Dad and I can take care of Axel again. I think he'll really like the way we cleaned up and Dad said we're going to have to fence in the yard for Willa's pug dogs. So Axel can run here with them. It'd be really funny to see them all play together."

I smiled at the thought of the dressed-in-clothes pug screamers running after Axel like a pack of zombies. "I think I can arrange that."

It was only fair to give her another go at Axel. A fence sounded like a big improvement on keeping him and his half-assed way of playing fetch from becoming an all day affair.

"Let's go eat." She pulled me behind her and was still very much in caretaker mode.

She made me toast and a scrambled egg.

"Where'd you learn to do all this cooking?" I sprinkled a touch of pepper onto my eggs.

"I have a class in school. They make us manage a budget, cook, pay taxes, and learn how to vote." She sat across from me with a plate of her own.

"That sounds like a legitimately cool class." I tasted the egg and it was great. "You can really do this, I'm so proud. Nice work. They never taught me any of this stuff when I came through school."

I took a bite of the perfect, tan toast with a touch of melted butter.

"Yeah, a rich guy donates money, but it has to be used to give us life skills. I think he does it in honor of someone. I forget the story they told us." She crunched her toast.

"That sounds awesome." Dad was long gone. I saw an empty spot where his car normally was. "Where'd Dad go?"

"He drives Willa to work. He walks her dogs, too. He'll be back in an hour or so." She started pushing her eggs onto her fork.

"So he's really into her, huh?" I added a bit of pepper to mine.

"Yeah. He's into her, you're into your new guy, and all I have is a dumpster. It went on fire once, too. I took a picture in front of it." She tapped her phone until she could show me the picture of her standing in front of the flaming dumpster.

She had some text underneath:

My life in one picture.

"You're a funny kid." I rolled my eyes as she tucked her phone into her lap.

"I got jokes for days, sister." She held out her fork and I toasted it with my own.

I was going to spend more time with her—that was a promise I was making right now.

IT CAME time for me to go back to school. Dad had questions about where I would be staying. The Loveville police told us that Roberta would be facing charges, as would her boyfriend. That was good, but I wasn't looking forward to a trial, if it came to that. I got ready to go back and it seemed silly but I did all the same things as I had before. I packed a bag, made sure I had my charger. Took the ride. All like I hadn't watched Endgame take his last breath.

When Dad parked the car in the metered spot, we had about a half an hour to do the transfer. Austin had asked me to meet him at Parker and Tinsley's place. Axel and Parker rounded the corner and instantly picked up the pace, whether Parker wanted to or not. Axel barreled at Raven. She braced herself like she was the bottom of a cheerleading pyramid and Axel launched himself at her like a rocket.

She caught him and I caught her. Dad steadied me.

"You big meatball. You're going to knock us all down, then who's going to feed you?" I petted his big thick head.

Raven captured him in a hard hug. He licked her whole neck and face in response.

Parker put his hands on his knees and breathed quickly while we all got acquainted.

Eventually, he reached out a hand for my father.

"I hope this isn't a surprise? That my sister is taking Axel home?" I felt bad for Parker. According to Austin, Axel was doing great with Parker's workout routine.

"It's not. Part of the reason we went for a run—I knew he

would have a hard car ride. Let me text the crew that you guys are here. They can bring down Axel's stuff."

Tinsley and Austin came down with two canvas bags full of stuff.

Austin shook my father's hand and Tinsley started showing Raven the stuff in the bags. "This bag has the normal stuff, his bowls and food and leashes and harnesses. This other one has the silly stuff. Hats, t-shirts, shoes, and toys."

I noticed then that Austin had a pink hair tie on his wrist. I felt my heart stop in my chest. Austin wouldn't meet my eyes. Cruel Pink. Now it was my turn to feel the pain.

I instantly tried to push away the fear. That it was just an oversight. That it was just a coincidence.

Raven grabbed a daisy petal hat and used the Velcro to secure it around Axel's head. He was content to have it on and looked at each of us with a wagging tail.

"So crazy that he ran to this place when he ran away." Dad gave me a smile. At least he's a ham," Dad commented. "He'll fit right in with Willa's pugs."

While the trade-off was happening, I noticed Austin didn't look me in the eyes. Bad things. Bad vibes. I wasn't wrong about our last conversation. Doomsday was settling over me. Austin grabbed my bag from our trunk and Parker helped get Axel in the car. Raven and I hugged. In no time, they were pulling away, Axel's head was out the window with his tongue wagging in the wind.

"They seemed sweet. How are you?" Tinsley came close and wrapped her arm around me.

I showed her my much more sensible bandages. "Healing."

I saw a bit of pity. She knew. Whatever was going down with Austin, she knew. My stomach dropped another notch.

I had the irrational thought to run away. If I left right now, the next part wouldn't be able to happen. We started walking up the stairs. When we got to the top, instead of coming with us, Tinsley and Parker left Austin and me at their door.

"Aren't you coming in for a shower?" Parker was always washing up after sweating.

"Actually, I'm going down to the park to do some stretching. Tinsley is coming, too."

Tinsley held up a book and wiggled it.

"Okay." There was no denying it now. Austin let himself in with a key and held the door open for me.

I followed him inside and waved to the departing Parker and Tinsley. Austin walked me through their very nice apartment. Second floor, huge windows, and lots of interior brick walls.

He led me to a door and opened it. Inside was a bedroom. All my stuff was carefully laid out. I had a desk, my computer, all the stuff I had left at Austin's.

I took a deep breath. None of his things were there. It was all me.

I sat on the edge of the bed, letting my bag fall to my feet. Now he finally met my eyes. I saw nothing but pain and regret there.

Hooking my index finger around the pink hair tie on his wrist, I slipped it off his arm. I purposefully pulled my hair up into a messy bun. And waited.

"I'm so sorry, Taylor. So sorry." His eyes filled up.

And then instead of dread, I had empathy. I stood up and wrapped my arms around him.

"No. You don't get to feel guilty about this." I rubbed his back. He held my hips.

"How could I not?" He shook his head slowly.

"Maybe that's the gift I get to give you now." I made a choice. "I need some space. If it's okay with Tinsley and Parker, I'll live here. You need to get some closure. I deserve to be able to move on from this."

The tears were flowing, and it was all lies, but I'd take this part from him—break my own heart so he didn't have to. I was wearing the pink now anyway.

He looked to the ceiling briefly before pulling me closer. He kissed my forehead and then my lips gently. "There's no one else like you on this planet. Never settle for anything. Ever. Whoever's next? If they don't build you a pedestal from their own bones for you to stand on, I'll kick their ass. Now for another hard part—I got offered a position in France from Stars Unlimited. For a year."

I moved his hair off his shoulders. The thought of someone else besides him was a jagged blade. I saw the brokenness in his eyes. The way he would staple all the responsibility for Endgame's death and breaking my heart to his soul.

"You should go to France, Austin Burathon." It was a lightning bolt moment. It all came together for me. "I've loved you my whole life. And I think it was so I'd be here for this exact moment. This moment right here. Let me treat you with love. I have so much. More than I'll ever need. It all belongs to you anyway."

Austin closed his eyes as if my words had hit him. It took a few beats before he responded. "I love you, too." He kissed my forehead again and then lifted each of my hands so he could brush his lips on them as well.

It was time to tell him. I had this information to share and he was clearly going to work things out.

"Before he died..." I sniffled at the thought.

Austin's eyes slammed through emotions in front of me. Anger, loss, fear. And then he nodded for me to continue, still holding my hands.

"Endgame said this: 'Tell him I ain't never loved anyone, but right now? All I can see is his face.'" I squeezed Austin's fingers, knowing that that information was going to haunt him and maybe change the course of his life. I prayed telling him was the right move. That Torin's final impulse was not to hurt Austin, but to let him fly.

Austin swallowed hard and looked at our hands. "Yeah. You're one hell of a human Taylor Fancy Boland. Thank you."

I raised his fingers to my lips, and kissed them goodbye.

Austin

Maybe this was the moment. Right here. She was in front of me, breaking her own heart. Stomping on it. I saw her then, for what she was really, really worth. And it was everything. I reached out for her hand. She gave it to me.

She would give me anything I asked for. Devotion, fierceness. She would live in disappointment if it made me happy. It almost took my knees out to see the pure reflection she radiated to me. Like a magic mirror. Her heart could twist my nightmares like balloon animals into something to be dreams. To be her dream.

"I love you. I love how when I come to you there is only love. When I need you there is only soft. I can't believe that I have to leave you. But I have to. I need to face the things I've done with him. To you. To him."

She was more than her beautiful looks. She was a bundle of kindness. Empathy. I could see her saving stray kittens and helping strangers. It was who she was. If she found someone else while I sorted myself out--that would be my greatest regret.

I left quietly. But the moment was thunderous.

29

Taylor was exceptional. She broke up with me when she read the scene. Took the pink from me. Then she told me she loved me and I believed it. How doing the right thing could feel so wrong was a mystery to me. Just like doing wrong things with Endgame could feel so right.

I had packed my bags already. Had everything stowed away. My apartment was empty now, a huge batch of it in storage. Being able to pick up and leave—all my business could be fit in a bag and relocated was a blessing. But it didn't feel like it now. My parents, siblings, and Pixie Rae were all there to see me off. We met just outside the airport at a restaurant to have a final meal.

I sat next to my mother who held my hand. "You look like you haven't been eating. Have you been eating?"

I rested my head on her shoulder. "No one cooks as good as you and Dad, you know that."

Teddi sat on my other side and Gaze was across the table. It'd be the longest I had ever been separated from them.

I needed it. Somehow I knew that fixing all the things that were shattered inside me would take my greatest resource: time.

Teddi wrapped her arm around me. "All I know is I better be getting French pastries mailed to me daily."

I lifted my head from Mom and set it on Teddi's shoulder. They were making mush out of my convictions.

Gaze leaned forward. "If your place has an extra bedroom, Pixie and I have never been to France."

"Always a spot for any of you anytime." I pushed a smile on my lips. This was good—plans and hopes. They were letting me go, too.

And that probably told me more than anything they knew I needed space.

Teddi rubbed my hand as everyone's dinners were delivered to the table. "How's Taylor?"

Maybe Teddi did know now that it had gotten real. So real for us.

"She's beautiful, empathetic, and giving." I felt numb coming from my throat.

"And devastated?" She gave me a sad look.

"I think we both are." I felt my shoulders slump.

"Peaches and I will keep a watch on her."

I considered my sister's beautiful face, then glanced at Ruffian. "You'll take care of her too, right?" I lifted my chin so he would know I meant Teddi.

"That's all I do. No worries." Ruffian stabbed his chicken with a fork.

And then I had to eat because my mom was watching. I knew she'd give me hell if I didn't at least put in an attempt with my food.

Afterward, Dad, Ruffian, Pixie, and Milt opted for dessert.

I picked up my fork and snagged a small bite of Milt's chocolate cake.

"You know, I have a virtual system working where I recreate house and building layouts. I could set up our house and give everyone avatars? We could still get together." He gave me a big smile.

I loved that Milt never gave up. He saw that we were all going to miss each other, and he figured out a solution. Granted, it was computer-based, but all of his solutions were that way. His thick swoop of black hair covered his crystal blue eyes. Looks of a model and head of a gamer. He was a fun conundrum. And despite how morose I had been feeling, they lifted my spirits.

My father stood up and came around the table to me. "Son, we're so proud of you. Always have been, always will be. Mom and I will come visit. As soon as we get our passports, we'll make plans."

I patted my father's hand. "Thanks, Dad. Means a lot to me."

Dad paid for the breakfast tab, even though we all tried to put in money. When he refused, Teddi suggested that he allow us to leave the tip. That server was going to be set for the day as we all tossed in the cost of our meals.

I walked over to the airport so I could take my flight to France. I was doing this. For me. And a little bit for Endgame.

Taylor

Watching him leave was horrible. I added it to the things that I'd continue to see in my nightmares.

When Tinsley and Parker came back in, I was still sitting on my bed, bag at my feet.

I was in shock, which considering how many feelings I had was probably not that surprising.

Tinsley had a shopping bag and Parker ran into the kitchen.

When she got to my room, she unpacked ice cream, candy, and tissues. Parker came in with three spoons.

"We're going to handle this like a pack of girls." Tinsley pulled me against her chest as she hugged me. Parker did an air hug from the door with the spoons in his hand spread like a deck of cards. "I'm going to shower, but I'll be ready to do whatever you ladies need."

He set the spoons on my dresser and rushed out.

Tinsley grabbed the spoons and two tubs of Ben and Jerry's ice cream. "Sobber's choice." She offered them to me.

I picked Chubby Hubby and a spoon. She had the Chunky Monkey. After she sat down next to me, we both started eating the ice cream.

When we had demolished about half, I was ready to talk a little. "Did you guys help him do all this?" I waved my spoon around the room.

She nodded. "Yeah. I handled your clothes and makeup and

they did the heavy lifting and sourcing the furniture. But Austin picked out the art and all the little touches."

There were four paintings on the wall, each more beautiful than the next. There were a few pieces of art on the tops of the dresser and near the window. I noticed the window had a reading nook, packed with some of my favorite books and some I had never seen before.

It was all too much. Thinking of Austin thinking of me while he prepped to move to France—it was overwhelming.

Tinsley rubbed my shoulder. "Baby girl, you were so good to him. So good for him."

I ran my tongue over my teeth and took another scoop of ice cream. "Not enough, though."

Parker returned to the room, hair still dripping wet. He was wearing cotton shorts and a tank top. "What'd I miss?"

He grabbed his spoon and then sat crisscrossed on the floor in front of us. He riffled through the brown grocery bag that was near my bed. "All I got was vanilla? Dammit."

Tinsley took a heaping scoop of her ice cream and plopped it on top of his as soon as the carton was open.

We silently ate the ice cream for a few minutes before Parker peered up at me in a way that reminded me of Axel. I gave him a spoonful of mine as well.

He mixed it up and took a bite. He said, "Heaven," around a mouthful of ice cream.

I fully intended on becoming a boneless, crying house hobbit for the rest of my days, but Tinsley and Parker seemed to have other plans.

And again, I thought of how Austin had literally given me his friends so I wouldn't be alone.

I loved him so much. I loved him still. And I'd always love him. I touched the hairband in my bun. I would change what pink meant to me. It would be about Austin now. Good things now. Love now.

30

W orking for Stars Unlimited in France was more than I anticipated. Instead of Paris or a big city, I was in a small village that the company's founders grew up in. I had a tiny cottage by a creek. In the morning, I'd hear the water and it helped settle me. It was different than the city noises. Coffee outside was a must.

Roberta and Peter were in the process of a trial. I'd asked

Taylor if she needed me to come back. She had told me that no, I was not involved in the investigations. It required her, the cops that had found her and the paramedics. A few low level people in Bullsen's organization had flipped on him. The trial took a long damn time. Luckily, they were both behind bars while they waited. No one would post bail. Which was good. I was able to focus on what I needed to do and know that Taylor remained safe.

It took me about two months before I was ready to spread Endgame's ashes.

I brought the triple bagged remains in an intricate box with gold foil. He probably hated it. The day had a slight mist to it. The cottage had a wall of ivy growing on it. In the distance I could see the hilly main part of the village dotted with orangey rooftops. It was scenic and lovely. And it made me miss Taylor.

But this morning was about this troubled man that I had loved in the past.

I set the box down on the wrought iron table that I usually had my coffee on and took a seat. My closest neighbors were a brisk walk away, so I had privacy.

"Remember when I said I'd take you to France someday?"

The only answer I had was my memory of the conversation.

Endgame smoking, leaning out the window of my place. "Why would we go there? Fuck that."

"I hear it's beautiful. Relaxing." I had come up next to him and placed my hand on his shoulder.

He scowled at my fingertips before grazing them with his lips. "You wanna go? Let's go."

The smoke had been pushed back into the room, the wind changing course. It was a short conversation, but it meant much more.

I had wanted Endgame to see what he was worth. Know that he didn't have to sabotage happiness because he was afraid to hope for good things. And now look where it got him.

"What was your first memory?" He and I were lying naked in

his bed. At that point we were broken up, but we had slipped back again.

"Oh, crap. Huh. I guess the first thing I really remember is getting ice cream with Dad. It was a special treat because my mom had to go visit her aunt. It was just the two of us. Had a great time, from what I remember. Probably helps that I've seen the pictures of it and everything."

He snorted. "Man, it's like we lived on different planets."

I had been almost afraid to ask, but I felt like I had to. "What about you?"

"My first memory was the inside of a dryer. Not sure where the hell it was because we didn't have a dryer. The cops were coming and my mom wanted to slow them down while she escaped. I was crying, and she stuffed me in the dryer and bolted out the back door. It was one of those little porthole ones, so I could see the whole thing. I was in there for a bit, probably not that long, but it felt like forever. I was so scared that I'd die in there. Not sure how old I was, but I knew cops and Mom were problems together.

"Then this cop comes in and I'm banging on the glass and crying. He opened the door, and he was like, 'Shit, our perps are so stupid. Instead of money laundering, they're sticking kids in dryers.' And the cop and his buddies laughed and laughed."

"That was your first memory? Ever?" I had turned over in bed to face him.

"Yeah. It worked. Mom got away. Didn't come to get me from the emergency foster home for a few months."

"That's heartbreaking." I had touched his face, running my fingers on one of his tattoos.

He shrugged. Shrugged away the pain of it. Shrugged away the horror. "Hate closed spaces. Shit, my worst fear is that someone will bury me in a coffin. There's not even a window in those." He had covered my hand and his eyes let me in, just a little.

"If I'm still alive, I'll make sure you're outside, where there's nothing to close you in." It was a toss-away promise, though I meant it.

I had no idea I'd be carrying out that exact thing a year later.

"I bet this bag sucks. This box sucks. But I had no other way to get you to France. I want you to be here, peaceful, unbothered." It took me two times to get up the guts to open the lid. When I did, I had to reach in and pull out the bag. The contents were more than I thought and somehow less as well.

Even though it was early in the morning, I went inside and grabbed whiskey. Instead of a fancy glass, I drank from the bottle. I hated whiskey, but Endgame loved it.

After I had a serious burn in my throat and a buzz in my head, I kicked off my shoes. I was wearing sweatpants and a pink t-shirt.

I stepped on stones until I was in the center of the creek. "Torin Rulle, I wish for you peace and I thank you for your life. I know you did the right thing, even though you knew it would end up like this. I loved you. I love you. And I believe the best part of our energies will blend again someday."

I set the bottle down and opened the bag. I took another drink of whiskey and then poured some into the bag, sharing one last drink.

The tears came as I upended the bag. The ashes flowed out and into the water, creating a thin coating on top. I took the bottle and poured it over the spot, over Endgame's remains.

When the bottle was empty, I slowly lowered myself into the creek, being surrounded by him one last time, hoping I had done something that mattered.

"If being loved by me means anything, you had that." And then I slipped under the water.

I had my dream guy, I *had* him, and now he was gone from me. Sure, we FaceTimed a few times a month, but it wasn't the same. It was stunted. He gently pressed me about dating again. I didn't want to, so I'd tell him things would happen in a few weeks. And those few weeks would never actually come. Wearing a touch of pink became my tradition. If he noted it, Austin didn't mention it. For me it stood for the time I loved him. Well, of course I still loved him. But he had said it to me. And then left. I needed to remember it. The small sliver in time when the planets had aligned and we were in love. Just a gasp of perfection.

I watched through the little screen as Austin got his confidence back. It was not all at once, but he was speaking French over his shoulder to others from time to time. I followed his social media and saw the growth there, which was crazy because he was already so talented.

Peaches and Teddi came to visit. Peaches way more than Teddi because she and Ruffian were busy with her new charity.

Peaches and Parker seemed to really click. She was actually the one to suggest that Parker walk/jog with shelter dogs. Turns out, Parker was super missing Axel since he had returned to my family, but he tried not mentioning it around me.

It was a great idea. Parker had the energy of a Jack Russell anyway. Tinsley seemed to empathize with how deeply I was affected by the loss of Austin.

Hence, tonight I felt like she was betraying me by forcing me to go to a dating service. Booty Camp Dating Service was coming to town and they promised to deliver your perfect match. One hundred ten percent guaranteed, which was obviously a scam, but Tinsley said the tickets were purchased so we were going.

I dressed up in a flowy black dress with a low back. Tinsley had on a pink number that seemed to accentuate every curve she had, and a few she didn't.

"Are those padded underwear?" I poked her left butt cheek.

"Yes! Amazing, right?" She slapped her ass with a satisfying whack. "They have these inserts that feel like raw chicken and I can make my booty bounce now."

She did just that, making me laugh. Parker had come out of his room, munching on an apple. He started twerking with Tinsley without hesitation. After getting my arm yanked on by both of them, I caved and started doing my best to make my booty pop, too.

Tinsley pulled her phone out and yipped. "Uber's here. We gotta go."

We left Parker twerking alone in the apartment and hurried down the stairs.

By the time we were at the event space, we had calmed down.

As we walked in, it was clear that this was an expensive, expensive event. I gave Tinsley a hard look.

When we were approached by a staff member, I saw a glimpse of the paper that Tinsley signed. A few thousand dollars had gone into our experience here. It included the pricey one-on-one time with the company's owner, Wolf Saber.

"Who paid for this?" I took a glass of champagne off a tray.

Tinsley bit her lips together and shrugged.

I tilted my head to the side in disbelief.

"Fine. You know who." She took a long sip.

"Austin paid for this? He wants me to find a match this much?" It hurt. I took a long swallow as well, until I had drained the whole glass.

"He just wants you to be happy, and this place has a great

reputation." She glanced around at all the dressed up singles. "There are a lot of hot guys here."

"He's Austin." I toasted myself as I realized how futile the rest of my life would be. I was madly in love with Austin. It was part of who I was.

A staff member appeared at my elbow. "Taylor Boland? Hi, I'm Shing. You have a VIP meeting. Why don't you bring that glass and we can get that over with before the event?"

I shot Tinsley a look, but she was already walking away. I was the only one with the VIP setup. Man, Austin really wanted to get rid of me. I was seconds from walking right out and taking a car home, but I couldn't leave a woman by herself even if she had half-sabotaged me.

"This is where Mr. Saber is basing his office in this city, so please, make yourself comfortable."

She indicated the red leather chair. I moved to it and sat down.

"He'll be right in." She was smiley, like a receptionist. The space wasn't fancy, and it had quite a few portable filing cabinets.

I waited for a few minutes, but before I could take out my phone from my purse, a man opened the door. He had piercing blue eyes and a very dominant demeanor.

I went to stand and he put out his hand to stop me. "Please, stay seated. I have no idea how you ladies walk around in those heels all the time. Take a load off while you can." He slid behind the desk and picked up a folder. I could see now that it had my last name on it.

"So what goes on here?" I wasn't getting a bad feeling, but it was definitely out of my wheelhouse.

"I come from a long line of matchmakers. Usually, it's the ladies that do it, but I have a knack for it. Hence, the business." He flipped through my paperwork and furrowed his brow.

"Matchmaking? I saw the advertisement for one hundred ten percent and all that. Seems a bit much."

He leveled his stare at me from over the paperwork. "Have you found any negative reviews?"

Whoa. It was a touchy subject for him, I was guessing. "No. I was gifted this whole thing from a guy I used to be involved with." I ran a finger in circles on the edge of my glass.

"Austin Burathon?"

My eyes snapped up at the mention of his name. Then I tried to hide my eagerness by looking at the floor. "How'd you know?"

"It's his credit card." He tapped the paper.

"Oh. So this isn't some sort of mind reading/psychic experience." I really should've done more research before coming here.

Wolf closed my file with a slap. "I'm canceling this. We can't do it."

I had a decent amount of self-confidence, but Wolf claiming he couldn't do for me what he one hundred ten percent could do for anyone else was a kick in the pants.

"Don't make that face. You're a gorgeous woman, but you're here under false pretenses." He grimaced at me.

Now I was getting insulted. I stood up and put my glass on his desk.

There was a light knock on the door and a beautiful woman walked in.

She read the room quickly and hurried over to Wolf's side. "What's up?"

"Can't do this one." He pointed at my folder with his pinkie.

"Care to tell me why?" I was ready to huff out.

"Hi, I'm Hazel. This is my husband and he sucks at speaking clearly to women sometimes. Please forgive him. He can do this for everyone so far, but if there's a complication, sometimes he needs to tell people." Her words got harsher toward the end of her sentence.

Wolf grumbled under his breath.

"Just tell her before she leaves." She grabbed his bicep.

"You've already met your match, and setting you up with one

of the guys here is just a recipe for disaster." He waved his hand in dismissal.

I sighed. "This is a hell of a scam. You have to give my friend his money back. Do you buy good reviews or get bad ones taken down? How does this work?" I headed for the door Hazel had recently stepped through.

Wolf crowded over to be in front of the door. Hazel pulled him backward.

"Always leave a lady a way out of a room, you caveman." I liked Hazel.

I appreciated that she cared about my comfort.

Wolf stepped back and appeared chagrined. "I'm sorry. I just... This one is a powerful connection. You *will* end up together. The universe won't have it any other way." He gave Hazel a look that was much softer.

She turned to him. "That strong?"

"Inevitable." He held my folder out to me. "I'll refund his money."

"Wait, you have to tell me who it is." I hugged the folder to my chest.

Hazel and Wolf regarded each other.

Then Hazel gave me a gentle touch. "You know, sweetheart. You already know."

"Austin?"

Wolf shuffled his feet. "Could it be anyone else?"

"Not for me."

"Then you have your answer. And your friend that you came with? She has, like, three perfect matches out there, which is another whole story I've never felt before." Wolf stepped back and I opened the door. Sure enough, Tinsley was surrounded by three guys, each talking to her in bursts.

"Oh yeah. That's going to be a problem." He frowned.

Hazel sidled next to me. "A problem or a hell of a night," she said, winking. My eyes went wide at the thought. Could Tinsley be that spicy? I wasn't sure.

Wolf hung back. "Just wait for him, okay? Don't force this."

I nodded. "Thanks."

"Yeah. Congratulations. We aim to please." He added one more thing, "Can you get your friend to go home? I need to spend some time with these guys and see what the hell is up."

"I can try." I drank a few more glasses of complimentary wine before dragging Tinsley home.

She was a chatterbox, showing me how she had all three numbers in her phone. Each guy was perfect for a different reason.

And my perfect guy was in another country entirely.

31

T eddi was sitting too close to the screen, but she was excited. "I'm so glad. This year has been a shit cake without you."

She was taking the news that I was done with Stars Unlimited's French program well. "You know we're doing *Everyone's a Damn Bride Day* again this year, and it's bigger than ever and a little later. I'll bring you an outfit and Ruffian and I will pick you up at the airport."

"Is Taylor coming?" I wanted her to be there. Honestly, I was going back to her. For her. She had always been there every time I called. Tinsley refused to tell me how the Booty Camp Dating Service went other than, "We got a lot of numbers."

The charge on the card never cleared. I hadn't asked her if she was dating anyone. She was incredible and beautiful and selfless. She broke up with me so I wouldn't have the guilt of ending our relationship on top of everything else I was feeling. And anytime I saw her on the screen, she was wearing pink. I hadn't asked her what it meant. So my butterflies in my stomach were legitimate.

Teddi looked to her side and then back. "I wasn't planning on grabbing her, but she'll be there. We were planning our dresses."

"I don't have time to get dressed up."

"Please, you act like none of us could possibly pick out an outfit for you. I could be you for Halloween and freaking kill it. Bet." She wiggled her nose at me.

"Fine. Make it happen, Bear." Delight reached her eyes. She was still my little sister and it was fun to make her happy.

"Send me your flights and stuff. I can't wait to see you." Teddi blew me a kiss.

She and Ruffian had visited a few months ago, and Mom and Dad had popped by right after the holidays.

I had run long enough. It was time. And I said goodbye to Endgame. I was trying to leave the guilt I felt where he was concerned in France as well.

My business had flourished. I had meetings set up back in the States almost immediately after returning. As I hefted my carry-on and boarded the plane, I kept thinking that I had to reset my brain without expectations as far as Taylor was concerned. She had a whole year without me.

I thought I'd be able to sleep on the plane, but I could only drift in and out. I was keyed up.

When I grabbed my suitcase from the carousel, it was seven in the morning in New York. On the sidewalk of LaGuardia Airport, Teddi flailed both her arms until I saw her. She took off running and I got ready for her. People would have thought we hadn't seen each other in ten years.

I scooped her up as Ruffian waited in the driver's seat of his car. "Teddi Bear."

"Austin Bear. I love you, thank you for coming back."

I set her on her feet and she started pulling my big suitcase. Ruffian was holding the fort, watching the policeman whose job it was to keep cars from lingering. The trunk popped open and I took my bag from Teddi and hefted it inside. She climbed in the back of the car and yanked on my arm until I sat next to her.

"We're going to the mall a few miles away and get ready for the Bride Day there."

She curled up against my shoulder after she buckled her seatbelt.

I held a hand over the seat to Ruffian after he was done merging back onto the highway. "My man."

"Big A. Good on you for getting back in the good U.S. of A." He smiled at me in the rearview mirror.

"Got to say, I loved France, though. So peaceful."

Teddi leaned forward so she could look in my face. "Where are you staying? Have you even made a plan yet?"

"No, my Type A sister. Some people just go places and hope it works out."

"That's fine." Her eyelid twitched.

"You can always stay with us. We have an extra bedroom." She motioned to Ruffian.

Ruffian snorted. "Yeah. I'm sure he'd love to bunk down in a room full of files and your projects. Plenty of room there to be comfortable."

"I'll be fine. I have places to stay, though I appreciate the offer." I pulled out my phone and checked the hashtag to see what kind of traction Teddi had pulled together.

#EverybodysABride wasn't trending like last time, but the actual social media posts were far more elaborate. Companies were even getting involved. Leave it to Teddi to turn something that was meant as an insult into an event that fostered more diversity and representation.

Ruffian put on his blinker and parked in the closest spot he could.

"Is this place open?" I had my doubts. It was still early in the morning.

"Yeah. They open it for walkers in the morning and they have a great set of restrooms and family rooms where we can put on our outfits. Then we will drive straight to the event."

Thankfully, Ruffian had borrowed my parents' minivan and we had plenty of storage space. Three outfits were on hangers and covered in dress protectors.

When we got inside the mall, it seemed like a whole different business than normal. The elderly were everywhere, laughing and stretching.

"Most of the people are from the retirement place down the street. You guys can go in there and I'll pop in here."

And just like that, I was left with my sister's boyfriend to help him into his wedding dress.

I put the finishing touches on my outfit, a crop top paired with a glittery skirt. I was a ball of nerves because I knew I'd see Austin. But I think dressing up as a bride brings out a special set of nerves that correlate with the white outfit combined with a veil. There was a pink barrette fastened in my hair.

Tinsley had on a Cinderella type number and Parker had on a bodycon white dress that was very, very see-through.

I came up behind him as he circled his own in the mirror.

"So handsome. So nipple. Yeah, baby." He turned around and added even more vigor to his motions.

"I feel like it's too early for this spectacle." I covered my eyes.

"It's a testicle festival." Parker rolled his hips.

"I guess it can be. Anyone is allowed to be themselves, as long as they're a bride." I tried to keep my gaze on Parker's face.

Tinsley legit looked like a storybook princess that fell from a movie screen. "Do you think doing this every year will make our actual wedding days less special?" She touched the tiara on her head.

"I don't know. I feel like we will figure out what styles we like best because we'll have had a few dry runs under our belt." I grabbed the purse I had for the occasion—a sweet rose with a zipper so it looked like a part of a bouquet.

"I just got a text from Austin. He's in town." Tinsley adjusted her crown.

I glanced at my phone and I had a message from him as well, and Teddi had sent a selfie with him.

Tinsley peered over my shoulder. "Lord, that man photographs like a damn dream."

He did. I had FaceTimed with him enough, and hell, been around him my whole childhood, but the way he could smolder at a camera brought out the feral part of me.

Once we all had water bottles and phone battery packs, we were ready to leave. Now that Teddi had a month to prepare, it was going to be an all day affair.

When we got to the sidewalk, it became a march to get downtown. There wasn't an official parade, though Teddi had her sights on that someday in the future. Instead, we were meeting in the park. It had acres of grass and rolling hills. It was great for photos and events.

Teddi had a band set to play, and there were a few speakers

and a lot of businesses that were providing "favor bags" for anyone attending.

The only problem was the dark clouds bullying their way into the crisp blue sky. Parker pointed at them with his middle fingers. "If they screw with my hair, I'm going to throw a fit. Bridezilla style."

Tinsley and I linked our arms in his and pulled him forward. He could fight the clouds after we got to the park. It was warming up, and the humidity was ticking up as well.

When we got to the park, it was decorated in white ribbons and balloons. Every company that had a booth contributed to the silver and white theme. It already looked like a great time.

In a wall of white dresses and veils, I was looking for him.

Austin. It had been a year since he left. A year since I laid eyes on him in person. I didn't realize how being near him calibrated my internal happiness until I didn't have access anymore.

The rain started. First, a mist, then in earnest. Tinsley and Parker went one way, and I went the other.

I found a large tree that was helping provide some cover, and I could see Tinsley and Parker hiding under a small pop-up canopy.

There were four other people under the tree with me. It wasn't the best, as the leaves started to bend with the weight of the drops.

A tall person with a white umbrella scurried underneath the tree, and when they lifted it to include me in the shelter, I was inches from Austin's face.

I felt my shoulders slide down a bit as release rolled through me.

Here. He was here.

"Hey, beautiful." The devious smile. The lined eyes. The plies of silver jewelry and silver painted nails. He had on white jeans, a sequin tank top, and a veil. The combat boots seemed to be a repeat from last time.

Last time. When Endgame helped Roberta and Peter kidnap me.

"Hi." He reached a hand out and I wrapped my fingers around his hand.

He turned and led me out from under the tree. Under the umbrella, it was just he and I.

"God, I missed you." I wanted to kiss him.

"Same here." He ran his thumb in circles on the top of my hand.

He pulled me close. Chest-to-chest so we were out of the rain as we could be.

"You didn't get a love match at the place I sent you to?" He looked down his nose at me.

"Did you find what you needed in France?" I tilted my chin up.

"Yes and no." He tilted his head. "I think I did what I had to do, so that I could finally be here with you completely."

"That sounds...promising." I put one hand on his shoulder and gave in to the need to lay my hand on his chest. He cradled me, humming while kissing the top of my head over and over.

The rain started to let up a bit. Downpours can only keep it up for so long. They're too dramatic, too damaging. As suddenly as it appeared, it was back to the mist. The whole event came back into view.

Soon, we weren't alone under the umbrella, with Tinsley and Parker crowding in to join our hug.

The welcoming hellos and joy were loud, and soon, Austin closed the umbrella and set it to the side so he could properly hug everyone.

"French guy! How was it? Are you back *back* or just sort of back?" Tinsley jumped on Austin and he supported her.

I had a hug from behind and wrapped my arms around my back so I could hug Teddi.

We had quite a group when we had all finished saying hello.

Ruffian, Gaze and Pixie Rae, and Milt and his cosplay business buds—everyone was there and in a version of white.

Austin welcomed everyone and then stood next to me. I put my arm through his.

He paused to look down at me. "Where's your boyfriend?"

I gave him a look. "There's no one. You know that."

"I still can't believe that's possible. Have you seen you?" He took me and twirled me around.

Everyone that had booths or tables in the park had to dry up. Luckily, it seemed everyone was expecting the fickle weather because there were a ton of towels to go around. Before long everyone was reset and the balloons floating back at full height. The band could even begin their sound check.

"You got Widowed Vibes to play?" Austin hollered up to Teddi.

"Hell yeah. Wait until you see who else we got to play. And I already have a wait list for next year." She started dancing and walking at the same time as the Vibes began playing one of their songs that had gone viral on social media.

Austin stopped where we were. "Can I have this dance?"

It was an upbeat song, and he passed his umbrella to Parker, who started using it as a cane. Austin held his arms out in a classic dance pose.

I pretended to curtsy and then took up in his arms. We were slow dancing to a fast song, but it didn't matter.

"Is it selfish to say I'm glad you're not dating anyone?" He twirled me into a dip.

I knew I was blushing. "I don't think so."

He pulled me back up. "Your face is just what I needed."

I rubbed the scruff on his face. "Same here. Every day I can't believe I made it through a year without you."

I had a touch of concern—maybe I was saying too much. He didn't know how big my love was for him. That I already knew he was my one and only. If I couldn't have Austin? Then I was content to just be Taylor on my own.

"I can't believe it was a year. It felt like forever, but also so quick." He rested his chin on my head briefly.

Teddi tapped me on the shoulder. "Can I cut in? I want to see if he learned any fancy moves in France. I need to up my game."

Ruffian held up both hands. "Now I need to watch out for fancy moves?"

I walked over to Ruffian and heard my name in the distance. Peaches was headed at me with a running gallop.

"Holy crap." I tried to step behind Ruffian, but he put his hands on my shoulders and held me in place. Peaches hit me like a happy little freight train.

"Taylor! Look at this nonsense! All because you and Austin rock." She hung off of me like a rowdy koala.

"Peaches! You're going to knock us over and then we won't be wearing white anything." I pointed to the squishy grass.

"I don't care." She kissed me hard on one cheek, then the other.

Once she had relaxed a bit, we ventured out to see what the vendors had in place. There were free favor bags with pens, pop sockets, and bubbles to blow.

When the Vibes ended their song, Peaches and I were looking at a flower crown display.

I felt Austin's presence next to me. Just having him near made me feel special and like the luckiest person in the park.

He grabbed a white rose crown and placed it on my head. "This is the one for you."

He touched my hip and pulled out his phone. "I have to get this."

Austin started taking pictures of me, and at first I tried to pose, but then just smiled at him with my full joy. He passed his credit card to the vendor to purchase the crown for me.

He led me up a small hill so that the backdrop would be all these brides and party decorations. He had me face away from him and look back over my shoulder.

"This. Just this. I want to capture the way you look at me. You amaze me."

I looked at his boots and then back at his eyes. I was easy to read. I wasn't ever going to hide it. I loved Austin and always would.

He took two steps so he could fix my hair, placing it over my shoulder.

After staring at me for a beat, he traced the small bit of skin that was showing at the base of my back.

"I can trace the water droplets here. Just like a signature." The pad of his finger was barely making contact with my skin, but I felt the rivulets of water the motion created slip under my skirt's waistband.

Austin leaned forward and gently licked my ear before whispering, "You are edible."

My nervous system shuddered with the sensation. He had barely been in my orbit for an hour and I was wasted for him.

I bit my lips together so I wouldn't kiss him. I still needed to process that he was here. There was a small part of me that had a concern that this annual event coinciding with Endgame's death would have Austin acting impulsively. Maybe forcing him to move on when he wasn't ready yet.

Instead of kissing me, he put his arm around my shoulder. "Let's see how many of these brides we know."

I agreed. I'd follow him anywhere.

Austin

I was coming on too strong. I saw that. When I breathed near Taylor's ear, I watched as she reacted. Her pupils dilating, her nipples perking. I had to be sure before we started this. I had to be in this space where Endgame and I had known each other and not have flashbacks.

I didn't want to use her as a Band-Aid to overcome the pain I had endured because she was worth so much more.

Hell, she broke up with me to save me guilt that I had no room to board at the time. She stayed in touch for a year, never asking for anything other than what I was ready to give.

And now, when I showed up at the Bride event, she welcomed my arms, my advances like she'd been waiting patiently all this time.

I knew she was waiting. Teddi told me that she and Peaches were getting ready to apply to a nunnery for Taylor.

But seeing her, it was a flood. She was so spectacular, that during some of the worst parts in my life, she still made me feel worthy of love. In the few short months we had been together, she had helped me heal from the cracks I had.

Here, one-on-one, where I could touch her and see her and smell her hair? It was better than I thought. I had clarity now. I had distance now. I might even deserve her now.

She kept looking at my face like I was a mirage that would burn off when the sun got high.

Teddi was making her way around to all the vendors and tables, thanking people for showing up. How she remembered all the names I didn't know. My sister had the demeanor of a well-respected debutante and the people skills of a movie star. If she said she wanted to be the president someday, I'd believe her. But even she was looking between Taylor and me.

Making time to watch us watch each other. At the next bay of tables, I spotted my parents. Two brides headed in our direction. God bless my father, he was carrying a huge pair of chunky heels. Instead of wearing the heels, he had on a set of satin slippers that I could read as he got closer.

Bride & Bride.

"You couldn't do the heels?" I held my arms out for their hugs. Mom beat Dad to it, but soon enough I was in the center of their double decker hug sandwich.

Dad was wearing a bridal gown that could have fit an NHL linebacker. "Where'd you find this beauty?" I lifted up the edge of the skirt. I saw now that there was a different lace pattern on the back of the dress.

My mom came forward and started pointing out seams. "I used two similar thrift store dresses and sewed them together to form a Frankenstein's monster piece. It worked and he looks super cute, so I'm happy."

"You're a good man, Dad." I touched dad's dress.

"I'm thrilled you're home. How's the day going for you? You came here straight off the plane?" Dad grabbed his skirt and did a little kick.

I saw that there was a photographer in the distance, and he was snapping pictures that had us framed in the background.

I spoke to my parents while watching the photographer. I was on high alert. "Yeah, Teddi was a task master. But I wanted to be here for Taylor."

My mom rubbed my arm. "That's good, sweetheart. That's good."

Maybe we were all past the sister's best friend taboo. This year had put something on our relationship that went beyond labels.

The day included pictures, games, and dancing. My parents left after dinner. Both Taylor and I had moments that were stressful. A popping balloon made us both flinch. I wouldn't let her out of my sight and she seemed to be gripping her phone tightly. This wasn't just a reunion, it was an anniversary of trauma. When we were all exhausted from the day, we headed home.

I held Taylor's hand and kept sneaking peeks at her face. She was glowing despite the blips of sadness in our day. I tried not to focus on the pink in her hair. Tried not to wonder what it meant.

The posse of friends that came back to Taylor, Parker, and Tinsley's apartment was overflowing. Teddi, Ruffian, Gaze and Pixie, a huge group of Gaze's basketball friends, and a few of Ruffian's crew from when he was on the streets.

I stood on the coffee table and held up my hand to get everyone's attention.

"Thank you. Thank you for coming here. I don't know if you all know the reason we're dressed as brides, but it's because my sister and brothers never let a guy stand alone, even if he's wearing a skirt."

The hooting and hollering picked up, and I stepped down from the table. Taylor's beautiful smile was like a beacon that I had to be near.

She was close to her bedroom door, and when I was in arm's reach, she pulled me inside.

The room was very her. It was soft and a little edgy and smelled like warm cinnamon.

I stepped up to her, now alone. "Hello, beautiful."

She tilted her head up at me. "Hello, handsome. I've missed you."

I put my hands on either side of her, as she put her back against the door. "I missed you, too. I've said goodbye to him. Finally healed. Finally."

"I'm glad." She straightened my lapels.

"Have you healed?" I searched her face, the pristine skin luminescent in the soft light.

Resolve built in her gaze. "I've grown, but the only healing I could do was learn how to do without you." Her voice dropped to a whisper. "And I failed at that."

I echoed her, "I'm glad." I leaned my head down and nuzzled her face, letting my nose trail up her jaw to her earlobe. "I learned that I wanted to feel this again. With you. I wanted a love that didn't hurt. I wear this color everyday to remember the moment in time when you loved me."

She took in a quick, sharp breath and held it.

I ran my thumb over her lips and then touched my forehead to hers. "Breathe for me." She exhaled and I heard the shakiness there. "May I kiss you? You can say no. I'm yours, no matter what. And I still love you. So let's allow pink to mean that."

Her eyebrows pushed together. She put her hands on either side of my face. "Say that again."

"I'm yours and I love you." I felt my smile matching hers. My heart swelled at her joy. I felt my soul matching hers.

Then she kissed my lips like I was the best treasure in the world.

Knowing I was waiting for Austin my whole life, and I was right about it, was a meteor landing. It was the miracle of flight. It was the beauty of him. The smell of him, the way his hands felt on my body. It was like a snug fit. A way I knew that I could make the world spin around us. Wait for us. Believe in us.

He put one hand in my hair and the other on my lower back, and then he dipped me into a deeper kiss. That was Austin, the most romantic. He could pull it off, and I was more than grateful to receive it.

After we kissed, he pulled me up and hugged me. I felt my heart slip from neutral to drive. I'd been waiting for this moment since he last held me.

AUSTIN HAD SWITCHED to water hours ago, when we finally decided to leave. I was still buzzing. I had a bag packed at his direction.

"Can we just stay here?" I offered.

"No, we can't. The thing I want to do to you needs privacy." His smolder said it all and I didn't argue.

We walked hand-in-hand to the expensive Hillshire Embassy. The doorman was there, smiling and crisp at what had to be four-thirty in the morning.

As we took the elevator, I had questions, "Did you get this hotel room because you thought you couldn't stay with me?"

Austin bit his bottom lip before responding, "Kitten, you've always welcomed me. That's never a question. You will always have options with me. You get to leave with never any bad feelings at all. You're free. I hope that freedom leads you to my bed every night, but my respect for you will come before my needs where you're concerned."

I realized that the hotel room was his way of being different from Endgame. Whenever Austin tried to leave, he was treated to mind games and fights. He didn't ever want to be that.

The elevator sounded its bell at the top floor. Austin pulled out his phone and held an app up to the scanner.

Inside, the plush penthouse suite was laid out to the city. It looked beautiful. There was a generous kitchen, dining room, and living room.

"Wow. This is a home, not a hotel room. Do they owe you money or something?"

"Actually." He chuckled. "I had a voucher for this room for, like, two years because I had done some social media stuff for them. I thought it would be a great wedding present for a friend or something. But..." He pressed an elaborate button in a frame on the wall that read "Call for Champagne".

There was a vacuum noise and then Austin headed to a small silver door on the cabinet. He opened it and cold vapors spilled out. He expertly popped the cork on the bottle and then covered the foaming eruption with his lips.

After he had it under control, he tipped the bottle backward and took a few swigs. He crossed the room to me and continued, "But, we've both been brides enough times now I think we warrant more than a few wedding gifts."

His eyes twinkled at me. He held the bottle up and gently poured a few sips into my mouth, watching the action with carnal eyes. "You're good at that."

I covered my mouth as he pulled the bottle away.

"I can't believe I get to have you back." I was still a little bit scared that I was dreaming the whole thing.

He set the bottle down and properly held me. "Always. I love you, Taylor."

Austin leaned forward and put his hand on my head, rubbing his thumb on my cheek while he kissed me. Between nips, he added his tongue and then pulled me even closer against his body.

I could wait no longer and started to pull at his clothes.

"Wait, first." Austin twirled me so my back was against his chest. He undressed me quickly and covered any new exposed skin with caresses or nips, depending how close it was to his mouth.

I could see our reflection in the floor-to-ceiling windows that formed the expansive view. When I was naked, he twirled me back. He was taking deep, labored breaths.

"Is this okay? Are you okay with this?"

Permission, always. I never expected anything else from his safe aura.

"I love you, Austin Burathon. Always have. Always will."

The carnal look softened as I watched my words touch him. "Kitten."

He stopped for a second and took me in. "I want to remember this moment."

I blew him a kiss from where I stood. He approached, touching my hips and then putting me on the dining room table. "And I want to remember how you taste, too."

I leaned back, lying spread for him. He disappeared for a moment and then was back, icy cold champagne bottle in hand.

"May I drink you?"

I laughed. "Yes."

Austin poured a little bit of champagne into my navel and then used his tongue and mouth to clean me up. My skin thrummed with his touch.

I had never wanted anything so much. He loved me. Austin loved me. And even though I thought I might be off the wall for waiting for him, it was true. He loved me.

The champagne trickle moved lower. First, my inner thighs, the top of his head grazing where I needed him most. Then he moved to my center, pouring and lapping me up. My spine arched and he set the bottle down so he could use both hands.

"Grab those beautiful nipples for me." I heard his words but felt his breath between my legs. I did as I was told. He matched the passion and sensation by nuzzling in deeply, finding my clit and sucking. His fingers massaged the outside of my thighs until I felt like I was an over-strung guitar. When his first finger slipped inside me, he increased his clitoris adoration. This man knew what I needed. Slow, steady, firm. He added fingers until I was full of him. He moved his lips and tongue in a way that made me think he could illustrate my body with his eyes closed.

Closer and closer. With other lovers, I would have called it quits or faked something to get away from the need that was building, but not with Austin. He wouldn't let me get away from an earth-shattering, mind-bending orgasm that started and didn't stop. And when I came, I was soaked. He grabbed the champagne and poured it as well, mixing it and drinking it from between my legs. His tongue lingered on my opening, circling it as I spasmed. My throat was raw from screaming his name.

I was panting as he climbed up me, still dressed, save for his unbuttoned shirt. He was hard as a rock and I felt him on my stomach.

Over me, his hair fell to the side, tickling my cheek. "That's it, kitten. Feel it all."

He moved to his waistband and I shook my head. "No. I'm gonna have you in my mouth."

Ignoring my plans, he started kissing me again, pressing me against the dining room table. I grabbed fistfuls of his hair and kissed him back.

This wasn't just sex. We loved each other, and I gave my all when I loved someone. I scooted out from underneath him and he lay back on the table.

"I've loved that scarf on you my whole life, and now I'm going to tie you up in it and deep throat your dick."

His hips rolled. "Oh my God."

I slid off the table and found his scarf. When I came back to him, his hands were above his head. I tipped the two chairs closer to him over and kicked them out of the way. I went to the head of the table and tied his wrists together. As I did so, he cradled between my legs. "What if I want more?"

"You'll have it. I promise." I stalled for a few minutes while he explored with his bound hands. I leaned forward a bit when the sensations caught me off balance. He took my left nipple into his mouth and nibbled and circled it with his tongue.

I had to use superhuman strength to pull away. When I did, I fastened the other end of the scarf to the leg of the table. I crawled on the table and straddled him. Amusement and lust colored his handsome face. I traced his face with both of my hands and lingered on his bottom lip with my thumb. I slipped it into his mouth as he smiled around it and then sucked it.

This man's face when he was doing something sexy would be my mind's wallpaper forever.

"Are you okay with this?" I had to offer him the same courtesy he did me.

"Please."

That was all he had to say. I made sure to unbutton his pants slowly. I slid them down and was faced with his erection. I missed it. I gave it a kiss on the tip and was rewarded with a grind.

I started my kisses just on the inside of his knee, making sure my breasts brushed his skin as I worked my way up. I took a pause to envelop his dick in my breasts and start licking the head.

The grind picked up. I cupped his balls gently and ran my fingertips along the sensitive parts there. He started cursing. The bottle he had used for me was still on the table. There wasn't much left, but I tipped it over him. The slow trickle was mesmerizing, and I challenged myself to keep every drop on his shaft.

"A finger, maybe?" I whispered.

He growled and nodded. I made sure to fill him up.

I knew I had had my orgasm a few times over, and I wanted him to be inside me for his.

The condoms he had brought over when he grabbed the champagne were sitting on the buffet just an arm's reach away, near his head. I worked my way up and was pleased to see his eyes had briefly rolled backward from pleasure. I could have slid off the table to secure the protection, but instead, I made a game of straddling him as much as I could until my knees were on either side of his head. While I reached for the condom, Austin's tongue tasted me again, in and out, in and out.

I forced myself to leave his talented mouth so I could give him the pleasure he needed as well. I shimmied back down his body until I pinned his legs under me. I ripped the wrapper off the condom with my teeth and slowly rolled it on him, making sure to pinch the tip a bit in preparation for his release.

"Ready?" I asked as I positioned myself over him, hovering.

"Sweet fuck, yes." He rolled his hips.

I let myself slide down his shaft one inch at a time until he was fully inside me.

The city night was my view, just beyond his long, lean, naked body. His tattoos, the ones I always lusted after, were on display. I ran my hands over them.

"Love you. Love you. Love you," I told him in time with the rocking of my hips.

His bound wrists were released. I didn't notice until the scarf I had used was tangled in my hair.

He used his strong arms to help move me faster. In the reflection of the window, I watched as my body rocked up and down.

"Changing it up." His voice was deep and growly.

I tilted my head back as he sat up to kiss my neck. He fisted my hair and licked from between my breasts to the inside of my mouth.

Carnal. Feral. Desperate.

And then we were off the table. Austin had straight manhandled my body to carry me. I was on the couch before I could get my balance back. He picked one of my legs up and wrapped it over his shoulder.

When he entered me, he made sure to put his hand between us and give me friction so I could feel full and ignited at the same time.

He was close to me now. He slid my leg off his shoulder, and soon we were chest-to-chest. Face-to-face. He slowed, and the strain in his neck told me it wasn't easy.

"You are everything."

"I love you."

We whispered things to each other. Promises, prayers, until he lost the use for words. I met him, thrust for thrust. He was sweating, and now, so was I. I was building to my orgasm, but he went before me. His thrusts slowed as he tensed. As soon as he was done, one more motion from his hand sent me crashing to my own release. I spasmed around him, hugging him from the inside.

Spent, he snuggled next to me on the couch.

We were boneless, stupid, and panting, but smiling. The look of pure satisfaction and adoration on his face made me glow.

It was the start of the forever I'd been waiting patiently for.

EPILOGUE

Austin

At Taylor's graduation party, I had to threaten a few guys to let me dance with her. Between Gaze's basketball teammates, my brothers, my father, and her father, she was a hot ticket to get a chance with.

I loved her ice blue form fitting dress. It was one of my first designs that was mass-produced. We were sourcing ethical fabric and workers.

The color matched her eyes, even to the ombre hues toward the hem.

"Kitten." I held out my hand to her.

We had on matching polish and our unisex makeup box had provided us both with eyeliner. I had been wearing a pink bracelet for all it symbolized for us. What it had been and what it was now. And I noticed she had on the same type today. I touched her wrist.

"I love you." She said it so much, so easily. I was grateful that I had the sense to realize I deserved this love. She gave with her whole heart and put me first, and I was doing the same for her. "We can do this together too. Remember him and celebrate us."

I adored her drive and her ability to make my dreams her priority, too. As we celebrated in my parents' backyard, I overheard her talking to Teddi about her degree.

"Just general studies. I just wanted the Bachelor's to open possibilities. I may go back for my business degree if our clothing line takes off."

Our clothing line. She was a force. All those years I blamed Teddi for having such a relentless drive, but Taylor was almost as fierce with it.

One boozy night soon after I returned from France, I had confessed to Taylor that I had dreamed of having a clothing line of my own. She had sat down on the floor, a wipe away marker on hand, and we drew out my business plan naked on the tile floor.

She had forced me to think in wider and wider circles until not only would I be doing clothing, but I'd also have makeup and a style page. She was an organizational wonder, and in her free time she'd organize all my files and made outfit boards as well.

Taylor was a true partner in crime.

I dipped her on the dance floor/basketball court, and Teddi, with impeccable timing, popped off an air cannon packed full with silver confetti.

We had reminisced just the night before about how far we had made it in just twelve months. The impossible was just a to-do list for us now. The brides' event was continuing and Teddi had reached out to friends all over the world, as had I. Everyone's a Damn Bride was reaching not only many parts in the U.S., but overseas as well. It was a mixture of Mardi Gras and New Year's Eve every year. We hoped it would only get bigger. Taylor and I stayed supportive and interactive with the community that I represented. LGBTQIA+ needed allies, and I was happy to help have a place where everyone felt comfortable to be themselves.

Roberta was due to have her early release hearing, as was Peter. It wasn't long enough for what they had done, but it was good that they'd have to tell employers in the future that they had a criminal background. They were horrible at making decisions. The judge in the matter made the restraining order a permanent fixture, legally keeping Roberta and Peter from contacting Taylor in any way.

Endgame lived on in my heart. He always would. The empathy and hope I had for him would color my views. Color the way I approached adversity. Taylor was always down to talk about it, and I took her up on it on many occasions.

Raven was already a sophomore in high school, and talking about attending college in our city. I could see her moving into mine and Taylor's second bedroom in a couple years or so.

Taylor's father had kept up his routine of keeping the house tidy. He'd even begun some renovations on the place. Having a therapist on the case was helping with any potential relapse. Willa and her pack of pugs still lived in their own place, but the back-yard became a puppy play zone that Raven was live streaming for subscribers.

I handed Taylor a box from inside my pocket. She opened the present quickly and gasped at the necklace I had for her. It was a gold charm of a champagne bottle.

"For the night I got you back."

I was gratified to see her blush, knowing she was remembering our reunion on the dining room table.

She turned in my arms and lifted her hair so I could secure it. I leaned over and spoke into her ear. "I love you."

She leaned back and responded, "I've loved you always."

WANT one more scene for free? I've got you covered.
Check out CRUEL PINK THANKSGIVING!
https://BookHip.com/BSCKWBW

ACKNOWLEDGMENTS

A huge thanks to you, the reader. I'm back again with another story and it is always humbling to know that I will find you letting it into your heart. My sincerest thanks.

To my beautiful family, T, J and D, I absolutely adore you and am so proud of all of you. Thank you for putting up with me.

A HUGE shout out to my parents, Steve and Valerie. I remember when we had the biggest RV in the early 90s and you two would be in the driver and passenger seats and Pam and I would sit on the hump so close so we could all chat. I love that even though we are states apart, we all manage to sit on the hump together. The longer I'm on the planet the more rare I realize you are. Bad ass, kick ass and incredibly kind—I come from amazing people. Sorry I write about sex so much. Thank you for all your incredible support.

Pam and Jim! Thanks for keeping my bedroom ready in NY I love you. To Jim's mom Cathy, you are incredible.

Helena Hunting, Man has this been 13 years yet? I know we are close. Our friendship is getting pimples and having an attitude problem and I couldn't be prouder of it. Thank you for this wild ride. I love you even though the entire country of Canada including you lie about the money smelling like maple. Hard truth.

Tijan, I feel like we have had the same conversation open for a decade. Like just existing next to each other, tossing out observations and news. My mermaid energy loves your guru energy.

Mom and Dad D, I can't imagine nicer humans if I tried. Thank you for saving Blackberry. You are stars.

All my Beta Beauties! Michele, Marty and Brandi, Amanda, Tessa, Carol S! You are an emergency swat time of awesome.

Debra's Daredevils! We've been doing this for so long, I am the luckiest.

Whole Brower Literary Crew—Amiee Ashcraft and Kimberly Brower Thank you so much for everything!

Aunt Jo and Uncle Ted—you guys are so cool thank you for the updates on your cross country journey!

BLACKBERRY the talking cat, thank you for all the directions given to me with a look of disdain. I had no idea how often you needed treats.

Bud: Erika— CVS forever, Jenn, Kelly B, Ashley S, LLL, Sarah Pie, Melissa love you guys!

Cassie S thank you so much for all your help

Paige Smith Editing— You make everything better and I am never happy unless you have seen what I've done!

Social Butterfly PR To the endless help and for so many opportunities! Love you!

ABOUT THE AUTHOR

Debra creates pretend people in her head and paints them on the giant, beautiful canvas of your imagination. She has a Bachelor of Science degree in political science and writes new adult angst and romantic comedies. She lives in Maryland with her husband and two amazing children. She doesn't trust mannequins, but does trust bears. Also, her chunky tuxedo cat talks with communication buttons. So that's fun. DebraAnastasia.com for more information.

Pretty please review this book if you enjoyed it. It is one of the very best ways to support indy authors. Thank you!

Scan the code below to stay connected to Debra:

ALSO BY DEBRA ANASTASIA

MY DAD

My Dad

******FREE BOOK PLATES******

Okay Daredevils. I have literally the cutest offer ever for you. My dad makes my swag down in Florida. He is freaking adorable about it and is very serious about his job. If you want a FREE signed bookplate(s) email my dad and we will send them to you and whatever swag he can fit in the envelope.

To receive an envelope sealed with adorableness and extreme efficiency email: debraanastasiaDad@gmail.com with your full name and mailing address (plus how many bookplates you need!!)